MISTRAL

Robert Cole

First published in 2025 by Blossom Spring Publishing
Mistral Copyright © 2025 Robert Cole
ISBN 978-1-0683266-9-1
E: admin@blossomspringpublishing.com
W: www.blossomspringpublishing.com

Chapter 1

"Bloody hell," Adam muttered, pulling up his coat collar and hunching his shoulders against the numbing chill. The ferocious wind rattled the wooden shutters and shredded the last of the brown and lifeless leaves from the trees. "What am I doing?" It wasn't the first time he had asked himself that. Grimacing, he thrust his hands deep in his pockets, cursing himself for not bringing enough warm clothing. His fingers curled around the postcard that had brought him to this part of the south of France in February. It had dropped through his letterbox in London just over a week ago, buried within the usual pile of junk mail. The front bore an enticing picture of a sunlit, bustling, Provençal market scene. With a jolt he had recognised the two-tiered fountain in the ancient main square of Uzès. The message on the back, scrawled in blue ballpoint, had said, '*Forgive me*'. That was all. There was no name or signature.

It must have come from her, but the writing looked hurried and he couldn't be sure it wasn't a cruel joke. He had heard nothing since she had disappeared, more than two years ago. He didn't even know whether she was alive, but he was becoming reconciled to their troubled past, and his sense of loss and betrayal. Those two simple words, though, had triggered the feelings of guilt he thought he had laid to rest. It should be him who was asking for forgiveness, shouldn't it? His role had been to shield his wife from the world — and protect her from herself. So why contact him now… after so long?

Adam's stomach clenched as he quickened his long strides across the cobbles towards the old square, willing the man to be there at his market stall. The stallholder might just be able to provide him with some answers. He wished he could remember his name. Adam joined the throng of early-morning shoppers being blown down the alleyways and side streets towards the central Place aux Herbes by the fierce gusts. The wind, like an angry serpent, wound its fury around the street corners, seeking out the dark crevices of the ancient square, whipping up leaves and debris from the market stalls, sending it swirling around the streets. "Christ... Bloody hell," he muttered again, wiping dust from his eyes. Most locals had the good sense to stay inside during the mistral.

The man he sought was a photographer. When Adam and Maryanne had visited that summer, some two-and-a-half years ago, he had been selling black-and-white pictures of Aix-en-Provence. His wares had also included wine and olive oil from a small *domaine* near Saint-Rémy-de-Provence, but Maryanne had been engrossed in the pictures. She had begun a long conversation with the photographer. Her French was almost fluent, but the man spoke good English. Maryanne had an easy manner with people and she and the seller quickly struck up a rapport. Fascinated by a photograph of a church in the old district in Aix, it had led to an animated discussion about the region and its turbulent religious history. Adam had left them to it and wandered off to browse the other stalls. Religion had always held little interest for him, but something about his wife's rekindled fervour for her faith had disturbed him.

Today, the market was quiet but there were still the thirty or forty stalls braving the chill. Multi-coloured lights decorated the bare plane trees surrounding the medieval square, lending a festive atmosphere to the grey morning. Adam squeezed through a crowd, drawn to a *poissonnerie* by the rich scent of saffron, garlic and seafood emanating from a large pan of simmering paella, and scanned the stalls for the photographer. He wasn't sure what he would say to him, but Adam believed the photographer was a piece of the puzzle surrounding Maryanne's disappearance. His only evidence was the postcard of the market, but he had few other leads. He ran his fingers through his thick, dark hair in frustration and stood and surveyed the market again until he spotted the stall in a far corner of the square. It was under one of the thirteenth-century stone arches that gave welcome shelter from the sun to the shops and cafés that proliferated in the warmer weather. The seller had his back to a customer, but when he turned around Adam knew he had found the right man, despite the upturned collar and thick woollen hat muffling his features. He hurried across the square and waited until the photographer had finished serving his customer. The man turned to Adam, looking up to meet his gaze and smiling.

"*Bonjour, Monsieur. Comment puis-je vous aider?*"

"*Pardon. Parlez-vous Anglais?*"

"*Oui…* Of course, *Monsieur*. How can I help?"

"I was here at the market a couple of years ago with my wife. We spent a long time at your stall and bought a couple of prints of Aix." Adam gestured at a photograph of the city.

"I hope you liked them. Perhaps I can show you some new ones that I have taken since?"

"I'm sorry, I'm not here to buy anything, but I was hoping you could help me in some way. You see, my wife went missing just after we visited here."

The man looked startled. His voice became less

assured. "I am very sorry to hear that *monsieur*, but I don't know how I can help."

"I'm trying to trace anyone she had contact with just before she vanished." Adam pulled two photographs from his coat pocket and handed them to the stallholder. "Here. That's my wife. You spent a long time talking to her. You must remember, surely?"

"*Non.*" There was a slight hesitation. His tone changed and the response now bordered on the gruff. "I am very sorry, *monsieur*." He shrugged. "I do not remember. I see so many customers. I cannot remember them all." He had barely glanced at the photographs. Instead, his gaze darted around the market, as though he were looking for someone he didn't wish to see.

Adam screwed up his eyes. What was he missing here?

"You must remember," he repeated. "You both spent a lot of time talking about your photographs of churches. I left you both talking. It was July. Two years ago. The market was very busy."

The photographer shook his head rather too vehemently. "*Non.* I cannot help you, sir. You must be thinking of someone else. There are others who sell pictures."

The man wouldn't look Adam in the eye. "I left you both talking while I looked around the market," Adam persisted. His only chance was disappearing. Surely the man remembered spending the better part of an hour with his wife. He had always been aware of the effect her striking looks, and her charm, had on men. Despite the knowledge that the man was lying, Adam searched his mind for any other detail that might help. "It was lunchtime. It was very hot that day. We also bought some of your wine… this wine here." He pointed to the bottles displayed at one end of the stall.

"I said I cannot help you. I do not know you. There is nothing more I can say." Behind the man's hostility, Adam also saw the fear flash in his eyes. "If you do not wish to buy anything, please go, *monsieur*. I have other customers." He turned away angrily to serve a woman who had just arrived at the stall.

It was obvious the man had recognised Maryanne and there was something he was not saying. Still, Adam had not expected such a response. He was, in turn, shocked, and puzzled. As he turned to leave, he noticed some black-and-white prints of the Saint-Paul mental asylum in Saint-Rémy, where Vincent Van Gogh had been hospitalised, just before his death. The prints had not been there two years ago. The photographer must have developed a passion for a new subject. Adam picked up a business card from the pile that lay beside the new pictures. Beneath the illustration of an olive tree, it read *Jean Gilbert, Photographe Artistique et Professionnel, Domaine des Oliviers, Châteaurenard*. The photographer had mentioned his farm was somewhere near Avignon.

Adam waved the card and called out, "*Au revoir,* Jean Gilbert. I will see you again… very soon." The man watched Adam as he walked away, a frown now darkening his face.

Despite the gesture of defiance, Adam couldn't fight the defeated slump of his shoulders, as he trudged through the market, not sure where next to turn. For more than two years he had feared his wife was dead, but still hoped to be proved wrong. Then the postcard arrived. He knew he had pinned too much expectation on the photographer providing a lead. Now he didn't know where to look next and he cursed his naivety. Adam had become used to suppressing his emotions during his marriage, but today he felt less than equal to the challenge. A brightly-lit bistro ahead beckoned and he entered in search of warmth and food to lift his spirits. Steam rose from the coffee machine at the end of the bar counter and condensation forming on the large windows at the front of the restaurant blurred the view of the market. He took off his coat. It was good to be out of the wind. Ordering from the *menu du jour* written on a small blackboard by the bar, he sat back and thought over the morning's events. Was he missing something significant about the market scene on the postcard? What had been in Maryanne's mind two years ago, when she had vanished from his life — for the second time? They had met at a party while at university in Exeter, where they were law students. It was his second year and her first. He was instantly charmed by her soft Irish accent, the light brown freckles that dusted her nose and cheekbones... and her easy welcoming smile. They had connected instantly, and it was not long before they became an item. Later, he had fallen in love with her intelligence, her sense of the absurd and her vivid imagination. She was different — and everything he was not. There was also a sense of other-worldliness about her that made him feel protective. He had wondered then what she was doing with someone like him and whether she would soon get bored? Was he just too reliable, too predictable? Probably, but they had enjoyed just being together — it all seemed very natural. They said they completed each other... and she was fun to be with.

"*Monsieur?*"

Adam was startled from his reverie by the waiter

arriving with his order. He ate slowly. Even in the early years with Maryanne, there had been clues to what was to come. But they were young and, if he was honest, he couldn't believe his luck that such a vibrant woman wished to be with him, so he had ignored them — and had continued to do so for much of their time together. Their relationship had been intense at the beginning, then Adam lost her for the first time after he graduated and began his first job in London, working for a large energy company. Maryanne had remained in Exeter to finish her degree and they had seen each other only at weekends, until the fateful Friday night when she had told him she had met someone else, through the university Catholic Society. The cold and dispassionate way she had broken the news had seemed so out of character. He had felt his world falling apart and he had barely recognised the woman who was shattering his dreams with indifference. Numbed by the news, he didn't even ask her about who she was seeing. Much later, he realised that it was as though she had been coached in what to say to him. They had then been reunited by chance years later, but the second time he lost her there had been no rehearsed explanations. She had simply vanished.

*

"Monsieur," the waiter was standing over him again, this time with a look of concern, *"avez-vous fini?"* Adam had finished his meal some time ago and realised he had been staring into space, turning things over in his mind. He had assumed it was his fault that Maryanne had left him that first time. He shuddered involuntarily at the memory of the break-up. No wonder the waiter was worried about

whether he was OK. He looked up and smiled, before asking for coffee as well as the bill. His gaze returned to the postcard lying on the table. Two simple words had brought him to Uzès, but, after his encounter with the photographer, what should be his next move? He returned the postcard to his coat pocket, shaking his head at the man's unexpected reaction.

Emerging from the light and warmth of the café, Adam wrestled with his coat in the strong wind. A short, stocky man blocked his way on the narrow pavement. Adam tried to pass, but the man stepped sideways and barged roughly into him. Adam's knee gave way and he slipped off the pavement, tumbling heavily onto the cobbled road. His thick coat saved him from significant injury, although the palm of his left hand was badly grazed on the frozen, uneven surface. His assailant, feet planted on the pavement, glared down at him, a challenge in his eyes. Adam scrambled stiffly to his knees and picked up the business card he had dropped in the fall. As he struggled to his feet, his attacker did not move to help him. There was something familiar about the belligerent air of his attacker. Adam had a feeling that he had come across the man before.

"What the fuck do you think you are doing?" He was shaken, but took a step towards the man, who stared back at him, his dark eyes below heavy brows filled with menace. Adam was a head taller, but his attacker showed no fear.

"You deliberately knocked me over. Why the hell would you do that?"

"*Je ne vous comprends pas. Parlez français,*" came the rasping challenge. His sneer revealed a missing front tooth, accentuating his disdain.

"I know you from somewhere. Who the hell are you?"

The man grunted, then turned and walked away. Should Adam follow? Before he could decide, the man had melted into the market crowd. Adam could only stare down the street. His hand was smarting now and bleeding freely. There were smears of blood on his coat. He fumbled in his coat pockets for his handkerchief and wrapped it around the wound. He needed something stronger than the coffee he had just drunk. That encounter had not been a coincidence. That shove had been deliberate. But how had his attacker known he was here? He must have been followed. He stood for a moment, staring down the street, half-expecting the stocky man to re-emerge.

The gloom of a winter afternoon was fast descending. There was little more he could achieve and Adam decided to return to the apartment. He tested his knee tentatively as he stepped back onto the cobbles of the square. It probably already needed surgery after a recent squash injury but, apart from a dull pain, it would hold for now. He would ice it when he got back.

"Shit," he said. He didn't need this. He was about to head away from the Place aux Herbes when he heard a voice calling to him from one of the few stalls that had not packed up for the day.

"*Monsieur*? Are you all right?" He stopped. His gaze followed the voice to a stand selling ceramic plates and bowls. It was overseen by a young woman with vivid, cropped red hair and a look of concern that reached her gentle blue eyes. After a morning where human kindness had been conspicuously lacking, it was welcome. He limped slightly as he approached the stall, clutching the bloodied handkerchief around his injured hand.

"*Merci*. I'll be OK. I'm just a bit shaken. Thank you for your concern."

"I have *un sparadrap*," she said, pointing to his hand. "Sorry, I do not know the correct word in English." She produced a plaster from a large bag. "Please. Come. Sit down." She gestured to a chair behind the stall and he was grateful to sink into it.

"My name is Vivienne. My husband is usually with me," she said, pointing at the second chair, "but he has had to leave early. Please have some coffee." She poured him a cup from a Thermos flask. "Perhaps you would like some brandy in it?"

"Thank you. Yes, I would, if you don't mind. It's been a bit of a day, so far." He hoped she understood the colloquialism, and she seemed to because she smiled. Adam applied the plaster to his hand and took a gulp of the strong coffee. The brandy warmed the back of his throat and he took a few more sips, allowing it to steady him. He asked about her business. She said that her ceramics were handmade by her, and she and her husband were regulars at the local markets.

"Do you know Jean… Jean Gilbert?" He showed her the now muddied business card. "The photographer, who also sells wine and olive oil. He had a stall over there today." Adam pointed to the now empty corner of the market.

"Only by sight, and to say hello to. My husband might know him better. Why?"

"It's just that I had a very odd encounter with him earlier, and I have a feeling he knows the man who just assaulted me."

"Oh? That is very strange." Vivienne's brow furrowed. Her concern and warmth encouraged Adam to open up about why he had come to Uzès. As he told her about his missing wife, she leant towards him and placed a hand on his arm. The simple gesture touched him. They talked for a while and, when Adam felt he had recovered, he thanked her again for her kindness and said he would be on his way home. Vivienne took his phone number and said she would call if she had any information.

Back in the apartment's warmth, Adam settled down with a glass of red wine and a painkiller. He phoned Caroline, a former work colleague, and a good friend, who had also owned the house where he and Maryanne had stayed two summers ago. Caroline lived and worked in London, but the house near Uzès was her countryside retreat. Since her divorce, a few years ago, she had spent more and more time in France. She had invited Adam to stay with her, but he hadn't wanted to be in a house that had unhappy memories. Anyway, he needed to be alone. He had promised to visit her, though, and they arranged to meet the next morning. Despite his reservations about the house, he knew he needed to, at least, see it again — briefly. It wouldn't be easy, but he might recall something he had missed at the time of Maryanne's disappearance. Everything had been a bit of a blur in the aftermath of that summer.

Later, Adam lay awake, bedside light on, for a long time. His knee and hand throbbed. His mind churned over the questions the day had thrown up. He was even more convinced that the postcard had come from Maryanne and that she must be alive. But why on earth would anyone be upset by his attempts to find her? It made no sense. It surely wasn't a coincidence that he had recognised the man who had barged into him. Where had he seen him before? Then there was the photographer...

Jean… His responses to questions about Maryanne did not add up. He had seemed on edge. A link between the two men at the market was possible. Then, there was the postcard itself. Was it meant to be a clue? Was the market scene significant, or was it the town, or even the time of year? Then, again, it could be something else. Adam had been struck by the photographer's scenes of the asylum in Saint-Rémy. Maryanne had been insistent on visiting Van Gogh's hospital, where there was a museum to the artist, but they hadn't made it there before she disappeared. It was a long shot but he might find something there. He would visit it soon.

Outside, across the road, the dim light of a streetlamp outlined a stocky man, huddled from the wind and rain in a thick coat and hood. His features were hidden in the yellow-orange half-light, but his head remained tilted up towards the lit apartment window, until it went dark. Sleep, when it eventually came to Adam, was fitful as the wind, which with each gust, threatened to tear the shutters from their hinges.

Chapter 2

Adam woke with a start as a bin blew over with a loud crash, its contents scattering. Tins rolled down the road. The commotion set off insistent barking from a dog. It was pitch dark, and the wind's force buffeted the building. His phone rang.

"Good grief!" Adam exclaimed, looking at his watch. It was only quarter past six. It had already been a disturbed night's sleep, with the rattling of the bedroom shutters. Sighing, he picked up his phone. The screen showed a local number.

"Hello?"

"*Bonjour Monsieur*." A man's voice.

"Hello?" He suddenly felt wary.

"Is that Monsieur Dawson?" The voice had a strong French accent.

"Yes. Hello. Yes, it is." He sat up. Outside, someone shouted at the barking dog. "Sorry. How can I help you?"

"Monsieur Dawson. This is Emile. I am the husband of Vivienne. You spoke to her yesterday... at the market in Uzès, *oui*?"

"Ah yes. Of course. She was very kind to me." Adam relaxed. "What can I do for you?"

"Vivienne told me you had been asking about *le* photographer. The one who sells his pictures in the markets, *oui*?"

"Yes, he sells his black and white photographs. Mainly of towns and buildings... and of churches."

"*Oui*. Yes. I know this man... well, I see him sometimes at the markets. Vivienne insisted I phone you before I leave for work this morning."

"That's very kind of you."

"*Pas de problème.* His name is Jean and I have only spoken to him a few times..."

"Yes. That is the man. His name is Jean... Jean Gilbert... but please go on." Adam was now fully awake.

"Of course. I haven't seen him for some time but recently... two weeks ago... he had a stand at our small market in Saint-Quentin... Saint-Quentin-la-Poterie. It is close. Nearby to Uzès. Then, last week, I saw him again, this time working in Saint-Rémy."

"Thank you, Emile. Do you know much about this Jean?"

"Ah. Well, only a little really. My friends at the markets have spoken of him, and of his brother. I understand they live near there." There was a pause. "My friend, I am afraid I have to leave now for the market in Beaucaire, but Vivienne has told me about your wife. I am so sorry to hear about your troubles and we both wondered if you would like to join us for lunch on Tuesday. We live in Saint-Quentin. I can then tell you what I know or have heard about this photographer."

"That's very kind. I'd love to."

"Good. Vivienne will be very happy. We will be there, at the market in Saint-Quentin on Tuesday morning. We always have a stall on market day. I understand you are in Uzès, so it is very close... ten minutes perhaps. The market is in the car park, right at the bottom of the village. You will find us. Normally in Saint-Quentin there are only a few stalls that sell ceramics."

"I will find you. See you then on Tuesday... and Emile, thank you. You have both been very kind to me."

*

Fallen branches and debris strewn along the rutted country lane slowed the car's progress. Frost glistened wetly on the hedgerows. When the house came into view, Adam was taken aback by how different the place looked in February, compared with his mid-summer stay more than two years ago. It was not just the bare trees. Winter had swathed the garden with a stark abandonment. Even the straggly clumps of snowdrops, huddled around the base of the fruit trees, were dying. A sense of decay cloaked the wind's destructive passage.

As he drove up the narrow drive, Caroline emerged from the house and waved enthusiastically. She was wearing jeans and a chunky green roll-neck sweater. He had known her for about fifteen years, ever since they had worked on a major infrastructure project together. Brought together by work, they had had a brief fling which had petered out when she moved to Scotland to work on another project. He remembered feeling a greater disappointment than he suspected she had at this outcome at the time. She was slim, of medium height, with shoulder-length brown hair gathered away from her face in a ponytail. Two years older than him, she was a very capable capital finance expert. He knew her to be fiercely loyal to her friends and they had always remained in touch, but their friendship had become harder to maintain after Adam had married Maryanne. Caroline had never really liked his wife. They were too different: Caroline's calm and pragmatic approach to life was at odds with Maryanne's more unworldly nature. They had clashed verbally on occasion. He suspected that Caroline viewed Maryanne as self-indulgent and irresponsible. She had hinted as much and, without being too blatant, tried to make Adam question whether it would be a good idea to marry a woman who had already abandoned him for someone else once before.

She greeted him warmly as he joined her on the terrace.

"Gosh, everything looks so different from when Maryanne and I stayed here that summer." He looked out on the frozen garden.

"Well, it would. And this year the *sangliers* have done a lot of damage to the grass, particularly around the trees over there." She pointed to an area that had been dug up recently.

Adam shuddered. "We had a run-in with one when we stayed here. I can't remember if I ever told you. It was the night before Maryanne vanished. We had had a barbecue... right here. We had just finished, and we were sitting at the table. Maryanne was on that side, nearest the driveway. It was late, but it was still very warm. All of a sudden there was a loud, deep growl and I saw the dark outline of a large animal in the driveway. I could even smell it. It had an awful odour. I'll never forget it."

"That sounds very much like a *sanglier*." She pointed to the hedgerow of oleander. "They come up from the water meadow and get through the fence. What happened after that?"

"It was terrifying. And it sounded aggressive. Maryanne almost vaulted the table in fright. Luckily, it was so startled by her that it just disappeared back into the night. I guess it was attracted by the smell of the barbecue, but we were shaken, I promise you."

"I can believe it."

"Can they be dangerous?"

"Well, you wouldn't want to take one on. I've seen some huge ones around here. Now, I'm more careful not to walk around outside the property at night. Some of the adult males can grow up to two hundred kilos and they do have razor-sharp tusks." She grimaced. "But they do have to eat and I would hate for all of them to be shot. Come on, let's go inside and get out of the cold."

Caroline poured them some coffee.

"You're limping. Are you hurt?"

He told her about his two encounters at the market, though he was economical with the truth when it came to the assault, describing it as an accident. He didn't want to worry her.

"So, in spite of being a bit battered and bruised, how are you, otherwise?"

"I'm OK. Not sure precisely what I am doing here, though." He pulled a face. "It doesn't help that it's freezing. I can't believe how cold and windy this part of France can get."

She laughed. "Well, it's not quite the Côte d'Azur but I like it. I was going to light a fire later. People who live here get used to the mistral and adapt. It's better, of course, to stay indoors while it blows. It should finish tomorrow, or possibly Tuesday, and then we'll get amazingly clear blue skies. It is almost worth the wait. You'll see."

"I hadn't bargained on arriving during the mistral. It wears you down a bit, doesn't it?"

"Yes… it can, I suppose. But there is a very positive side to it. It helps in creating the wonderful climate we normally have down here." She then added, "The fierce wind also clears the air. You'll see when it finishes. As you know, the resulting light was precisely why so many of the Impressionist painters were attracted to the area."

"Ah, I see. So, really, it's a good thing?"

"I know it doesn't feel like it now, but yes. It is also supposed to have health benefits. And then, on top of all that, it is claimed locally that the mistral improves the vines somehow to produce some of the best of the Côtes du Rhône wines. So, definitely not all bad."

"Well, I am all for that." He sipped his coffee. "I'm curious, though. Where does it get the name from?"

Caroline smiled. "When I first bought this place, after the shock of my first mistral, I read up on it so that I could learn to understand it, if not quite to love it like the locals." She chuckled. "Perhaps love is too strong. However, people here do treat it as being animate, almost human." He had forgotten how her whole face seemed to light up when she smiled. This time, though, he noticed the fine lines that traced from the corner of her green eyes.

"And the name?"

"Ah, yes. It comes from the word '*mistrau*', which in the local dialect — Occitan — means 'masterly'. That refers to its strength, which occurs when high atmospheric pressure in the north runs into a low-pressure system around the Bay of Biscay. The flow of the cold air gets stronger as it travels south. It is then compressed as it is funnelled between the Alps and the mountains to the north of us, the Cévennes. That's what creates the ferocious winds that you've felt these last few days. Usually, it gets up to about sixty kilometres an hour, but it can get up to three times that — the force of a hurricane. And that is when it becomes destructive."

"I can believe it." Adam smiled. He was familiar with Caroline's knowledgeable diatribes on a range of diverse subjects and was reminded what a good mind she had. Some of their past discussions had continued well into the night. He was glad, now, of her earthy, no-nonsense outlook and her wisdom, which went well beyond meteorological phenomena.

"Next time you drive through the countryside, look carefully at the old farmhouses… the *mas*… as you go past. Most are built facing south, with their backs firmly to the wind for protection from the mistral." She smiled. "Anyway, you're not here to talk about the weather."

"Well, it's hard to ignore at the moment. I was just thinking. Your description of the contrasting faces of the mistral does remind me of her… of Maryanne. On the bad days she was difficult to be with but also difficult to ignore. On her good days she was an absolute joy, and she filled my life with a similar light."

Caroline was silent for a while before asking him, "And, how's this search going?"

"It's a bit like hunting for a needle in a haystack, as you can imagine. I believe she is alive and I'm sure she contacted me for a reason."

"OK?" she sounded dubious.

"But that's it. Beyond that I don't really know what I'm meant to be looking for."

"I guess there's still no point in my asking whether it'll all be worth it." Adam had always been reluctant to talk much about Maryanne's disappearance and, knowing her friend, Caroline had deliberately never pushed him to open up.

"I don't know." His face sagged and his shoulders slumped. He looked defeated. "I still can't get it out of my head that it was something to do with me… that I wasn't good enough or I didn't protect her enough. Essentially, that I was the reason she left."

"Jesus. Don't even go there. You've always stood up

for her. Maryanne was often her own worst enemy."

"You're probably right, Caroline. But I do question whether I could have done things differently, which might have led to a different outcome. But who knows?"

"You know, I wouldn't be a friend if I didn't say this to you. I know her disappearance hit you hard. I remember how haunted you looked after she first went missing, but over the last year or so, your old sense of humour has started to come back. You'd almost become the person I first knew, all those years ago. Now... I don't know."

Adam looked at the floor. "I know where you're coming from, and you mean well. And I have always had this tendency to take things, including myself, much too seriously." He sighed, spreading his hands, "I need to do this. I feel she's around somewhere, nearby."

"Adam, of course I'll help in any way that I can."

"Thank you," was all he could say.

"And Abi? How is she?"

"Ah, Abi. She's fine. She's great, actually. Doing really well in her new job and I am, of course, immensely proud of her. But you probably hear from her as often as I do."

Abigail, Maryanne's daughter from an earlier relationship, lived in central London, not far from him, and each, in their own way, had helped the other through the aftermath of her mother's disappearance.

"She's a good kid... well... young woman now. It's funny how we get along so well, despite her..." Caroline didn't have to finish the sentence. "Anyway, I believe I owe her a phone call."

"Good. She would like that."

He paused. "Getting back to why I am here, I'd like to

have a look around your place, if you don't mind. I can't work things out in my mind and, you never know, it might just jog a memory."

"Of course. Help yourself."

"Thanks. I'm not sure I told you precisely what happened during our stay here, particularly in the days just before she vanished. The more I think about it, the more I believe that, somehow, these events were all linked. They might help you understand why I need to go through with this."

She smiled. "I know why you have to go through with this. You have always felt this responsibility for her. But, go ahead. We spoke a few times just after she vanished, but, of course, it was still very raw then. I know you found it difficult to talk much about it, so, no, I didn't know all the details. I thought Maryanne had disappeared after going for an early-morning walk along the lane outside?"

"Well, yes, and no. There was a lot I didn't piece together at the time and a great deal I don't know now, but it would really help to share it with someone I trust, even though I know your views on her."

"I'm happy to listen and I do really want to help you. I'm sorry I didn't really get on with your wife, but I don't want to see you suffer." She poured them some more coffee and sat back and patiently waited for him.

He frowned. "Now I look back, things started to go wrong when we visited the market, though, obviously, there had been a lot that was not right before that — I sort of half-knew and didn't understand. The holiday was intended to try to sort things out between us." Adam's grin was rueful. "That's why I went back to the market yesterday to find the photographer. Somehow, it all seemed to begin with our visit to his stand in the Place aux Herbes that Saturday. I thought he might be able to help, but he acted so strangely with me and I've no idea why. I know he's hiding something. He said he didn't recognise Maryanne, but I could tell he did."

"That's odd. So, what happened when you and Maryanne first met him?"

"Well, Maryanne spotted his stall — she was drawn to the street scenes in a lot of his photographs. They were good, evocative and he was clearly talented. The stallholder — his name was Jean — seemed pleasant enough. Taking pictures was his passion. He told Maryanne that they were mainly taken in and around Aix-en-Provence. He specialised in monochrome images, which were more evocative. He used a French word for this. He was good with us. Very patient. He said that the old part of the town still had 'so much soul and depth', which immediately intrigued Maryanne. She was particularly taken by images of churches — the one where Cezanne was baptised, if I remember correctly, and also the cathedral in Aix. She bought a couple and then got into a deep discussion about baroque architecture. Then they moved on to Provence's religious history. I confess I got a bit bored, and she suggested I take a walk around the rest of the market. She wanted to stay and chat. So, I wandered off. Also, there was something about her focus on the religious side that day that put me on edge. Religion, as you know, has always been part of her, but its importance to her, its intensity, went up and down. I've sometimes wondered if this impacted her illness, or whether it was a symptom. She had started having those mood swings of hers and I was worried that things were flaring up again. I'd asked her a couple of times in the weeks before the holiday whether she was taking her medication, but it didn't go down well."

"No, I'm sure it didn't. So, you were already worried about her?"

"Yes, but I didn't say anything to anyone. It would have felt disloyal. Anyway, when I got back to the restaurant where we said we'd meet, she was still deep in conversation with Jean. When she finally spotted me, she left, but not before, and I remember this distinctly, they exchanged *three* kisses.

Caroline snorted, "God, don't take too much notice of that. I'm always losing track of what's appropriate here."

"Over lunch, she was withdrawn and seemed distracted. I tried to lighten things by asking what they had been talking about. She said Jean had been inspiring. He knew a huge amount about the churches in the area. He'd also said his brother was a scholar of early Christianity across the south of France and it was all very fascinating..."

"So, this religious thing, this interest, was affecting her behaviour at the time?"

He nodded. "Yes, it really was." He frowned. "Apparently, they also shared a connection with a place... a coastal town in the Camargue where she stayed for a time, years ago. She spent a few months there with Abigail just after her mother died. She said it had been a strange time, but she told me she wanted to go back to visit the crypt of a saint in the cathedral in the town. Of course, we never got there."

"So, you think this Jean had a past connection with her?"

"It's hard to believe but yes... yes, I think I do. She had been in such a good mood when we set off for the market, I was beginning to think things might be OK between us. Then, after she met the photographer, she just withdrew. It felt that she wasn't really present. She spent a lot of time lost in her thoughts and I couldn't get much out of her. At the time she put it down to the heat. Then, the day before she disappeared, as I said, we went to watch the Tour de France pass through the town and I've got this idea that's where I met the guy who bumped into me yesterday. I recognised him from somewhere and now I'm fairly sure it was there. He was with a friend."

*

Adam was looking forward to the event. He had followed the race for as long as he could remember, but he had only seen it live once before. He had been an enthusiastic cyclist when he was younger. Nowadays, the congestion of London streets made cycling around the capital almost an extreme sport. The Tour de France stage would be winding its way along the back roads from Nîmes to Uzès, before turning back on itself and ending back in Nîmes. The town centre was buzzing with excited fans waiting for the arrival, but they had somehow managed to find a table at a small pavement café beside the route. Even in the dappled shade, the temperature had hit forty degrees by midday as the caravan of the Tour began its noisy procession through the cobbled streets. The caravan was the preamble, with the first of the cyclists due an hour later. The heat was overwhelming, as though a heavy woollen blanket had been pulled over them. Adam wondered about the wisdom of the walk they had planned the following day to the Pont du Gard to watch the start of the next stage.

As they waited for the cyclists to appear, a tall gaunt man in his late forties or early fifties, with a long greying beard, came over to their table and gestured a request to sit at their table. Adam had noticed him earlier, sitting on the stone steps behind them with another, more heavy-set, man. A large black dog on a lead lay on the cooling steps beside the shorter man. Adam had guessed they were homeless from their unkempt appearance. He wasn't thrilled at the idea of sharing the table, but indicated to the stranger that it was fine. Pulling up a chair, the man muttered something and disappeared into the bar behind them. Reappearing with two large glasses of beer he gave one to his friend on the steps, before returning to the table. Adam felt uncomfortable, and not just because of the sour aroma of unwashed clothes that the man brought with him. There was something unsettling about his manner. Maryanne didn't seem to mind, though, and the stranger sat next to her. After a while Adam noticed that the man was talking to her in a low voice. Adam's French was inferior to hers and he soon gave up trying to understand what was being said. The man spoke no English. If he had a name, he shared it only with Maryanne.

The volume of the excited race commentary increased, heralding the arrival of the cyclists, and he turned back to watch the race, thrilled at the prospect of watching the Tour. He was lost in the theatrics of the event: the build-up, the caravan, the anticipation of the race itself. The atmosphere, the sense of history and the hysterical French commentary electrified him. Two riders from the powerful Dutch cycling team, Jumbo Visma, had formed a small breakaway. Three minutes after they had passed, the crowd lining the street stood and roared as they identified the leading French rider, towards the front of the *peloton*. When the applause died down, he saw that the stranger was still talking to Maryanne. She had to lean in to listen above the din of the crowd and the PA system. Adam saw her nod occasionally and wondered what they could possibly have to talk about. Then, there was a sudden commotion from behind them as the large dog on the steps growled at a black-and-white terrier that had ventured too close. Its owner snatched up her dog and exchanged a few heated words with the man on the steps. As Adam turned back to watch the last few stragglers coming up past the flower shop on the corner, he saw the man pass Maryanne a slip of paper. Adam couldn't see what was written on it and turned back to the race. When the last rider had passed through, the clean-up of the streets began almost immediately. The heat had become overwhelming. As they got up from the table, Maryanne turned back to the man and said something Adam could not make out.

"Did you know them?" he said, as they walked away.

"Of course not. Good heavens." Adam was not convinced. He wanted to ask about the note but sensed that now was not a good time. He had been walking on eggshells with her a great deal recently — her behaviour had become more and more unpredictable.

"What on earth did you find in common to chat about?"

Maryanne shrugged. "Oh, nothing much. He asked if we were tourists and where we had come from. That sort of thing."

"Hm… OK." He was still far from convinced but knew there would be no point in persisting further. He had learnt to recognise when Maryanne was done with a conversation, but when a strange man hands your wife a note, it's not something you're going to ignore, he thought. He would ask again when things were better between them.

He didn't get the chance because the next morning she vanished.

*

"That note probably held a clue to what was going on, but I never found out what it said. I should have persisted," he said ruefully, running his hands through his hair. "Maryanne and I had been having problems, as I said — it's why we needed to get away and spend some time together, here at your place. It had all been looking promising, though she was still behaving oddly."

Caroline nodded, her expression sympathetic, but she remained silent, letting her friend talk.

"Of course, later on, things just became weirder—" He was interrupted by Caroline's phone ringing in the kitchen.

"I'm sorry, let me just see who this is." She left the room. On her return, she looked worried. "It's my mother. Adam, you remember meeting her at my place in London a few years ago? I apologise but I am going to need to take this. She's not been well recently—" She turned away to answer. "Hello Mum, is everything OK?" After a while, she turned back to Adam, hand over the phone, and said, "This is going to take some time. Mum had a bad fall the other day and she's struggling a bit. You mentioned you wanted to look around the house and garden. Why don't you go ahead and do that while I speak to her?"

Adam wandered through the house, remembering the few days they had stayed there. He went out onto the terrace, now covered in dead leaves from the vine. He still shuddered at the memory of the encounter with the wild boar and how shaken they were. Even now it still felt very real. He felt a sudden feeling of apprehension of being back, and he shook his head.

With the cold of the wind and the frozen ground crunching below his feet it was hard to imagine the fierce heat at that time. A large black crow flapped its wings noisily as it prepared to leave its night's refuge. The sudden sound intruded on the memory. He walked further into the lifeless garden and looked around. He was shivering and stamping his feet to get rid of the frost and grass. Something might come back to him later. When he went back inside to say goodbye to his friend, she was still on the phone, but was gazing out of the lounge window, looking thoughtful. Adam caught her eye and gave her a thumbs-up.

Caroline whispered, "Sorry about this. Let's meet up again in the next day or two. I'll give you a ring."

As he drove out of the property, he had an impulse to drive to the nearby Pont du Gard, rather than return to the quiet of the apartment. He had last visited the world-famous site some years before and, of course, their plans to revisit it two summers ago had been tragically dashed. Adam felt hungry and he looked at his watch. He remembered there was a restaurant on the Remoulins side of the Gardon river, overlooking the aqueduct. He would see if it was open.

When he arrived at the site, he was surprised that, despite the wind and freezing weather, there were quite a few visitors, including a number of large tour buses. He walked up the path from the car park and, suddenly, there was the amazing structure spanning the gorge over the river. The yellow stone of the Roman aqueduct making a striking contrast to the blue-green of the water below and the grey of the sky above.

After a warming lunch at Restaurant Les Terrasses, he walked down to where the river flowed strongly through the huge arches. Standing on the stones beside the water he looked up to the pedestrian walkway, where two more tiers towered high above. He felt very small and alone.

At the modern tourist centre, the museum was closed, but the gift shop and café were open. He bought a guidebook and, after ordering a hot chocolate, he removed his coat and settled down at a table in the corner.

His reading was interrupted by the sound of someone exiting the gift shop. He had only a glimpse of their back, but there was a sense of something familiar about the figure — was it the clothing or the way they had moved? Standing abruptly, he strode across to the café window as the man disappeared from view. By the time he had reached the door, the figure had vanished. All he could see was a young couple with two small children playing nearby and an attendant sweeping up the leaves that had blown into the museum entrance.

He must have been mistaken. He should not let his mind play tricks on him. He must focus. He returned to his seat in the nearly deserted café and tried to relax. It was starting to get dark when he finally emerged: most visitors had already left the site. By the time he reached his car, the icy raindrops were stinging his face. It would be good to get back to the apartment in Uzès, out of the incessant wind and the rain.

That night the disquiet that had not left him since he

had arrived, and which had increased each day, troubled him. Perhaps it was the mistral. Was it the constant howling of the wind, or perhaps the change in air pressure, that was making him jumpy? The mistral was reputed to have the ability to drive people mad. Adam felt uneasy and began to question what he was doing, and why. He finally fell into a disturbed sleep, only to wake from a nightmare, drenched in sweat. He lay there, with his heart racing. He and Maryanne had been running through a dark, dense forest, with a group of snarling *sangliers,* blood dripping from below their snouts, on their heels. The wind had whipped branches across their faces as they fought to keep ahead of the ferocious beasts. Just as the largest of the *sangliers*, a huge male, caught Maryanne, dragging her to the ground, he had woken up, her screams still ringing in his ears.

Chapter 3

The small hillside town of Saint-Quentin was a short drive through barren fields of darkened vines. High above, a lone buzzard circled the brown and lifeless countryside. He arrived to find just a dozen or so stands at the market, which occupied the covered parking area in the town centre. He looked around, cautiously. He wasn't expecting to find the photographer here, but he was wary after his confrontation with the man on the pavement. It didn't take long to see that there were no stalls selling pictures. Most seemed to be laden with fresh produce and the enticing aroma of roasting chestnuts drifted from an equally alluring open fire in one corner. A crowd had gathered around it. Adam immediately recognised Vivienne, her shock of short, bright-red hair singling her out. She and Emile looked to be in their early thirties. Her husband was slight, with a full dark moustache exaggerating his mournful expression. Taking off one brown woollen glove, he shook Adam's hand vigorously.

"*Bonjour. Bonjour, mon ami.* I think these temperatures have discouraged a few people. There have been very few sales, so we will be packing up soon. Then we can have lunch. Have you been to our little town before?"

"No, I haven't. It looks very pretty."

"*Oui. Bien sûr.* It is quite famous for its pottery, which of course explains the name. The town has about twenty-five *ateliers céramiques* which are normally open to the public. At the moment, perhaps ten or so are open, but we do also have a museum of pottery, as well as an art gallery, in the town. Why don't you have a look around and then come to our house? It is much too cold to be standing around outside here for long. Lunch will be quite simple, I'm afraid, but we would like to be able to help you in your search if we can."

Adam was moved by the generosity of these people that he barely knew. Vivienne told him how to find the house, so he set off up the hill on which the old town perched. Dotted among the stone buildings were others, walls painted in vibrant Provençal terracottas and pinks, bringing a welcome warmth to the winter day. He made his careful way through the narrow, cobbled streets, conscious of the stiffness he still felt in his knee. As the streets wound their way upwards, he passed ancient wooden doors and houses decorated with sculptures. Signs for pottery studios were everywhere. Despite the weather, and the season, a number of shops were open. Adam was content, though, to just browse the vibrant window displays as he wandered slowly through the maze of streets. Nearing the top of the hill, he came across a gated entrance to a courtyard and the museum. A glass-fronted gallery was currently hosting an exhibition of modern sculpture by local artists. There were only three other visitors. As ever with sculpture, it worried him that he was never really sure what he liked, or what qualities he was meant to appreciate. Much just left him baffled.

Vivienne and Emile's small, terraced house was on the corner of a narrow, tree-lined square. A pair of wooden benches sat back-to-back in the centre of the square. Next door to the house was a shop front displaying white ceramic plates and finely decorated bowls. At the rear of the shop was a little studio and Adam was impressed by the quality of the work he saw.

"Vivienne is the real artist," said Emile. "I do some of

the pottery, mainly the bowls and vases, but now I concentrate more on the marketing. And I do most of the selling at the markets. I enjoy getting out."

"Emile is being very modest about his abilities," said his wife. "He taught me everything."

"Ah, but very soon I could see how much better you were than me, *chérie*. Now, while I go off to the markets in the mornings, Vivienne works in the studio at the back. She also runs this shop. Saint-Quentin is well known to visitors and we have orders for our ceramics from all over the world."

Vivienne smiled and put her arm around Emile. "We do work very hard, but we make a good team. We have a nice life." She looked up fondly at her husband.

"Come, let's get warm next door and have something to eat," Emile said.

"This is so kind of you," Adam responded gratefully. In truth, he felt humbled by the quiet care, and kindness, this couple offered each other.

In keeping with the rest of the town, their two-storey house was more than two hundred years old. The small rooms were cosy and the dining room, at the rear of the house, overlooked a small courtyard garden surrounded by ancient stone walls. An open wood fire warmed the room. One of Vivienne's vibrant vases, brimming with early daffodils, sat at one end of the old oak dining table. Over *coq au vin* that Vivienne had prepared the night before, Emile said he understood that Adam was looking for his wife. That she had gone missing in the area some time ago.

"Yes, she disappeared while we were on holiday in Uzès, over two years ago. It still feels like a bad dream."

"I am so sorry." Emile's large brown eyes were filled

with sympathy. "I can imagine how you must have felt." There was a quiet sadness about the man, Adam thought.

"She vanished one morning. I thought she'd just gone out for a walk, but she never returned. The police could do nothing and now I believe she's still classified here as a 'missing person'. Neither I, nor any of her friends, have heard anything from her since, until I received a postcard with a picture of the fountain in the main square in Uzès. That's why I came back."

"So, you think she is still in the area?" Vivienne prompted.

"Yes, I have this sense that she is still around here... somewhere nearby. All I can do is try to locate anyone she spoke to just before she disappeared — they might know something and provide me with a lead."

"And Jean, the photographer, is someone who can help?"

"I thought so, but he said he did not remember her and became angry when I pressed him."

"All I know about him is that people think he is a bit odd," Emile replied. "Well, he has a brother who is definitely strange. The brother occasionally helps Jean out on the stand, but he is not popular among the other stallholders. They try to avoid them, particularly the brother. He is known to have a temper and sometimes he is very abrupt with the customers. Emile turned to Vivienne. "You did meet them once, here in Saint-Quentin."

"Yes, I do remember now, I felt very nervous around the brother. He has an unsettling look. I did not like him."

Emile nodded. "I do not know for definite, but I think the brothers may live together. They have a *domaine* somewhere towards Saint-Rémy. A *domaine* is really a

34

small farm," he told Adam. "I have heard they live quite like… how you say it… like hermits there?"

Continuing, Emile said that the photographer had stopped selling his pictures at the markets for a while. "Whether he had been away, I do not know but I heard from some of the other stallholders that the brother was unwell for a time. Perhaps Jean had to look after him. I believe the brother is also a priest and works for some church in the south, I think around Marseille. Perhaps that's where Jean had to go to."

"I wonder if that's why he takes a lot of photographs of churches?" Adam said he had one hanging on the wall of his bedroom at home.

Over coffee, Emile asked what he was now going to do next.

"Well… I think that Jean… Monsieur Gilbert… is due another visit from me. This time, at his home. I have the address of his *domaine*. You mentioned that there is a market tomorrow morning in Saint-Rémy, will you both be there?"

"Unfortunately, no. Not tomorrow." Emile smiled at his wife. "We have to go to the hospital in Nîmes. It is a just a routine appointment — a check-up — for Vivienne. We have just learnt that she is pregnant."

"That is wonderful news. Many congratulations."

"Thank you. As it is our first child, we are both nervous, as you can imagine… but we are also very excited."

Adam left them with the promise that he would keep in touch and drove back to Uzès. He was startled to find that, when he turned the key to the patio door at his apartment, it was unlocked. He remembered locking it that morning. He glanced up and down the street. There were no stocky figures lurking in the shadows outside, so he entered cautiously. A table lamp was glowing in the corner of the living room, and the apartment was warm.

"Hello, Adam. It is so good to see you."

He stumbled, startled. A figure, curled on the couch, turned towards him.

"Shit, I am so sorry I made you jump. I was waiting for you, and I think I must have dozed off in the warmth."

"Christ, why…? What on earth are you doing here?"

She sat up, shaking the off the rug. "It's a long story. I should have phoned you first. I did try last night after I had made my flight booking but your phone just rang."

"I saw I had a missed call, but I didn't recognise the number."

"Ah. I must have phoned on my work phone."

"How did you know where I was?"

"I heard you might be here, so I phoned Caroline. You know we've always got on well. I knew she was in Uzès so I figured she was likely to know where you were, if you were in France. She gave me directions to where you were staying."

Adam switched on another light, as he tried to make sense of this.

"Anyway. I was sitting outside on your patio waiting for you and it was starting to get dark and cold. I was about to drive down to Caroline's house when a kind neighbour noticed me. She had a key to the apartment for emergencies and took pity on me. To simplify things, I said I was your daughter. She let me in. Then I fell asleep in the warmth on your couch."

Adam winced as he sat down; his knee had stiffened after the climb through the little town. "Well, I suppose you'd better tell me why you're here."

"OK. Let me get us both a drink and I'll explain. I picked up a couple of bottles of red wine at the small supermarket in the town as I came through. Is that OK?"

Adam tried to think when he had last heard from Abigail. Perhaps three or four months ago. She reappeared with two large glasses of wine and sat back down on the couch, opposite him. He had always liked her. Circumstances had pulled them apart.

"Christ, you look like shit, you know that?" She was peering at him closely.

"Ah, thank you for that. I know and can explain… well, some of it… but I think you should go first."

"All right, I'll keep it as brief as possible. As you know, Mum and I have not seen eye to eye for years… maybe as far back as when I turned sixteen. The last time I saw her was when she came to see me in London just before I went to back to uni. It was about nine or ten months before she vanished, so that must be three years ago. We had a huge row and she stormed off."

"I remember. I also remember how upset and sorry she was. She wasn't herself at that time."

"Well, be that as it may, I've heard nothing from her since that row. Not one thing… until—"

"Neither has anyone else," he interrupted gently. "Well, not since she disappeared. But what are you doing here?"

"Caroline said you were here looking for Mum. She was worried about you. She thought you'd got your hopes up that she might be found."

Adam wondered how much he should tell Abi. "Just under two weeks ago, completely out of the blue, I got this postcard." Reaching across to his coat, he took it out and passed it to Abigail. "See, it was sent from Uzès. I know it's from her and I think it's meant to tell me something. Quite what, I'm still not sure."

Abigail studied the picture of the market scene, before turning the card over, carefully, as if it were delicate. A tear traced its way down her cheek and she wiped it away. Putting the postcard on the coffee table, she looked up at Adam, eyes brimming.

"You believe it's from her?"

Sounding more confident than he felt, he said, "I do. It's why I am here. She's around here somewhere."

"And if she is, do you think she wants to be found?"

"That I don't know. If the postcard's from her, she could just be telling me that she's alive, or perhaps just that she's OK. But I couldn't forgive myself if I didn't try to find her... if I hadn't tried to help when she needed me."

Getting to her feet, Abigail came across to Adam and hugged him tightly. "She doesn't deserve you," she said quietly, releasing him. "She never has."

The hug felt good. It was what he needed to keep positive. "Look, that's not true. There is an awful lot that you don't know... she kept a lot from you to protect you. But this is just something I have to do." Getting up to refill their glasses, he winced again as he stood.

"You're hurt. What happened?"

"It's nothing really. First, tell me why you are here, then I'll fill you in on things here." He handed her a glass of wine before lowering himself carefully into the armchair, waiting.

"OK. Well, I got a phone call on Sunday evening. The number was blocked. There was a silence and then I heard a strange voice. A male voice with a French accent. He asked if I was Abigail. I said I was and he then said he had someone who wanted to speak to me, and, I was to do what she said." She took a deep breath. "That's when Mum came on the phone. I am sure it was her." Tears started falling again. Adam didn't know what to say. Could it be true? His blood pounded in his head as he waited for her to continue.

"She called me Ab... and said how sorry she was... that she loved me and missed me. She asked me to forgive her..." Abigail broke off and looked into the distance, composing herself.

"She repeated it again... that she was sorry... for everything. I hadn't said anything at this stage. It's hard to describe, but she sounded calm and a bit distant, maybe a bit hesitant, as if someone was there with her and she had to be careful what she was saying. Anyway, she said she was OK, but that they just wanted to be left alone." She stopped for a moment before continuing, sounding hesitant. "I don't know how you will take this, but she asked me to tell you to leave her alone, to go back to England. To stop looking and to forget about her... and... and she also said she realised she could never return to her old life. Those were pretty much her exact words. I must say, I didn't really know what she meant by that. She asked if I understood and would I make sure I did that for her. She was quite deliberate about that. It struck me as strange and I... I just didn't know how to respond. There was then a bit of a silence. Oddly, in the silence I thought I could hear some distant bells. They were muffled but they didn't sound like bells you would hear in England. When I eventually felt I could talk, I asked her where she was. And, what was going on? The phone was taken away from Mum and the man came back on. He said her family needed to respect her wishes.

But it sounded more like a threat."

"I have to ask this, Abi, but are you sure it was her?"

Abigail paused. "Yes." After another silence, she said, "Yes... I am sure. Her words sounded a bit forced, as if someone was standing right next to her, right at her shoulder, but I recognised her voice."

Adam felt disoriented. There had been so little to go on, for so long. It had been hard to sustain hope. Could it really be true that she was alive? "Go on," he said eventually, barely able to breathe.

"Another thing. She called me Ab, not Abi or even Abigail — which was usually when she was cross with me. She hasn't done that — call me Ab — for years. She would only call me that when we were really close. I know it was her."

"I believe you. Are you sure that Maryanne actually said 'they', rather than 'I' on the call?"

"Yes, I am pretty sure that's what she said. I didn't ask her what that meant or who 'they' were. But she also said only that she was 'OK', not that she was happy. Even that didn't sound convincing, but I guess you never really know with Mum."

Adam thought for a moment. The postcard had not been a cruel trick. He felt his breathing returning. "So, she knew that I was over here... looking for her?"

"I suppose so. That's what I presumed, and why I phoned Caroline."

"And the man didn't introduce himself? Or give himself a name?"

"No. I'm sorry. I should have asked."

"You've done well, Abi. How are you feeling? Are you all right?"

"Yes, I am now. You know, my first thought after the

phone call was, 'Mum, what have you now got yourself involved in?' It was getting late, so I phoned Caroline the next morning... yesterday... and when she said she had arranged to see you I booked a flight to Montpellier as soon as possible. I had to speak to you. I realise I should've phoned you first... but I didn't want you talking me out of coming." She stopped to think, concern etched on her face. "I didn't want to upset or worry you needlessly. And I really wanted to speak to you face-to-face... to determine your reaction. I didn't know how you would feel... after all this time. Caroline kindly said I could stay with her while I am here."

"No, you must stay here. Please, there are plenty of bedrooms. One way or another, we are both in this together. And, besides, I'd quite like the company." He smiled.

"Thanks, Adam. I'd like that as well."

"How long will you be staying?"

"I've told work where I am going, saying it was a personal matter, and asked for some time off. I said I would probably be away for about ten days. I haven't booked a return flight yet. In any event, it's easy for me to work from home here. If you don't have wi-fi, I'm sure there's a café in the town."

"There's a good signal here. I made sure of that, so I could do the same while I'm here. I've booked the apartment for just over three months... to early June."

"Perfect. Although I suspect I'll need to be back in London in a couple of weeks. Now, old man, tell me what has happened to you."

He laughed. "Much less of the old, please... although I have felt better. That reminds me, I need to put some ice on my knee."

"Let me. You stay sitting down and I'll see what we have here."

Abi found some ice cubes and wrapped them in a tea towel. He stretched out his leg and held the ice against his still swollen knee and, in the warmth of the lounge, Adam explained everything that had happened since arriving in France. She listened intently, interrupting only to get more detail on the man who had barged him off the pavement earlier.

"And you are sure that it is the same man you saw two years ago?"

"Yes, I am pretty sure it was. He looked slightly different from when I saw him before. Then he looked scruffier… more down and out, but I am almost certain it's the same man."

"I don't think all these events are coincidence. And if they're not a coincidence, then I agree with you… they must be somehow linked to Mum's disappearance. And perhaps there is a connection between the man who attacked you and the photographer you saw earlier. Is it worth going to the police with this?"

He told her that, frustrating as it was, there was little point in going to the police at the moment: he had no concrete evidence, just a feeling that the photographer was somehow involved in the disappearance and that he might have met the man who had barged into him before.

She looked across to Adam. "Perhaps there is a connection, though, between these men. The one obvious thing is that they were both in the same town, at the same time."

"Yes, I was thinking the same thing."

"It would also seem that they, whoever 'they' are, know that you're searching for her. That's obviously why

I got the phone call on Sunday. You're starting to make them feel nervous."

"You say that, and over the past few days I have had this uneasy feeling that I'm being watched."

To hide her concern, she got up and opened the fridge, saying that she would make them something to eat. When they sat down to eat the omelette Abi had produced from the limited ingredients she had found, Adam gazed at her over the table. There was no mistaking the resemblance to her mother. She was not quite as tall as Maryanne, but no less striking, with long auburn hair that tumbled down past her shoulders. Before she began to eat, Abi had swept her hair behind her ears with both hands, in a gesture that still reminded him of his wife. Maryanne always did the same when she was serious or thoughtful. They shared the same laugh, too, but there the similarities ceased. Perhaps that was the reason the two women had clashed often, sometimes dramatically. Maryanne's emotions were huge and unpredictable. One moment she would be captivating, loving… full of life and positivity. The next she could be uncommunicative, sullen even, and was often wracked with self-doubt. Despite this, he had loved being with her: the good times had more than compensated for the bad. It was easy to fall for Maryanne. You became carried away by her vivacity and the excitement of living in the moment, but it had been exhausting. By contrast, Abigail was calmer, more focused and considerate of others. She placed large value on care, and on consistency, and would expect similar from others. Despite the unwillingness on the part of both women to accept and accommodate their differences, Adam had believed that a huge residue of love remained between them.

Abigail had lived with them for four or five years, before she went off to university. Apart from the rows with her mother, she had been easy to have around. Always diligent at school, she was also practical and helpful around the house. He had seen her occasionally since her falling-out with Maryanne, and she had stayed with him for a week after her mother disappeared.

"How is the job going?" he asked. Having graduated as a biologist the previous year, she was working as an environmental consultant with a prominent charity, before going on to do a doctorate.

"It's going well. I'm surprised at how much I'm enjoying it. I just need to decide on my thesis. I had been prevaricating, but then, just last week, there was some talk of a secondment to Geneva for six months, at the end of this year. It would also give me a chance to get away for a bit."

"Abi, that sounds wonderful. I'm so pleased for you. You've worked so hard."

"Thank you, Adam. You've always been supportive of me."

"That's been very easy to do," he assured her.

"Going back to the phone conversation with Mum, why do you think she phoned me and not you? If she was so concerned about you looking for her, why not phone you directly?"

"I was wondering that, too. She could have phoned me at any time over the past two years. Why send me a cryptic postcard, rather than just picking up the phone?"

"The postcard does sound just like Mum. I don't know why she never phoned you, though."

"She left her phone behind when she disappeared. I don't know if that was deliberate or not. I handed it in to the police at the time, but I don't know what they did with it… or even if they still have it. All I can think is that her access to a phone is controlled. You said you had the distinct feeling that when she phoned you someone was close by. Perhaps she's being closely watched… or maybe she really does want nothing to do with me. Perhaps she meant to leave me after all."

"I hate to say this Adam, and she is my mother, but we both know she has a long history of suddenly ending relationships. Christ, this wouldn't even be the first, or even the second, time that she has left you. Shit, I'm so sorry," she said, immediately realising what she had said.

"Don't worry. I know you're right. I had thought, though, that she was past that. That she had finally settled down. I thought I had actually helped her."

"I'm honestly not trying to be hurtful, but I had to live with the consequences of her erratic behaviour for pretty much my whole life. When she disappeared, I wasn't entirely surprised. At the time, I didn't really understand why you even bothered to look for her. Why you continued to hold out hope that you would find her, that she would come back to you."

"I loved her," he replied simply.

Chapter 4

Abigail stifled a yawn. Her eyes were drooping but it was late. Adam glanced at his watch and saw the time. "Gosh Abi, you must be exhausted. You must have been up most of the day. Go off to bed," he gently exhorted. "Take the bedroom at the back. I'll see you in the morning." She climbed the stairs gratefully but stopped halfway up.

"Oh, I forgot to tell you. When I spoke to Caroline on the phone, she said that your visit the other day had triggered a memory for her... something that happened shortly after Mum vanished. She thought it might be related. We're going into town tomorrow, why don't you come as well?"

Adam was tired also, but he was buoyed by Abigail's arrival. He poured himself another drink and sank into the armchair. What was it that Caroline had remembered? Sighing, he reached over to his coat on the chair next to him, and took from the pocket the photographs of Maryanne he had shown to the photographer. One had been taken on the Spanish Steps in Rome, a few years ago. It had been a cloudless spring day and she looked so happy... almost carefree. He loved this picture. Was it an accurate portrayal of her general state of mind? Probably not, he had to concede. She certainly hadn't been happy in their last year together.

Looking at the photographs brought home not just his sense of loss but his bafflement at what had happened. He had to know what happened... and why. He felt ashamed to realise that it had become easier to believe that she was no longer alive. He had almost come to accept that. Now, he didn't know. Could she really be alive? After all this time? He could not move on until he had these answers.

He took another sip of his drink and shook his head. What was it that had led them to this point? Was it something deep within her... or was it really him? Had he forced her away? If so, was there anything he could have done to change things? Or was he missing something else entirely? He felt all the old, familiar doubts begin to resurface and found himself, once again, thinking back to that last day. Just how many more times would he relive those hours?

*

After watching the Tour de France, they had made their slow way back, on foot, down the winding hill to Caroline's villa. The afternoon heat had radiated off the road and the surrounding cliffs and they were drenched and exhausted when they eventually returned. Maryanne said that she had a headache and would have a lie-down in the cool of the bedroom.

It had been well past midnight and they had finished eating more than an hour earlier. Both were now sitting companionably at the outside table. The heat was still unrelenting, bearing down on them, despite the hour. There was not even the hint of a cooling breeze.

The wood table was situated at the kitchen end of the vine-covered terrace that ran the length of the villa, close by the gravel driveway. Oleander bushes flanked the drive, separating the property from a water meadow, with the river and woodland beyond. The embers of the barbecue had almost cooled. Pausing in their conversation, they noticed how quiet the night was. Aside from an earlier cry from an owl, there had been no other sounds in the stillness of the night. They were sitting quietly, gazing out down the length of the darkened garden, when there was a sudden rustling within the nearby vegetation. It was quickly accompanied by two loud guttural growls close by. The stillness amplified the otherworldly sound and a large grey shape suddenly materialised from the bushes onto the drive beside them. Maryanne screamed and leapt up, nearly turning the table over in her terror. An almost empty wine bottle toppled and rolled off the edge, crashing to the concrete floor. Adam grabbed Maryanne and held her close, protecting and calming her. There was another, higher pitched, grunt and then a crashing through the undergrowth, then silence.

"It's probably a wild boar. Your scream must have startled it. Come, sit down here on the other side of me."

"God, that frightened me," she said. "It was really close. It just came from nowhere. Do you think it has gone?" He was surprised at how shaken she was.

"I think it has. I'm sure it has left. It's probably all the way back in the woods where it lives."

"It was so close I could even smell it."

He could feel her heart pounding against his chest. "You know, it was probably as startled as we were. It won't be back." He tried to sound reassuring although he also had been alarmed. The shape had been huge — much bigger than he had expected. And there was also the powerful smell. It was of something rancid and primeval. He didn't feel up to checking the garden at that moment. "It was probably attracted by the smell of the barbecue."

They both sat down shakily. "We are in the countryside here," he continued. "The locals hunt the wild boars with dogs and guns. I know they are meant to be quite dangerous, but I suspect it was more scared of us. Come on, try to relax. It's gone. Let me clear up the glass off the floor and get you another glass of wine. Or perhaps a coffee?"

Maryanne shook her head, trying to smile. "No, I don't think I can relax now and I really don't need anything more to drink. Rather, give me a hand to take everything inside. I'll just tidy up a bit in the kitchen and then I'll join you upstairs."

Once Adam had helped clear up, he said, "OK. If you are sure you're alright. I'll see you upstairs." As he turned to go, he reminded her, "Don't forget to close up down here."

"No, I won't. I'm just going to sit for a moment when I've finished here." She still looked shaky.

"OK. If you are sure you will be alright?"

Maryanne didn't reply immediately. Eventually she nodded her agreement. "I will be."

Adam started to climb the stairs. "Good. See you in a bit. Don't stay too long" he added.

Lying down in the cool of the bedroom, he quickly surrendered to his weariness, as well as the effects of the alcohol, and was fast asleep within seconds.

The morning was etched in Adam's memory. Reliving it was still painful. It was the stuff of bad dreams.

Awakening with a heavy head, he had turned over slowly to lie on his back. The ceiling fan was still whirring, but it was the heat of the morning that penetrated his consciousness. Feeling groggily for Maryanne beside him, he had been surprised to find that she was already up. The heat must have woken her. She must be downstairs. He had lain quietly for a moment, taking stock. Had he really drunk that much the night before? They needed to try to cut down. He glanced at his watch; it was still quite early. Adam was tempted to turn over and go back to sleep. There was plenty of time to get down to the Pont du Gard for the start of the next stage of the race. If only his head would stop pounding. He thought of calling out for Maryanne downstairs to bring him some painkillers, but his head was too sore. He had to lie still for a bit until he could summon the energy to attempt to stand up. He really didn't feel well.

Ten minutes later, he navigated the stone stairs with care and went into the kitchen. Everything was spotless. There was no evidence of the debris from the night before. Pouring himself a glass of water from the tap, he turned, noticing that the door to the patio was open. Maryanne must be sitting outside, and he called out, "Do you have any paracetamol with you?" There was no response. Puzzled, he went out and looked around. No sign of her. He peered down the garden. She might be picking more berries from the fruit trees at the bottom of the garden, so he sat outside at the wooden table on the terrace and waited for her. When she didn't appear, he assumed she had gone for a walk. She had had difficulties sleeping for as long as he had known her and was often an early riser.

Inside, her mobile phone sat on the kitchen counter, still on its charger. Adam forced himself to have a lukewarm shower and, once shaved and dressed, called her name again. They were going to be late for the build-up to the race. There was still no sign of her downstairs and the first doubts nagged away in his mind. He had to go and find her.

It still had that early morning feel as he walked down

the driveway. The birds were already in full song, although it was too early for the cicadas to begin their insistent hum. Despite the hour, it already felt that the temperature would be a few degrees cooler than the inferno of the past few days. At the end, he turned onto the narrow country lane, away from the main road that led into town. Maryanne was more likely to have chosen to walk in the peace of the countryside. There were few other houses around and the lane skirted a wooded area.

After about twenty minutes, there was no sign of her. They were now in danger of being late. He turned back. Maryanne must have taken the other way after all.

She wasn't back at the villa. He thought he would phone her, only to remember that she had left her phone behind. She could be so irritating sometimes. Surely, she had not forgotten the race today, although it wouldn't be the first time. An hour later, his annoyance had turned to worry. There was now no hope of getting to the Tour stage on time. Had something happened to her? There was no sign of anything in the kitchen. Looking about him everything from the night before had been washed and put away neatly. Adam now regretted his actions in not waiting for her to finish before they both went to bed. He got in the car and retraced his earlier route up the lane. Still no sign of Maryanne. Turning around at the dead end, some two or three kilometres from the house, he drove up the winding main road to Uzès, expecting to see her around each corner. The place was starting to get busy and he did one circuit of the road through the town centre before returning.

There was nothing else to do but wait for her to come back. He checked his phone. There were no calls. He phoned a good friend of Maryanne's who said that she had not heard from her for over a week.

Adam waited for most of the day. Tired of pacing around the house, and unable to distract himself, he made another trip to town, leaving her a note on the kitchen door in case she returned whilst he was out. He parked and wandered the town blindly, hoping somehow to find her ambling around the narrow streets or even sitting at a café. She could be unpredictable.

There were no calls to her mobile, so that evening he phoned some of her friends, as well as mutual friends back home. No-one had heard from Maryanne for days. It was time to report her disappearance to the Uzès police. Her passport and clothes were still at the house. The police were polite. They took her details and a copy of her passport, but said, beyond circulating the information to regional and national police, there was little else they could do. Could she be considered a vulnerable person, they enquired. Adam thought about this, then shook his head. "No," he replied. He did not believe so.

The police then asked how long he and Maryanne had been married and, if perhaps, there had been a row between the two of them — they suggested sympathetically that these things happen all the time. Had anything been troubling her recently? Was there anything at all odd about her behaviour in the previous few days? Again, Adam thought about this before replying. They had their ups and downs much like other couples, married or not. He felt, though, the police's level of interest waning. He suggested she might have got lost on her walk. She could have fallen down one of the many ravines that he passed on the way into Uzès. After all, she had not taken her phone or any clothes. Could the police search the area? She couldn't just disappear. They were sympathetic but said it wasn't practical. The countryside was wild and it would be almost impossible to find anyone. Alas, they did not have the manpower for such a search.

As a last resort, he told them about the incident with the wild boar. Was it possible that Maryanne had gone for a walk and been attacked by one of these creatures? They shrugged. *"Bien sûr."* *Sangliers* were large and dangerous and people who lived in the area knew to avoid them, particularly at night. There were a lot of them around at the moment and, yes, they had been known to attack humans, mainly when they were injured or cornered, but it was unlikely. The police reassured him that it was likely that Maryanne would turn up over the next few days. They were polite but firm. He should just stay at home and wait for her to contact him.

That was over two years ago.

*

"Have you ever been here… to Uzès, or this part of France?" Adam and Abi were on their way into the town centre to meet Caroline. The rain of the last few days had petered out and clear sky outlined the grey scudding clouds. The cold wind remained. A smell of decay and dampness lingered around the narrow streets of the town.

"I don't think so. Caroline did invite me a year ago, but I couldn't make it then. I was in the South of France when I was young with Mum, though. It can't have been too far from here because we flew into Montpellier. Mum took me around the region. I remember Avignon and Arles, but I don't think we came here. Why? Is it nice?"

"You will see shortly. It is very old. Actually, I am sure you will like it."

"Good." She took in the narrow street of stone houses with olive-green shutters.

"I have a book on the town back at the apartment. And there is a very good tourist office here, just at the end of this road. But I am happy to show you around the town myself."

"That would be great. I'd like that."

He turned to her. "Abi, you know... it is very kind of you to come out here."

"I was worried about you. I wasn't sure if you really knew what you might be getting yourself into. I came for you as much as anything."

"Thank you. And you're right, Abi, I'm not sure I have much idea what's going on but I'm glad you are here." He squeezed her hand. They walked on. "With everything else I forgot to ask yesterday, how's it going with... is it James?"

"Oh, that finished some time ago."

"I am sorry. I didn't know."

"It's not a problem." She shrugged "We just wanted different things. But there were no hard feelings. We still see each other from time to time. In fact, he gave me a lift to Gatwick yesterday."

"And is there anyone else? I don't wish to pry."

"No, there isn't," she laughed. "And you are not prying. Anyway, you are family. I am just concentrating on work for the moment."

They passed an old lady on her way from the shops. She was struggling to control her young Jack Russell as its lead became entangled around a lamppost. Abigail bent down to help the woman free the trapped dog. As she handed the wriggling animal back to its grateful owner she received a frantic lick from the puppy as a reward, and a grateful, "*Merci, mademoiselle*" from its owner.

Crossing Rue Gambetta, its one-way system teeming with morning traffic, they continued up the narrow street to the central square. Caroline was sitting at an outside café, among a handful of other customers, in a corner of Place aux Herbes. Her face was turned to the weak morning sun that filtered through the plane trees. She wore a fleece, and a rug was spread across her lap. The two women greeted each other warmly. Their relationship had always been a source of surprise to Adam. Despite everything — their difference in age, Caroline's inability to disguise her enmity for Maryanne — there seemed to be a genuine bond between them. He gave them time to catch up while he checked his phone for emails and gazed out across the quiet square. In summer, it would be heaving with tourists. Today, despite the sunshine and the hour, most restaurants and shops were firmly closed.

The coffees arrived and the women paused their conversation. They seemed surprised to see Adam was still there. He smiled and looked at Caroline.

"How is your mother?"

She sighed. "Not great. She's got to an age where she is not really coping with everyday things and I'm not sure what we do next. I am going to have to go back to the UK in a week or so and try to sort something out. Perhaps it is time for her to move out of her house and into something more suitable."

"I'm sorry. I remember how determined she was to get on with her life after your dad died."

"I know. She has suddenly started struggling. The fall has rocked her confidence."

Abigail placed a hand on her friend's arm. "Please let

me know what I can do to help when I'm back in the UK."

"I will, thank you. But now you are here to support Adam," Caroline replied. "Let me know how I might help you both whilst I am here."

"Sure. Thanks, we will. On the flight over, I was thinking it through and I've this feeling that, once again, Mum might have got caught up in something that's out of her control. A bit like when I was a kid in Ireland, with some of the people that drifted in and out of the old Dublin house." She sighed. "I'd thought this was all well in her past," and looked across at Adam for acknowledgement. He didn't respond but he sat up and focused carefully on her words. "I never got used to it when I was young and, at the time, I didn't understand why Mum put up with it. I know now that it probably gave her some sense of purpose or belonging... outside of our normal life. But, if I'm honest, I found most of the people a bit creepy."

"That must have been hard for you."

Abigail pushed her empty cup away. "Most, not all, but most of our arguments were really centred around all of this. I'd get worried about her. Normally I could tell the signs. She'd start to look lost. Then she would say she'd expected more from life... that sort of thing. She would then get more self-absorbed. It wasn't that she was necessarily unhappy... she would just decide to go off into her own world." She looked skyward. "That was part of what our last row was about."

"Maryanne was inclined to be self-absorbed." Caroline frowned. Adam shot her a warning look. "I just feel that she should have focused more on those around her, the ones who actually loved her."

Adam shifted his chair. "I understand where you are

coming from Abi. Certainly, she'd become more distant, and I think more secretive, before she disappeared. But I'd got used to that side of her personality and I really believed that she'd put all of this behind her." He looked uncomfortable. "She never really talked about all that stuff — well not to me."

Caroline started, "After you came round on Sunday, I remembered something strange that happened at the house. Just a few months after Maryanne disappeared…"

Adam was willing to hear anything that might shed light on the disappearance. "Carry on. Please. I… we've so little to go on at the moment."

"OK. I'll tell you." A waitress passed their table and they asked for more drinks. Caroline took a deep breath. "It was autumn, possibly October, or early November. I do remember it being quite misty. Anyway, I came down one morning and there were these two strange men just wandering around outside, in the garden. I went out to ask what they thought they were doing. They were quite rough looking; one looked around his late forties, the other in his fifties, I'd guess. The older one was stocky and quite muscular. He had a dog on a lead, a big black thing. The younger one was thinner, taller. It might have been my French, but they didn't respond to my questions. They just looked at me. They weren't scared and didn't seem that surprised to see me. They didn't seem inclined to leave either and, if anything, were a bit threatening."

"God, what did you do?" Abigail's eyes widened.

"Well, I didn't have my phone on me, so I told them to leave. I pointed towards the gate. They just ignored me and continued to look around, muttering between themselves. As you know Adam, there's often no-one staying there. Anyway, I became quite nervous and went inside to call the police. When I came back out, they'd disappeared. I've never seen them since, but it was unsettling at the time. The police came but found nothing. They suggested that I keep the gate locked if I was worried." She laughed. "I am sure it's just a coincidence and has nothing to do with Maryanne."

Adam wasn't quite so sure. He recalled that, on the day they had watched the Tour, the stranger who had started up a conversation with Maryanne had a friend with a large dog. They were sitting on the steps of a building behind them.

"Can you remember what type of dog they had with them?"

She thought for a while. "I think it was quite big, and dark — like one of the street dogs you see around here. I don't know much about dogs, but I think it had some Rottweiler in it. Why?"

"I just might have seen them, and their dog, in Uzès. I told you what happened when we went to watch the Tour de France. The man who joined us at our table, had a friend who had a black dog. It was large. At the time I thought the men might be homeless."

"Yes, I remember. Perhaps it was that that jogged my memory."

"What on earth would they be doing at your house, though?"

Caroline shrugged. "I haven't a clue. But it was unnerving. I make sure my gates are kept shut now."

Adam and Abigail looked pensive.

"I guess the point is… what are you both intending to do now?" Caroline fixed her gaze on them.

"I will continue to look for Maryanne — now with Abi's help." He turned to Abigail for confirmation.

"Despite the fact that she has asked to be left alone, particularly by you?" she asked.

Sighing, he ran his fingers through his hair before replying "I know, I understand that. And I would respect her request if I believed it. Despite everything, I still feel a responsibility for her. For the last two years, I have felt that I somehow failed her: I could have looked after her so much better. I know her strengths, and how resilient she can often be. But I should have been more attuned to her weaknesses. If something was going on, then I should have spotted it. I should have helped her more."

"If something has happened, there would've been nothing that you could have done about it. Just look at her history." Abigail's voice was soft. "It was always difficult to change her mind once she'd decided on something."

"That is true," he had to acknowledge. "But I need to do something. Doing nothing would be much worse: it would feel like I was giving up on her."

Aware that both their eyes were on him, Adam called for the bill and suggested they take a stroll to enjoy what sunshine there was, and to show Abigail around the town. Abigail reminded Adam that she wanted to buy some groceries for the apartment.

"No problem," Caroline informed them. "I can incorporate the local *Petit Casino* in our walk. It should be open."

"Why don't you come back to the apartment with us, Caroline? I will get some things for a light lunch," Abigail said.

"This all looks delightful." Caroline gestured to the spread of two local cheeses, a creamy Bleu de Mazon and a Pélardon des Cévennes, a crisp salad, some early-season asparagus, a black-truffle pate a local *saucisson,* and fresh baguettes. As they tucked in, Adam said he wanted to drive to Saint-Rémy to visit the mental asylum that Vincent Van Gogh had been treated in before his death. Something about Maryanne's reaction to a Van Gogh exhibition they had attended nearby had triggered a thought. More urgently, though, they would pay the photographer a visit to his studio on the way there. He took out the business card, still stained with traces of mud and dried blood. "He lives in a town called Châteaurenard. I assume it's near Avignon."

"I've actually been there!" exclaimed Caroline. She sat up straighter. "It's somewhere off the main road from Avignon. The town's actually quite picturesque — its sits below a hill dominated by a ruined castle. The castle was pretty much destroyed by local villagers during the French Revolution, leaving not much more than a couple of high towers still standing. If I remember correctly, the last pope of Avignon stayed there."

"What if the photographer is there?" asked Abigail, her brow furrowing.

Adam fetched another bottle of wine from the fridge. "We just say that we're visiting his studio. That we're interested in his pictures. I am sure he'll recognise me from the other day, but we just need enough time to have a look around. I know he's lying about Maryanne. I'm certain he remembers her and I have this feeling that he knows something about where she might be now. I'm not sure what to look for but there must be some clues — maybe enough to then go to the police, if they'll listen. You never know, perhaps she's even there, at the farm, being held against her will."

Caroline offered to accompany them. "My French is

better than either of yours. Abigail and I can somehow divert his attention while you look around. Is it just a studio or does he live there as well?"

"The address on the card calls it a *domaine,* so I presume it's like a small farm. Well, something big enough to have a small vineyard and some olive trees. Maybe you could get him away from the studio. Say you are interested in buying some of his wine. Maybe even ask to see the vineyard, although there won't be much to see apart from dead-looking vines."

"Do you know if he has a wife, or perhaps some children around?" Caroline seemed to be enjoying the whole idea.

"I know very little about him. I think someone did mention a brother, though."

Abigail looked pensive. "You know, if I hear his voice, I might be able to tell you whether it was the same man on the phone the other night. His voice was quite distinctive."

"Great idea. Then we'd also know that Maryanne is somewhere nearby." Adam was suddenly animated.

Abigail cleared away the lunch and brought out the *tarte citron* that Caroline had picked up from the *patisserie* to finish the lunch. "More wine? Or would you like some coffee with this?"

Caroline said she would give both a miss. She wanted to get home whilst there was still some light, but she would see them tomorrow, bright and early.

After seeing Caroline out, Adam sat down again at the dining room table. Abigail said that she had been thinking about their visit to Jean Gilbert.

"As Caroline's now coming with us, why don't you stay out of sight when we arrive? Let Caroline and I deal with him. We can make out that we were just passing. Perhaps we can say we were looking for some wine or some olive oil, but we'll also keep our eyes open for anything unusual."

"OK. That might work. I'll hide in the back of the car until you and Caroline have got him away from his studio. If he is there, just promise me, that if he starts getting at all suspicious, you'll get back to the car and we'll just leave. I don't want to put either of you in danger."

"We will do. Strangely, I'm looking forward to it." Abigail looked thoughtful, then she smiled. "At least we'll be doing something positive."

"I agree, though it might be a dead end."

"What did you mean earlier when you said that Van Gogh had triggered a memory? You said it had something to do with a hospital."

"I did, didn't I? It's to do with an exhibition we went to, just before Maryanne disappeared." He screwed up his eyes in frustration. "I don't know. It's all rather hazy but it might be relevant. The hospital's not far from the photographer's studio." He sighed. "I think I need to pay it a visit."

Chapter 5

They found the entrance to *Domaine des Oliviers* down a quiet rural road, just off the Chemin des Lonnes, as they approached Châteaurenard. Caroline's hire car did not come with satnav and resorting to old-fashioned navigation methods resulted in a number of wrong turns. Eventually a sign, beside a dilapidated farm stall, still advertising last year's *cerises* and *fraises fraîches*, confirmed that they were indeed entering the outskirts of the town.

It didn't look promising. There were few dwellings along the long, winding lane, and most were crumbling inexorably into the countryside. The land mainly comprised empty farmland, with the occasional field of hard-pruned darkened vines, olive trees and bare fruit trees. They drove slowly, examining each track and entrance for signs of the *domaine*.

"There." Abigail, in the front passenger seat, pointed to the left. A faded sign on an old iron gate depicted an olive tree. *Oliviers Vignoble* was painted in black below it. There was no mention of *la photographie*, nor the name of the property owner. From the back seat, Adam looked down at the photographer's business card.

"This must be the place," he said, slightly doubtfully. "We're on the right road and the sign is of an olive tree."

Caroline pulled up onto the grass verge and Adam got out of the car to examine the entrance. The ground was spongy underfoot with the rain of the past few days. Rusted barbed wire was strung across the top of the closed gate. It had also been used to reinforce the fence that surrounded the property. The gate was secured to the rust-stained gatepost with a sturdy padlocked chain. A notice, scrawled on cardboard, said the property was '*Fermé. Ouvert le vendredi.*' He hadn't expected this. They had been focused on what they would do and say once inside the property. Unsure of what to do, he reached through the gate to test whether the lock was secure. A large black dog, alerted by the sound of the chain clattering against the metal gate frame, appeared from the side of the rutted gravel driveway that led to a barn.

"Shit!" Adam pulled his hand back from the gate, as the snarling dog threw itself at him. He was glad that he was on the right side of the fence.

Adam retreated to the car and got in. "That bloody dog is definitely not friendly. It looks like there's no one at home. The dog is there for a purpose."

Abigail turned to him. "Perhaps your photographer is away at another market," she replied. "It looks pretty shut."

"Let's just wait and see if anyone comes out to investigate all the noise. There's what looks like a barn fifty yards up the drive, but I didn't see any movement anywhere. If there is anyone around, the bloody dog will surely have alerted them."

The dog kept up its urgent barking, directed now towards the parked car. Caroline said, "You know I mentioned those suspicious characters on my property. Well, that dog looks like the one they had with them."

"That's interesting." Adam looked at the dog. Was it the same one he had seen that day in Uzès? He couldn't be sure. It was about the same size, certainly.

"I wonder…" He was interrupted by the sight of a man at the gate, shouting at the dog to stop its barking. The man, hair unkempt and dressed in shabby dungarees under a dark green weatherproof jacket, leaned on the gate examining the car. Adam was confident he had not seen him before.

"Let me go and have a word with him." Caroline opened the car door. As she approached the gate, the dog barked furiously.

"Arrête!" The man held up his hand up to the dog. The barking was replaced by a low whine.

Abigail and Adam heard Caroline greet the man in French. He gripped the dog by its collar and replied in a low voice. The conversation seemed amicable, although they could only make out fragments of what was being said. At some stage, the man turned back to point at a grey farmhouse they could now just make out in the distance, down a gravel driveway past the barn. They continued talking for a while, then Caroline returned to the car.

"It is the right place: the owner is a photographer and his studio is up there in the farmhouse. You can see just a corner of it up the driveway. The man at the gate is a sort of farm manager who looks after the grounds."

"Did he say who lived on the property? If there was there a woman there?" Adam leant towards Caroline.

"No, he didn't mention a woman. He did tell me though, that the photographer lives there, sometimes with his brother. If I understood him correctly, the brothers inherited the farm and vineyard from their father, who died some years ago. He himself has worked here for more than twenty years. Anyway, it seems our guy was called away this morning, on some urgent business. He'll be back on Friday."

As they drove away, Adam looked out of the rear

window. The man was still watching them from the gate. "All that barbed wire. I wonder why it's needed if the place only sells prints and the occasional bottle of wine or olive oil. It doesn't make sense."

"I know. I thought that," Abigail said. She looked pensive. "And the dog looks like part of the security. I wonder what they're protecting?"

"Or indeed, what they're hiding. Are we OK to come on Friday? I've a strange feeling about this place: that we'll find something if we can somehow get inside the property."

"I did tell the man that we might try again," Caroline confirmed.

"That's a good idea. Hopefully, the photographer will be here then."

The car's occupants lapsed into silence, each with their own thoughts. After a while, Caroline looked in the rear-view mirror. "Now, where do you want to go to?"

"You need to get back onto the Avignon road." Adam looked at the map. "Turn left when you get there and head for Eyragues." He spelt out the name of the town carefully. "Then, take the sign for Saint-Rémy. The Saint-Paul hospital should then be signposted."

"What are we meant to be looking for when we get there?" asked Abigail.

"Well, the hospital is a mental asylum where Vincent Van Gogh spent a year as a patient, just before his death. A few days before your mother disappeared, we visited a sound and light exhibition about Van Gogh in an old limestone quarry in a gorge just below Les Baux-de-Provence. I've been desperately trying to remember that day and some of it has come back to me. Huge images of Van Gogh's paintings were projected onto the high walls, ceilings and even the floor of the quarry, to the accompaniment of jazz and classical music. Many of the projections were animated, some with twinkling stars or fields of corn that swayed gently in the breeze. It was amazing."

"I went to a similar exhibition in London a couple of months ago!" Caroline exclaimed.

"Halfway through the exhibition, I lost her. It was quite dark, and she must have just wandered off. It was impossible to make her out in the kaleidoscope of constantly shifting images. I admit, I panicked until I found her, towards the end of the show, just when the exhibition was showing pictures of Van Gogh in in his last years in the Saint-Rémy sanitorium.

Adam gazed out of the window at the passing countryside. "She was sitting, alone, transfixed by the projection of an old black-and-white photograph of the artist who was standing and staring, looking out from his hospital room. The window had bars across, with what little light there was filtering through. It was very atmospheric. It was such a sad photograph, with the iron bars casting this shadow across his face and tunic. Maryanne was there, on her own… crying. The photograph made the room look like a cell. I recall I sat down next to her. All I could hear her say over the music was that it had reminded her of something, something in her past that had affected her. I felt her trembling. I thought at first she was cold — it was chilly inside the quarry — but it was something else. I put my arms around her and held her for a while. Then, when we left, she was insistent that we come back and visit the sanitorium."

"Poor Mum," said Abigail softly. Her eyes glistened.

"What do you think was going on with her?" asked

Caroline.

"Heavens knows." He shrugged, scratching his head. "I've thought about that. Perhaps something happened to her, something very personal in her past. Or, that she identified with Van Gogh's mental health problems. Deep down I suspect his feelings of isolation and sadness did have a resonance with parts of her own life."

Abigail nodded in understanding. "I think you're right."

"All I'm hoping is that by visiting the hospital, I can get some insight into what she was going through at that moment in the exhibition. Some clue to what had upset her so much. Maybe it was something in the room itself." He shrugged again. "Perhaps all Van Gogh really saw through his window was the lack of hope."

*

The sun had come out, brightening the contrasting landscape. Even so, the sign for the Saint-Paul-de-Mausole hospital, now unsurprisingly renamed *Clinique Van Gogh*, was easy to miss. Passing a sign for the quaintly named Parc D'Amour, they realised they had gone too far. Turning around, they retraced their route until they saw a faded red sign for the clinic. They pulled into the gently curving road that ran through the park. The road was bordered by towering cypresses that fringed groves of olive trees. Mont Gaussier, part of the ragged black Alpilles range, rose beyond the rock-strewn fields and trees. At the end of the road, the grey outline of the high forbidding walls of the hospital finally appeared. Parking, they paid for their admission and walked down the long gravel entrance towards a small chapel. On their right was a high wall separating that part of the hospital still functioning as a psychiatric clinic. They could hear distant voices and laughter emanating faintly from the hospital grounds, carried on the breeze.

They entered a draughty stone hallway leading to a cloistered internal garden, open to the elements above. Entering the small gift shop, they asked the way to the museum. Looking up from a magazine the woman at the counter pointed. They went through a doorway and up a set of ancient worn stone steps, clearly part of the original monastery. At the top, they entered the museum. To the left was a display of old photographs of Van Gogh's stay at the hospital. Glass cabinets on the other side contained a range of medical instruments in use at that time. Large boards mounted on two walls provided descriptions, in both French and English, of conditions in the hospital during the late 19th century.

Caroline was drawn to one of the wall displays describing the artist's life before he arrived at the clinic. Reading from the description she said, "It seems that, after he cut off part of his ear, he was hospitalised in Arles. On his release from hospital, he returned to the famous Yellow House in Arles, where, you probably remember, he had been living with Gauguin. He clearly was still not well and started to believe he was being poisoned. Apparently, it caused such alarm amongst the locals that they described him as the '*fou roux.*' That translates to the 'redheaded madman'. Under pressure from the locals, the police closed his house and he was forced to leave the city. It was then that he admitted himself to the asylum here."

"I didn't realise that," said Adam. "Clearly, he understood that he needed help."

"I really feel for him," added Abigail, shaking her head. "There was so little understanding, or tolerance, of mental illness in those days."

In a dimly lit corridor was a doorway leading to what had been the artist's bedroom. They waited until they had the small space to themselves. The room was dark with bare walls and a small window.

He cast his mind back to Maryanne's look of utter desolation when he had eventually found her at the exhibition. There was definitely something about the room itself that had affected her deeply. Looking around, grey daylight filtered through the iron bars that were secured across the window. In all respects the room resembled a cell, a place of incarceration rather than recovery. In one dark corner was an iron bedstead, with, to the one side, a small wooden desk and chair. Beside the small window stood an old easel. There was a pervasive sense of darkness and futility that he found profoundly unsettling. It had similarly affected Caroline and Abigail. The featureless room measured eight foot square. How could such a creative genius manage to conjure inspiration in such a space? He gazed out on the view that had been afforded the artist more than a century earlier. Walls enclosed the garden, with cypress and olive trees dominating the countryside beyond.

What had Maryanne seen within that old image of the artist and the room that had so unsettled her? Directly below the window, he could see the herb and lavender beds. Bare trees framed one side of the garden, alongside a path leading away from the building. Small groups of visitors walked slowly along the paths, some occasionally looking back up at the window from which he looked out. He could imagine the sense of isolation and imprisonment that

Van Gogh must have felt. He shivered, feeling an overwhelming urge to leave the darkened space.

"Let's take a walk around the garden." Adam felt suffocated up here and needed fresh air and daylight. The hospital grounds might also provide some answers. Retracing their steps carefully down the old stone stairs, they passed the gift shop and found themselves in a corridor. Pushing open a heavy wooden door, they were met by a blast of cold air.

Emerging onto a gravel pathway, Adam looked about him. A couple of visitors walked ahead, avoiding a painter sitting crouched behind an easel. Van Gogh had painted the herb and lavender beds, as well as the part of the garden set aside for spring poppies. Now everything, the bare earth, the trees, looked forlorn, waiting for life to emerge. They traced the perimeter of the garden. They saw the figure at the easel was a woman, bundled up against the cold in a thick padded coat. She was painting an almond tree, set against the background of the hospital building. Her stillness, the dark of her clothes, blended with the grey of the walls. Above the tree were the barred windows of the patients' rooms. Adam stopped and, looking upwards, saw two people standing at the very window they had looked out of only moments before. The couple seemed to be talking. One of them turned to gaze out below, directly at Adam. With a shock he realised who he was staring at. He was sure it was her: he would recognise that hair anywhere. The figure stared back at him without acknowledgement, not moving. Then, slowly, she moved from view. The man standing beside her replaced her at the window. It was dark inside the room, too dark for Adam to recognise her companion. Rooted to the spot, looking upwards, he felt a cold dread slowly spread through him. Trying to shake it off, he looked around.

"Just wait here!" he shouted to Abigail and Caroline and rushed to the wooden door. At the same time, the three visitors they had encountered upstairs arrived at the doorway. Apologising, he pushed past them, ran through the gift shop and took the stairs two at a time. His heart was pounding. Reaching the bedroom, he stopped. Inside, an elderly man, wearing heavy brown-framed glasses, was taking photographs of the interior. He was not the man he had seen at the window. Adam rushed into the large treatment room opposite, but it was empty. There was no sign of Maryanne.

He was breathing heavily from the sudden sprint from the garden and up the uneven stairs and his knee had started throbbing once more. He stood still and listened for a moment. The only sound upstairs was his ragged breath and the clicking of the camera in the next room. Surely, if there had been anyone else upstairs, he wouldn't have missed them. Had he imagined seeing Maryanne at the window? Had it just been a trick of the light? Was it a shadow passing, or was it only wishful thinking?

"Excuse me. There was a couple here, a man and woman, just a few moments ago. They are both quite tall. Did you see where they went?"

The old man was startled but replied in a thick German accent, "I saw no one. Perhaps they are downstairs."

Adam suddenly felt unsteady and grasped one of the cold metal bars. He stood looking out, feeling disorientated. He looked down from the window and caught Caroline and Abigail looking up at him, their brows furrowed. He had better go down and explain himself.

Back in the gardens, he gave them a wan smile and slumped onto a cold wooden bench. "I'm sorry. I thought I saw Maryanne. Up there." He pointed at the window above. "In Van Gogh's room, looking out. She stared down at me."

The women looked up. The window was now in shadow and, what sun there was, had been replaced by dark scudding clouds. A breeze had got up.

"I thought it was her. That she recognised me. I was so certain it was her." He shook his head. "She was with a man I didn't recognise." Abigail sat down next to him and took his hand, a look of concern on her face.

"I ran back up but there was no-one there. Well, just one guy taking photographs. No one else. She must have left when she saw me… or else I imagined that it was her. Did you see anything?" he asked.

Abigail looked up at Caroline. They shook their heads.

"Sorry," Abigail said. "Just you staring down at us."

"Adam, are you OK?" Caroline tilted her head and looked at him intently.

"I was so sure." His shoulders slumped. "Shit, perhaps I really am starting to imagine things."

A cold and penetrating drizzle began. Adam brushed away the rain from his face and stood. Abigail suggested that it was time to go. As they walked through the gift shop, Adam hesitated and then approached the assistant who was unpacking a box of Van Gogh diaries. She looked up with a start. Adam apologised and asked whether she had just seen a couple leave. Caroline, realising that the woman spoke only limited English, provided a description of Maryanne in French.

The assistant had recognised Adam from earlier. Looking away from Caroline, she replied to him directly "You were in a big hurry. But I am sorry, *monsieur*, but I see no-one today that looks like that."

"*Merci, Madame.*" Disappointment was etched in his voice. He must have imagined it all, then.

It was getting dark and there were only a few cars left in the car park. Adam looked around in the vain hope that he might see Maryanne, or, at the least, someone who looked similar. They headed back to Uzès. From the rear window, Adam watched shapes form and drift at each turn as the lengthening shadows combined with the glare of the car's headlights. He sighed, "I don't know what I saw. I guess I was just hoping it was her."

*

Back in the apartment, Adam turned to Abigail. "I don't understand why I didn't recognise the man I saw with Maryanne. They seemed to know each other — they were deep in conversation."

"Did you see enough to be able to describe him?"

"Well, as far as I could make out, he was wearing a darkish coat with its collar up." He paused for a moment. "He looked older than Maryanne, quite a bit older. And it looked like he had a bit of a stoop." He frowned. "The stoop… I wonder…?"

Abigail's eyes narrowed in thought. "And how was Maryanne… Mum… acting towards him?"

"I don't know. They were just talking. Well, he was talking, bending slightly, and she looked like she was listening closely until she turned and looked down. It seemed that she was deliberately directing her gaze on me." He sighed. "That's all I have. It did look like her. It was probably nothing... just my imagination. Just two ordinary people, one of whom I mistook for Maryanne." He shook his head. "I had this strong feeling that, by visiting the hospital, particularly that room, that some clue would leap out at me." He sighed again.

Adam smiled at Abigail. "Don't worry. I'm not losing my mind. At least I don't think I am." Actually, he wasn't so sure of this. "It feels like I have a million things going through my head at the moment and they're all jumbled. I may not have actually seen Maryanne, but now I can feel her around."

"It's not surprising, Adam. There have been so many unanswered questions for so long. I'm amazed you've kept your sanity."

"Well, it may not be fully intact right at this moment." He paused, running his hands through his hair. "Can I tell you something? Something I should have told you years ago."

"Of course. Go ahead."

"You mentioned the big row you had with Maryanne. It was caused by—"

"Her involvement with people who turned up at the old house in Ireland?" she finished.

"Yes, that. I remember when it happened, when you had that row. I'm not sure if you knew, but Maryanne would never talk to me about the disagreements that you had. Each of you could be just as stubborn at times and, perhaps naively, I felt it wasn't really my position to take sides. But I do know how upset she used to get. She may not have shown it to you, but they did affect her... quite deeply."

Chapter 6

It was late the following afternoon and Adam had spent the day with Abigail showing her around the town. They were now sitting back in the warmth of the lounge, chatting companionably. "You know I once met your grandmother... at the house in Dublin where you grew up. It was not long after I met your mother at uni. At the end of the term Maryanne came up to London to meet my parents and then the following Easter, we both drove across to Wales in my battered green Mini. I remember we caught an early ferry from Holyhead across to the outskirts of Dublin to meet your grandmother, your grandfather having died of cancer some years before. Perhaps my first impression of her should have provided some early clues. However, my initial impression was that she was very welcoming." He smiled. "She was also charmingly disorganised, and resolutely bohemian."

"You are, of course, Adam," he recounted. "I have heard an awful lot about you. You are very welcome here. Let me show you around," she'd said, taking his arm.

A potter, and by her own admission an enthusiastic but very average poet, her rambling rundown house was testimony to her lifestyle, with its eclectic and chaotic mix of interests and skills. He remembered he had immediately liked her and, over the course of the four days of their visit, he saw how close mother and daughter seemed.

"I know now, of course, that was a bit of an illusion. But, in some ways, they seemed like sisters."

Maryanne was determined to show him around

Dublin. Frequently all three of them went out, often arriving home from a restaurant or one of the many bars, quite drunk. She also managed to introduce Adam to a couple of her close friends, one a folk musician, one an aspiring actress, both of whom he immediately liked. As Abigail had said, there were others that seemed to come and go at the house that he was less sure of.

He did also remember asking her why she had not chosen to go to Trinity College and staying in her home town. They were sitting in a comfortable pub in Camden Street. "You would surely have got in."

Her reply that "I rather needed to get out. I needed to get away," had surprised him then.

Both women were similar in looks... as of course were Maryanne and Abigail. Catherine was perhaps an inch or so shorter than Maryanne, but both were slender, with the same flaming red hair. As he described Abigail's grandmother, he saw that she was listening intently, occasionally nodding.

In contrast to her bohemian lifestyle, Adam was surprised to find that Catherine was deeply religious. Wooden crosses adorned most of the rooms. He already knew that religion was a part of Maryanne's life: she had belonged to a Catholic group at university. Beyond that, though, she was fairly private about her beliefs, rarely introducing the subject. She occasionally attended church during their time together but had never pressed him to join her.

"I remember that house as if it were yesterday," Abigail quietly murmured. "Sometimes with mixed feelings."

Adam looked across to Abigail, a question forming. On both sides there were things that had been left unsaid. He knew he needed to talk more to someone about

Maryanne. Perhaps now was the time for them both to open up about her. He asked carefully, "Are you all right with us talking more about your mother?" He looked up. "Perhaps we should have had this conversation some time ago."

She drew her knees up under her and reached for her wine. She knew what he meant. And, she understood Adam's need to talk. Looking up she replied slowly, "OK. Why not start from the beginning?"

"Thank you." He felt quite emotional. He wasn't sure whether he had had this conversation with anyone else.

"Let me rather talk about the last nine or ten years, from when I met your mother again. From when you entered the story."

"All right." She thought back. "I must have been thirteen at the time, just starting my teenage years. I was a bit of a brat then, I remember. Go ahead Adam. I'll try and fill in any of the areas you didn't know."

*

The problem with Maryanne was that she naturally stood out. It was of course what had attracted him in the first place. Somehow, she seemed to demand attention and Adam thought that that had not always been a good thing.

He wondered just how to describe his subsequent life with her, and what he should tell Abigail and what might be better left out... for now, at least. "I think you know all about when we first met at Exeter. So, let's move forwards to a summer's day in London, many years later." He could feel the intensity of Abigail's attention as he thought back to that day in late July.

It had been one of those rare and glorious English

summers. He could almost see the cloudless blue sky, patterned with vapour trails of the incoming planes to nearby Heathrow. It was a Sunday afternoon and there was barely a breath of wind. He vividly remembered the smell of freshly mown grass as he walked past the old cricket ground on Kew Green. Taken by the tree-lined border of the ground, with its quaint old cricket pavilion in the corner, he made himself comfortable on a bench at the boundary's edge. With the last wicket falling, he navigated his way through a crowd of drinkers spilling out from the front of a nearby pub, all enjoying the early evening sunshine. The open doors and windows created a welcome through-breeze. Unsurprisingly it was less crowded inside, although he still needed to queue to be served by the overworked bar staff. As he stood patiently, he idly looked around.

Maryanne was the last person he had expected to see. He had neither seen nor heard from her since their break-up fifteen years before. He felt uncertain whether to approach her: would she even remember him after all these years? She was with a group of friends. They were chatting and laughing, and he felt strangely nervous as he moved towards her. Maryanne was talking to the man next to her and Adam waited, not wishing to push in. She looked up and saw him. He smiled and mouthed a hello. Her eyes widened in sudden recognition.

"Good heavens!" She grasped his arms before throwing her own arms around him, holding him tight. He still remembered her fragrance. Letting him go, she took a step back and looked at him for a long while. "I can't believe it, Adam. After all this time." She continued to hold his gaze. "This is amazing. It can't be true, surely?"

Up closer, he could see only the barest of hints of the

intervening years — perhaps a few fine lines traced around her eyes and her mouth, her hair slightly shorter than he remembered — but she was, unmistakably, Maryanne... and still stunning. "Can you stay for a bit? I would love to catch up with you. Find out what you have been doing with yourself. Come and say hello to everyone."

She took him by the arm and guided him into the group, introducing him as a close friend from university. Not an ex-boyfriend, Adam noticed wryly. Was she there with a partner? There was no wedding ring and he wondered, strangely, how he felt about that. There was no one that he recognised, but everyone was friendly enough and welcoming. It wasn't long before he established that most were work colleagues. He just wanted to talk to Maryanne and had to wait until, one by one, they gradually drifted away as the evening wore on.

Finally, it was just the two of them. She smiled and took his arm. "Come, let's grab a seat somewhere. My feet are killing me. Besides, I'm starving. I haven't eaten anything since early this morning."

Finding a table in an alcove, they sat down and looked through the menu. Adam went up to the bar and ordered the food as well as more drinks.

When Adam had sat down again Maryanne turned to face him. "Well, how do we even start this? It has been a lifetime... it must be all of thirteen or fourteen years."

"Fifteen years, I believe, but hey, who's counting?" He took the initiative. "Why not let me start? There's not a huge amount to tell you, really." Keeping things unemotional, consciously avoiding the hurt of the last time they saw each other, he explained that, following university, he had moved into the field of business consultancy. "I think law left me rather than the other way round."

He then had moved away from central London, which had allowed him, a few years ago, to buy a comfortable house in the suburbs, in Ealing, just a stone's throw from the common. Continuing, keeping things as light as possible, he explained that he had been married, not for long, six years, and it had ended reasonably amicably three years earlier. No children, he added somewhat ruefully. It just had not happened for them.

In turn, Maryanne had gone on to complete her law degree. It had been a wrench to leave Exeter, she felt more protected there, but she had accepted an offer to join a well-known, prestigious legal firm in London. Adam was unsurprised by this. She was always going to succeed, he thought. The tone, though, gradually changed. She revealed she had struggled to settle down, particularly following the birth of her daughter. The relationship with the father had been unexpected and brief: he had not wanted children and had been shocked when she became pregnant. They had not married, and he had left Maryanne even before the birth.

*

Adam suddenly stopped, aware of Abigail listening intently. He looked across. "I'm sorry. I think you probably know all of this but, please say if you feel uncomfortable."

She smiled and shifted her position on the couch. "No, it's fine. I'm fine, Adam. Mum never really felt comfortable talking about my father. I know that he did not accept the pregnancy and wasn't able, for whatever reason, to take on any parental responsibility. Please carry on."

Before continuing, Adam said to Abigail, "All right, if you say so."

*

Maryanne said it had been hard. "It was a tough time. He didn't support me, financially or otherwise, even before. I didn't expect anything afterwards. He didn't have much money and it was not something I pushed, anyway. We had some contact for a while. I haven't heard from him in some time and, unfortunately, Abigail has few memories of him," she said.

"Abigail. That's your daughter? It's a very pretty name."

"Thank you. Yes. Most of the times I just call her Ab or Abi. She's thirteen now, a fully-fledged teenager. With all the delights that naturally come with that." She laughed.

Their food arrived. Maryanne ate while she continued. "Early on I found I really struggled with motherhood on my own. Actually, I probably still do." She gazed absently around the room before focusing again. "I don't think I was ever a particularly good mother. I tried hard. I really did, but it just didn't come naturally to me. My law firm had a Dublin office, much smaller obviously than the one in London. I realised I wasn't coping well, so I rented out my flat here, went over to Ireland, and moved back in with my mother. You remember her, don't you?" she asked.

"Yes, I do. She was hard to forget." Adam smiled.

"If anything, Mum was so much better with Abi than I ever was."

*

Adam looked across to Abigail. She was engrossed, and nodded for Adam to continue. He recounted what Maryanne then said.

"Mum was a godsend at that time. I think in London I had become a bit crazy, what with worrying about my ability to look after Abi on my own, and with work. I felt I couldn't strike the right balance. In fact, I really couldn't concentrate on anything for long."

"It must have been hard for you. I am so sorry. I had no idea."

"Thank you. Of course, you weren't to know. Gradually I did get better at coping, at balancing things, although there was a period that still remains hazy."

Maryanne looked away and was quiet for a while. This was a different woman to the one Adam had thought he knew. Maryanne continued. "Anyway, I had Mum to help me. I also had some old friends from Exeter, as well as a couple of good friends from when I grew up in Dublin. In their own way they all helped me through this. I preferred being back in Dublin and it was good for me to get out of the rat race that was London at the time. I felt more secure there."

Coffee arrived and Maryanne went to the ladies' room. Adam sat there quietly, digesting Maryanne's story, trying to work out his own feelings.

Returning, she apologised, "I didn't mean to bore you with all of this. It is just that I feel I can open up to you."

"You haven't bored me. Whilst you were describing what happened, I had this strange feeling that I should have been there to help you. Even if only at the end of a phone."

"That's so sweet of you. I kind of wish you had been. Anyway, let me finish this and then we can talk about happier things. I got distracted. Help me, where was I?"

"You were back in Dublin, with your mother."

"Ah, yes. Living back with Mum."

Brushing her hair back in that characteristic way that Adam remembered well, Maryanne continued her story. "I was working out of Dublin, but I still had to come back to London once a week. Some of my clients were based in Europe, particularly in France, and I had to travel there at least a few times a month. Mum looked after Abi while I was away. I think, certainly in her early years, that Abi regarded her grandmother as more of a mother than she did me."

After a few years, she had met and married Peter, a lawyer in Dublin. He was quite a bit older, recently divorced, no children. They moved into a big house that they had rented outside of the city, with a view of the sea. Abi was enrolled in a local school and for a while they were happy. "We took days out over the weekend, going to the beach or up to the mountains, all that sort of thing." Like Adam's own marriage, it had not lasted. "Abi was four when we met. It turned out in the end that he couldn't cope with a child. He expected to have my undivided attention most of the time." She sighed. "I think I struggle with all of that.

"And then Mum got sick. She had cancer, a small cell lung cancer, and she went downhill from when she got the diagnosis. I employed carers to help Mum. Abi and I then moved back to the city to also help out towards the end. I had to resign from my job. I couldn't do all of it and I was struggling to cope. When Mum passed away, I needed to distance myself. I took Abi out of her new school and we left Ireland for a while and stayed with friends."

"I am really sorry." Adam found her story hard to hear. "I know how close you were to your mother."

"It took some time for me to get my head around things. After a time away, I returned to Dublin and started therapy. I still wasn't working and so I just took things day by day." She smiled ruefully. "Over time, bit by bit, I did start to learn again how to cope."

It was now late and the pub was starting to close around them. As they left, Maryanne asked "Are you walking to the Tube?"

"I am. I change at Turnham Green for Ealing."

"Perfect. I'm a bit further… Notting Hill. We can walk together… it's such a nice night and I've so enjoyed myself."

As they walked through the quiet streets of Kew, Adam asked, "And how long have you been back in London?"

"I moved back two years ago. Luckily, I still had my old one-bedroom flat, just off Kensington High Street, but I had to sell it and buy something bigger as I now had Abi. I was fortunate because I'd found a job as a partner in a legal practice… I still had a few good contacts here. I bought a three-bedroom place in Holland Park, just a short walk from Notting Hill tube. Of course, it meant I acquired a large mortgage at the same time... and then a French au pair for Abi," she added. "I've been happy since I came back, though," she said thoughtfully, surprising herself. "Life is strange, isn't it? Perhaps I have just got older — and wiser."

The train arrived and they both boarded it. "Can I give you my card with my phone number?" Maryanne asked.

"I have so enjoyed seeing you. You haven't changed. Do you think we could do this again?" She suddenly looked hesitant. "I have probably just bored you. If so, please just throw the card away."

Three months later, Maryanne, Abigail and their au pair had moved into Adam's house in Ealing.

*

A brief few years after their marriage, Adam and Maryanne were on holiday on the tiny Greek island of Skiathos. Adam had visited Skiathos once before, many years ago, and was keen to show Maryanne its sandy, pine-fringed beaches and its picturesque, whitewashed, main town, winding its way down the hill to the old port below.

They were sitting in a taverna beside a small crescent-shaped bay, a couple of kilometres from Skiathos town. It was evening. They had been told that the taverna served the best, and freshest, seafood on the island. It was early for evening diners, with only one other table occupied. It was still warm, even with the gentle breeze. Adam and Maryanne had caught the regular bus that ran the length of the island each hour, from outside their sea-front hotel.

The sun had started to dip behind the pale cliffs and they could hear the gentle lapping of the waves on the beach. Maryanne was wearing a light blue top and white skirt. The top showed off her striking hair and the freckles around her nose that had returned with her tan. Drinking his ice-cold Mythos beer, Adam sat back, enjoying just looking at her. She looked so well and happy. On the recommendation of the waiter, Maryanne had ordered a bottle of chilled Assyrtiko wine from

Santorini to go with the red snapper they had selected to be cooked for them.

"Please, you like? Very good choice. Yes?" the waiter asked, indicating the wine, as he lit the candle on the table. It was romantic in every way. They were both feeling pleasingly relaxed, having spent a lazy day at the beach.

"Cheers, my darling. This is so nice. I'm so glad we have come here to this beautiful island." Maryanne raised her glass to Adam. There was a glow about her.

"Cheers," he replied, finishing his beer. He could not remember the last time she had looked so content. Probably all the way back to the first time they had been together, at Exeter. They had needed the break. Ever since Maryanne and her daughter had moved in, more than two years before, they had not stopped. Her work still took her all over Europe. He had started a new contract and there was now Abigail to look after when Maryanne was away. It was an altogether new experience for him and he found, much to his surprise, that he was enjoying the shared responsibility it had brought. Besides, he found that Abigail was self-contained, for a teenager. She was also informed and well-read. They were able to enjoy mature conversations when it was just the two of them. She was currently staying with a friend of Maryanne who lived in nearby Acton whilst they both enjoyed their break on Skiathos.

As the evening darkened slowly into night, the conversation had turned from an amiable discussion of their past travels and experiences to that of past relationships. This was surprising to Adam, as this was not a topic they had comfortably navigated before. Where questions had formed in his mind, he had sensed a reluctance to delve into this part of her past: she would skim over the detail before skilfully changing the subject. Possibly, he thought, it was an issue of trust, and she was just not ready. Perhaps that evening it was the wine, or the setting, but this time Maryanne seemed more willing to open up.

Adam had seen a few women since his divorce. He knew he was not particularly good at relationships. Most had not lasted the distance, coming to a natural conclusion, through choice or circumstance. One had more substance and they had both decided to live together. However, after three years, he had finished it. "Emma kept on asking where I believed the relationship was going. I know that she was looking for more certainty, and security, and that was fair enough. But when I really thought about it, I just could not see a long-term future. It was difficult."

Maryanne poured them both some wine. The moonlight was now silver across the bay. Putting her wine glass down, she looked across at Adam, as if determining what she should say. Finally, it seemed she made a decision to open up to him. She started hesitantly. She said she had just finished with an Italian businessman, from Milan, before meeting Adam again. They had met through work — she had been in Milan advising on a contract. He was the Marketing Director for a Milan-based manufacturer of Italian kitchenware. "As you can imagine, the kitchenware was high end, and very expensive. Italian expensive. A number of us went out for a meal in Milan to celebrate the end of the negotiations and we had a good time. Imagine my surprise though, when he asked me out. He then came over to London every couple of weeks. It turned out though that he was not quite as separated from his wife as he had claimed he was."

She smiled ruefully, "Or else something got badly lost in translation at the very start when he explained that, sadly, it was all over, and had been for years. I only found out when she phoned me to ask whether Matteo was with me. We had an interesting conversation, as you can imagine. In hindsight, I can only be grateful, as I might not have run into you again."

Adam then asked her about the guy that she had left him for all those years before in Exeter... he didn't know his name but he had been part of the Catholic community at university.

"You have a good memory," she acknowledged. "He was half-Swiss. If I remember, his mother was English. Frowning, she added, "Looking back, I think I felt I was losing you, and he was there. He was also supportive..."

"I'm truly sorry. I didn't realise at the time how you were feeling. I guess when I moved to London I got caught up in the freedom and excitement of London... and of working there. I should have been more sensitive, and supportive. I don't think that I understood women very well then. I'm probably not much better now," he grinned, ruefully.

"I didn't handle it well either," she replied softly, taking his hand. "I should have talked to you about my feelings. He was insistent that I end things with you and said that the finality would help me. It's no excuse, I know, but I did find him different to other people I had met. He had all these compelling arguments about life, which challenged me at the time. I got so caught up that I started to rely on him too much." What she'd said had held a resonance with him and he remembered pausing for a moment.

"It took me a long time to get over you," he simply said.

*

Adam's re-telling of Maryanne's explanation was not lost on Abigail either, although she kept quiet, as he resumed the story. Maryanne had apologised, saying that she knew she had hurt him. Sensing that the tone needed lifting, Adam smiled and offered, "I guess we were both young. We really knew so little about life then."

Later, towards end of that same holiday on Skiathos, they were sitting in the welcome shade of a small taverna on Troulos beach. It was after midday and they had spent the morning walking the beach, swimming and reading. They were due to fly out the next day: Abigail had been happy to inform them earlier that it was damp and cold back home. Adam looked across at Maryanne. Despite their imminent return, she still looked so relaxed and healthy that she almost shone. He fervently hoped it would last. Over lunch he recalled her saying that, after her mother's death, she and Abigail had decided to get away from things. She had told him that they left Dublin for a time.

Maryanne looked up from her salad and considered him. She had tensed and there was a return of the previous wariness. He instantly regretted raising it and wished he could take the question back. She took a drink of her sparkling water and looked out over the sea shimmering in the bright sunlight.

Sighing, she said eventually, "It was a long time ago. I have not thought about that for so long. You have to understand it was a very difficult time. I had to get away. We went to southern France. To a friend's house in the Camargue. I was not well... and things got quite weird. Shit, I thought it was all behind me. I feel so ashamed, but I was helpless." She stopped and her eyes started to water. "I'm sorry. I can't. She shook her head and looked imploringly at him. "I just wish I—"

"Maryanne, leave it. Please. I'm sorry I asked," he interrupted urgently. Adam leant across the table and gently put his hand over hers. "Let's change the subject."

*

Adam looked up at Abigail. "And that's where we left it." A hopelessness was reflected in his eyes.

Chapter 7

"I never did, you know," Abigail finally interjected, after what seemed like hours, shifting her position on the couch.

"Never did what?" he asked, not quite understanding.

"Replace the friends that I lost when we moved in with you. It was a big deal for me and I thought you were being very selfish... both of you."

"Abi, I'm so sorry. We didn't realise what a wrench it would be for you."

"What you probably didn't know at the time was how often I had moved by then... or been palmed off onto people... sometimes even strangers. I never seemed to stay in one place, or at the same school, for more than a couple of years... often a lot less than that. I never really managed to keep close friends and I guess I thought there was little point in trying to make them in the first place. It was difficult... and I felt lonely."

Adam's phone interrupted them. It was Caroline, reminding them that she would be there early the next morning, and she would again bring her car. Adam thanked her and rang off.

"Sorry, you were saying, Abi."

"I was just saying it was not easy having to always make new friends. I know it often wasn't Mum's fault but remember... I had only known you for a few months. I thought you would turn out like some of her other friends. But there were times, though, when Mum could have made different choices. I know I can't blame her for me not properly knowing my dad. That was his choice, after all," she conceded.

"It doesn't make it any easier though, does it?"

Sighing she said slowly, "No, it doesn't. You still feel unwanted. As far as I know, he never wanted to be a significant part of my life."

"I thought there was meant to be a vow of celibacy for Catholic priests?"

"Yes, there is. Mum said that she met him just when he was still studying for his theology degree. Mum has told me that, at the time, he was still unsure whether to continue on into the priesthood. I suspect I was an accident. Conveniently, when he heard that Mum was pregnant, it seemed to have made his mind up."

"But does that explain why he left, why he distanced himself from both of you?"

"I guess so. He chose his career and abandoned both of us."

"He sounds very callous. Not the obvious person to represent the Church!" Adam exclaimed.

"I suppose not," she conceded.

"In the end, it is very much his loss."

"Thank you, that's nice of you."

"But it's true. He must have some regrets. If not now, I am sure he will in the future."

"I don't know. Mum said that he did see me periodically when I was very young, but he never showed more than indifference towards me. I don't really remember this, but I could have been anyone's child."

"I'm really sorry, Abi."

"It's old history now. I used to ask Mum whether she had any photos but she said... claimed... that she didn't. She doesn't even know where he moved to. I didn't miss him when I was young," she continued. "I guess I didn't know anything different. And I had Grandma. She was always around. It was only after she died that I began to feel different, particularly at school. Not only did I not have a father, but I could not even describe anything about him."

"You know that I regarded you as my daughter. I still do," he said quietly.

"I can't tell you how much that meant... that still means... to me. You were so accepting... and I know I wasn't easy... and you never took sides in my arguments with Mum. I could see how you tried to be as supportive as you could to her, but, importantly for me, you never attached blame for things that happened between us."

"I did try my best. I tried to treat you as an individual in your own right. Not as a teenager, or as Maryanne's daughter. And you were, you are, a lovely person to be around. You were always polite and considerate, which I remember thinking was unusual for a teenager." He smiled. "I could also see that you cared about things... not just the people who meant something to you, but other things... animals, the environment. Obviously, I knew that you had not had the easiest time when you were young."

"Thank you, Adam. I am glad to have you in my life," she replied simply.

He looked up, moved by her candid acknowledgement. "Good. And I'm not going anywhere."

Resuming her recollection of her early life, Abigail continued, "My first memories seem only of growing up in Dublin, of living with Grandma...Catherine. I can remember nothing of living in London, or of the old flat." Not for the first time Adam was reminded that there remained a trace of the Irish lilt, not as noticeable as her mother's, but no less endearing.

"Grandma provided the stability in my early life and for that I will be always grateful. But it was her who introduced Mum to a lot of the people that came, and went, in our lives with regularity. They were an odd mixture. There were of course the artists, and then there were the religious ones — always Catholics, of course." She smiled. "I understood the potters and the painters — who I largely liked — but I never could see why she was so drawn in by the others. I didn't even know how they even found their way to the house."

"I suppose, at that time, Dublin was booming," Adam replied. "A lot of people from all walks were attracted to the opportunities there."

"Thinking back," Abigail said, looking pensive, "I don't think these people were really friends. Rather they found Grandma useful. But their enthusiasm, or fervour, gave Mum an escape, particularly when she was down on herself... when things got tough. Certainly, I think it got her off the hook of trying to be a normal mother. And I am not trying to be hard on her. When I was younger, I used to think that she was indulgent, and that I came a distant second in her life. That is what I often accused her of... which one way or another led to most of our arguments. Now I understand that, really, she just struggled."

"As you say, I understand the artists, but less so all the others," he concurred. "It does all sound a bit odd."

"I know. But both Mum and Grandma were spiritual. Some form of faith was always central to them. They needed to believe that there was a higher purpose. It didn't have to be conventional religion. Both were always attracted by the energy of new ideas... and to the more bohemian fringe groups who challenged traditional interpretations. They were both hippies at heart. Of the two though, it was Grandma who was really into this stuff, and Mum I think less so. It was Grandma who introduced Mum to most of these people. And, of course, some of the men made it quite apparent that they found Mum attractive. Most I just found pretty creepy, and I tried to avoid being with them as much as I could."

"I only knew a bit of this," he admitted. "Maryanne kept that part of her life quite closed. I think she felt that I lacked a spiritual side: that I would not understand. She was probably right," he acknowledged.

Abigail continued, her brow furrowed. "At Grandma's house, you never knew who would drop in. One or two of these people even stayed in the house, sometimes for weeks. She didn't seem to mind. And there was one man, in particular. Whenever he was there, he seemed to have a hold over her. He was unpleasant, with a quick temper. She was probably scared of him, and I never understood why she allowed him to stay. There was also a strange look about him — he had a thick beard and long hair... and these staring eyes. I sometimes felt him watching me. I am sure that Mum noticed, but I tried to keep away from him as much as possible."

"Maryanne would never have let anything happen to you," Adam said quietly.

"No, you are right. But I found it hard during that time in Dublin, living in that house with everything else..." Her voice faltered momentarily. "Don't get me wrong, though," she offered more brightly, "Grandma was good to me... and she was also fun to be around. I think it was her who taught me to respect all life, and not to take things for granted. And, to give Mum her due, when she was around, she used to take me often to the coast or up to the Dublin mountains." She explained to Adam that that is what Dubliners call the part of the Wicklow Mountains nearest the city. "I would go with her along the Dublin Mountains Way, all the way to Rathmichael Wood. It's near Shankill."

Adam had to admit that he didn't know the area.

"Other times, when we didn't feel like going too far, or when the weather was poor, we would just take ourselves off to the zoo at Phoenix Park. Those times were precious, and I remember that was when I was happiest... with no-one else around apart from the two of us."

"And later..." Adam gently prompted.

"Eventually we moved out of Grandma's and went to live by the coast — in Dalkey. Mum had just married Peter and everything was fine for a while... for a couple of years. I know Mum says that they split up because Peter couldn't deal with her having a child to bring up, but I think there was more to it. I know he didn't fit in with some of her friends at the time — he felt that they still exerted too much influence over her, even after they were married."

"Maryanne was... is," he corrected himself, "cautious about talking about her past but she mentioned Peter to me," he conceded.

"I don't think he was a bad guy. He just struggled with a family, like some people do.

"Anyway, soon after Peter left, Grandma got sick and we went back to the old house to help look after her. I didn't want to go back there. I remember being upset that I had to leave my new school. I was probably a bit unfair on Mum, but I think I realised then there was a pattern to my life. And then Grandma died, and we went away again…" she sighed.

A loud beep suddenly issued from the German-made kettle in the kitchen. Steam billowed from its angular spout. Abigail got up to make herself a tea, asking Adam if he would like something hot.

Returning with the drinks, she sat down again, confessing that she was again starting to fade. The room downstairs had become quite warm and Adam himself had started to struggle to keep his eyes open. Abigail, however, insisted that, before she took herself off to bed, there were a couple of important things that she needed to tell him whilst she could still clearly remember them.

Adam knew he should hear what it was she wanted to say. He smiled, "Yes, of course. I am listening."

Sitting upright, she looked to one side, focusing on the Belle Epoque painting on the far wall showing two young women wearing white dresses against a red background.

Refocusing her gaze back on Adam she said, "When Grandma died, she left instructions that we scatter her ashes in Blessington. It's a lake just outside of Dublin." Before the Catholic Church banned the practice, she explained. "Anyway, it was just the two of us, which was a relief, and, one Sunday afternoon we drove up there, to Blessington. I remember how still the day was, but it was very cold. Afterwards we sat on some rocks beside the lake for a while, wrapped in our warm coats, watching the ashes slowly spread out across the water. Mum looked out over the lake and then started reminiscing about Grandma, telling me things that I didn't know. I think for her this moment was a kind of release.

"Grandma was darker, and much more complex, than I ever knew. She had always been caring towards me. But she had treated Mum very differently, particularly when she was growing up. I got the feeling that there was not much love early on; and what little there was provided really to reward compliance. That is why Mum was so keen to leave Dublin at the first opportunity: when she got into university. Granddad had died whilst Mum was still young. But, according to Mum, she remembers him as a remote figure in their lives."

"When I met Maryanne, in Exeter, she seemed exotic, and completely wonderful." He laughed. "I can still picture her then." Adam had been surprised that he had not noticed someone so striking before around the lecture halls or library. He remembered, despite the fast-fading light outside when he first met her at that party in Exeter, the light brown freckles dusting her nose and her cheekbones. He had found her immediately attractive. As striking as she was, though, what he had found surprising about Maryanne was her genuine modesty. She displayed little recognition that others found her beautiful. If anything, she would be embarrassed if anyone referred to her eye-catching looks. He had found this humility, together with a strange lack of self-belief, oddly endearing in those early months.

Abigail smiled. She was keen, however, to finish her story. "As a single parent, Grandma was very strict. Perhaps she had to be or maybe she knew no other way. Mum, for instance, was rarely permitted to bring friends home. Faith was a dominant theme in their life. Her upbringing was, in a way, very old-fashioned: if she did rebel or challenge things, she was locked in her bedroom for hours at a time. They had little money when she was growing up after Granddad died. Grandma owned the old house in Dublin but, as an artist, never sold enough pictures or pottery to provide much for them both. She would, from time to time, rent out the spare bedrooms in the house to provide some additional income.

"This was how Mum grew up — surrounded by older people that she often hardly knew. Mum did say that she benefitted from the energetic discussions that defined the household. She tried to explain it to me. She learnt from an early age how to respond, how to craft arguments to support her own ideas. This all helped her in her subsequent legal career. But the flip side was that she often felt an outsider: that most relationships seemed transitory."

Adam got up to turn on a light beside Abigail. "As I said, she never told me much of this. She did sometimes allude to her upbringing, that it was not easy for her to talk about these things. She was very closed about her childhood. But I did meet your grandmother once. and what you are saying does surprise me a bit." Sitting down again, he continued, "She was always kind, and generous, to me."

"Thinking back, she was good to me, but she did treat Mum differently. Even I could see that in Dublin."

"Perhaps with you," he replied, thinking, "your grandmother was trying to make up for the past: for the tough time that Maryanne had experienced. Showing that she had learnt from earlier mistakes. As I said, Maryanne was never critical of your grandmother with me."

"That's possible," she conceded. "The other thing that Mum tried to explain was more difficult for me to understand. It seemed like a confession, and it took me a number of years to understand what she was saying. She said that she had often felt controlled by those around her: by Grandma to start with, but then by others. She believed that she had been complicit in this: that she had somehow invited it." She shook her head. "It was a long time ago. But I hope I am giving a sense of what she was trying to say. I think that's why religion was important for her. It provided a set of rules and a direction. Mum said that you were the first person who did not try to change her: the first person who loved her for herself. I remember her saying how unsettling that was."

"I had no little idea," he confessed. "I suppose that explains a few things. When you first meet her, she seems so confident, so vibrant and welcoming. After knowing her as I do... as I did... I understand now that that was not the real person underneath, well, the confident part at least. I knew that she would withdraw at times, into herself. But I never got the impression that she lacked direction, that she was reliant on others to get through life. Just the opposite, really."

"That says more about your relationship with Mum," Abigail replied kindly. "You were very good for her. You always were. But there was the other side to her."

She paused for a moment. "You told me that she got upset when you asked about leaving Dublin after Grandma's death. I was eleven, almost twelve at the time. Let me tell you what happened when we went to stay in that cottage in France."

"OK." Adam hesitated, before saying, "All right."

"You're sure?"

"Yes, go ahead."

"The house was quite pretty, but a bit neglected — it looked like a holiday home. It was in a small seaside town called Saintes-Maries something. It's down in the Camargue. I remember the house smelt musty, and the first thing we did when we arrived was throw all the windows open. It felt that no one had stayed there for quite some time. But it suited the two of us. It was simply furnished and close to the town and the beach.

"It was May, I remember, and getting quite hot. In the beginning it was magical. I clearly recall the white horses, all the marshlands and *etangs*, and the lagoons fringed with the pink of the flamingos. When we weren't driving around looking at the sights we rented some old bicycles, and spent a lot of time cycling along the paths and lanes — being the Camargue, it was all very flat — and swimming in the sea. We often just lay on the beach, reading and chatting. Like friends almost. Sometimes we would just watch the people walking up and down. It was wonderful and it felt like Mum and I were finally getting to know each other. She was more relaxed than I had seen her in a long time, perhaps ever.

"Mum and I talked like we hadn't ever before... or since, come to think of it. She told me that, with Grandma dying, she felt different, refreshed."

"Do you know what she meant by that?" he asked softly.

"They're probably not the exact words that she used. My understanding was that this had provided her the opportunity for a new start. To start her life over again.

"We had been there a couple of weeks and then these people arrived. They were the owners of the cottage. A few days later another friend... I think from Marseille... also arrived. He was known to Mum. This was the same man I told you about. In Dublin. That I remembered feeling frightened of years earlier. He was... unsettling. He was the one with the beard and the long hair... and these strange eyes." She shuddered. "They had all come over to attend a festival that was held each year in the town to celebrate a local saint. I remember that she was known there as the Black Madonna.

"People came from all over the world to attend the festival. The body of the saint is buried in the crypt of the cathedral. Each year an effigy of the saint is paraded through the streets, all the way down to the sea. Then, after the parade, horse races and bull fights were held around the town. There was even flamenco dancing in one of the squares."

She smiled at the memories. "Mum even dragged me into the square to try it. I was very shy in those days and it was difficult to follow the moves. Anyway, getting back to the point, it would all have been wonderful if these friends had not arrived. They were fervent about the festival, and I could see that Mum was slowly coming under their spell. I am sure they had no ulterior motive, that they had arrived purely for the festivities, but bit-by-bit, Mum changed. She became caught up in it all. It was very powerful. There was no shortage of the saint's followers, or indeed followers of associated cults.

"The town — Saintes-Maries — is the place where Mary Magdalene, together with this saint and other disciples, were meant to have come ashore in Europe, after they fled the Holy Land after the Crucifixion. The cathedral in the town is dedicated to the saint but, of course, there is also a cult dedicated to Mary Magdalene, who is the patron saint of Provence.

"Mum got caught up in this and I could see her changing. Together with others, she would go to the church two or three times a day for prayer and, once again, she became more removed from everyday life. Our wonderful trips into the countryside became a thing of the past. Sometimes she would take herself off for the whole day, only coming back the next morning. And she always she looked completely drained."

Adam felt surprise and concern. He wasn't sure what to say. He asked Abigail what happened to her during this time. Whether she had been alright.

"I became quite unsettled. I was concerned for Mum, of course. She became this different person and it was difficult to talk to her. I didn't like the other people who were there, and I no longer enjoyed staying in the cottage. I would take the bike and cycle off somewhere on my own."

"What then happened?" he asked gently.

"Five or six days after the festival had ended all three of the friends left. By that stage most of the festival goers had also gone. One day I came back from a cycle ride to the beach and found Mum just wandering around the house in a daze, not making any sense. It was then that I started to feel frightened. It was now just the two of us and I didn't know what to do. There was no one to help.

"The weather changed suddenly. Before, and during the festival, it had been sunny and hot. As the festival ended, the clouds had started to build, not from over the sea but inland, from the north. There was a strange air about the place. God, I still remember it so vividly." She shuddered involuntarily. "It started with a thick sea mist that crept in with the tide. Smelling of salt and sea kelp it slowly filled the narrow streets and seemed to billow around the church in the centre. I've never experienced anything like it. It was as if the mist was a living thing. Then this freezing wind started up. The locals there in the town called it *le mistral*. It blew in from the north, across the plains and the salt marshes, and the temperature suddenly plummeted. It became quite cold. Eventually the wind turned into a gale. It was unrelenting. All the inhabitants of the town were forced back into their houses, closing their shutters to the strong wind."

"I know the mistral," confirmed Adam. "I've experienced it. It was blowing very hard when I arrived here and has only just stopped."

"It lasted for three days and by the time it finished there was hardly a soul around," she continued. "It seemed to have cleared the town, leaving virtually no trace of the festival, apart from a few tattered posters on walls and outside shops. I went into the town a couple of times, but it felt eerie. Even the people selling crosses and other religious bits and pieces were gone. I mainly stayed in the cottage reading: Mum spent most of the time just sleeping. This must have done her some good because, gradually, she became more coherent. And gradually more aware of her surroundings and me."

"Did she seek out any professional help there?"

"Not at the time. We stayed on for another ten days or so. I felt that I didn't want to leave Mum, so we mainly stayed inside the house, only leaving to go to the supermarket. Then one day, Mum announced we were going to return to Dublin. We couldn't have just stayed there. I had already missed a lot of schooling and I was starting to get worried about that. So, we left and came back. Mum was better by then and I went back to school — I never knew what Mum had told them about why I was absent. Day by day, normal life gradually resumed."

Adam remained silent for a long while, eventually confessing, "I'm sorry. I don't quite know what to say."

"The whole episode frightened Mum as well. So, one of the first things she did when we got back to Dublin was to seek help. It was then that she realised she could not deal with things on her own."

"I know about that. She told me when we met up again that she had found a psychiatrist in Dublin who helped her a lot."

"Yes, she did. She improved hugely. When we moved away from Dublin, to London, she had a referral to another psychiatrist there."

Adam looked thoughtful. "She's been on medication since we met up again. She was very open about this. And she still sees the doctor from time to time. Sometimes, though, she stops taking the medication: she says that dampens her senses: she describes it as feeling that she is packed in cotton wool. I know it also makes her feel tired — I can normally tell when this happens. I had started to worry that she had stopped just before she disappeared."

"I know," Abigail replied. "I used to have the same thing with her. She would get cross if I asked whether she had taken her tablets."

He smiled, remembering similar battles, which he never won. "She was always headstrong."

They were quiet for a while. Abigail then stirred herself. Getting up from the comfortable couch, she said "Right, that's enough for one day. I am off to bed. Don't forget that we have another early start tomorrow."

Chapter 8

Caroline had to dodge deep potholes as she manoeuvred the hire car up the farmhouse's narrow rutted drive, past clumps of early daffodils. This time there was no evidence of the dog as they entered the *domaine*. A hundred yards along, they passed a dilapidated barn, one of its doors hanging open. She parked away from the building. Adam sat in the back seat. They hoped the tinted glass of the rear windows would hide him.

Caroline and Abigail got out and walked towards the entrance to the main building. No-one had noticed their arrival but, as they neared the door, barking came from inside the house, followed by a man's voice shouting at the dog to be quiet. The sign beside the door said *Domaine des Oliviers* and instructed them to press the bell.

It was a while before door opened and a man stood there. From behind him was the sound of muffled barking, and the scrabbling of claws against a door. The man, who was in his forties, ran a hand through his unkempt dark hair. Of medium height and build, he was dressed in jeans and a heavy green sweater. He was unshaven and, under one eye, was a livid purple bruise. He looked surprised to see visitors.

"*Bonjour*. How may I help you?"

"*Bonjour, monsieur.*" Caroline held out the stained and crumpled card for the *Domaine des Oliviers* that Adam had taken from the photographer's stand. "You are Monsieur Gilbert?"

"*Oui*. Yes." he smoothed his hair. "And how may I help you?"

"You were recommended to us for your prints… your photographs around Provence." The photographer returned the business card and smiled. Caroline wasn't sure whether she had seen him before. The man with the dog who had strayed onto her property two years before had stood some way off, while she had spoken to the other man. Gilbert seemed not to recognise either woman, but when they stepped forward to enter the house, he gave Abigail a more searching look.

"Excuse me, but have we met somewhere?' he asked, eyes narrowing. He seemed disconcerted by her.

"I don't think so," she replied. "I have only just arrived from England to stay with my friend."

"I am sorry *madame*. You just looked familiar."

"We're interested in buying some pictures," Caroline reminded him. "We saw some of your work at a friend's and she gave us your business card."

"Ah, I see. I understand and I am of course very flattered. Have you come far to find me here?" Gilbert was now smiling.

"I have an apartment in Avignon. We were visiting Saint-Rémy, so thought we'd stop off here on the way. Could we take a look at your pictures?"

"*Bien sûr…* But of course," he offered. "My studio is inside, at the back of the farmhouse. Please, follow me. And do not worry about the dog. He is shut away."

Caroline and Abigail followed Gilbert inside and down a narrow passageway, dimly lit by a single unshaded light bulb. The dark green wallpaper, which was peeling in places, added to the gloom of the interior. They passed a sparsely furnished kitchen and both women glanced inside. It was spartan. The house lacked a feminine touch.

"Not many people visit the farm. Normally they find me at the local markets."

They passed a dark wooden staircase and came to a large bright room. Gilbert gestured for them to enter. "Welcome to my studio," he said proudly.

It was scattered with metal cabinets and trestle tables, mostly covered with photographic prints. Picture frames and framing equipment occupied a table in the corner. Despite the size of the room, it still felt cosy. To the one side stood a wood-burning heater, emitting a glow through a glass panel. Instead of wallpaper, the walls had been painted an off-white colour, adding to the brightness. Two large windows looked out over an unkempt garden, with a small grove of olive trees beyond. A weak winter's light streamed in over an old oak desk, piles of papers, assorted cameras and camera lenses covering the surface. One whole wall of the studio provided a gallery of his work, displaying dozens of framed pictures of varying sizes.

"These are most of my pictures. The prices include the frames, but I also sell them unframed, if you prefer. Is this what you were looking for?" he asked.

"Yes, very much so," Caroline smiled. "They all look wonderful." And they were good.

"As you see, they are mainly landscapes or architectural studies of buildings that have interested me. I like the detail of old buildings. Mainly my photographs are in black-and-white for the contrasts, but I do have some colour copies. All the pictures are taken around here, in Provence and the Languedoc. I have some prints, which I have not yet displayed, of the dunes of the Camargue as well as a study of le Pont du Gard. They are on that table," he pointed, "if you have an interest in these."

"Thank you, *Monsieur*. We will look through all of these." Caroline crossed the room to the gallery and pointed to a cluster of photographs. These are Aix, aren't they? I recognise the Cours Mirabeau. Ah, and these are taken in Avignon. This one... is it the Église Saint-Didier?" she asked.

"You are quite correct, Madame. You know these towns well."

"Your pictures are great. You don't mind if we take our time looking through all of these?"

"Please take what time you need," he offered.

Abigail saw a pile of recently printed wine labels. She picked one up. "Do you make your own wine here on the farm?"

"Yes, of course. It is only a small vineyard, but it is old. It was planted originally by my father and the vines are mature. Naturally, we have a nice Côte-du-Rhône-Villages, and also a good rosé. It is full-bodied and made from the Grenache grape. My brother is more the winemaker than I am, but he is away at the moment, unfortunately. He would explain things better. But I can show you around and give you a tasting, if you are interested."

Caroline nodded. "Yes, thank you for your offer. That would be very kind. Once we've looked at your pictures, we would love to try some of your wines."

Abigail, standing the other side of Caroline, shifted uncomfortably. The photographer was again staring intently at her. "*Madame*, I do have this strange feeling that I know you."

"*Monsieur*, you are mistaken. It is not possible." She turned away from them both and looked back at the pictures. "I live in London and it's the first time I've come to visit my friend in Avignon."

The women made a show of taking their time to look at each of the prints. They were really good. Abigail was drawn to the landscapes, particularly a series showing scenes of rolling sand dunes. They struck a sudden chord. She turned back to him. "Were these all taken along the Camargue coast?"

"Ah, yes. They were taken around an area called Salin de Giraud last summer, between *les plages* Beauduc and Piémanson. It is a wonderful place to visit, but perhaps not at this time of the year."

"I think I know them... both those beaches. They are lovely. A number of years ago, when I was young, I stayed nearby at a seaside town called Saintes-Maries."

"Ah. You know the town. Saintes-Maries-de-la-Mer. That is normally where I stay when I take these photographs. I have some friends who sometimes let me stay in their holiday house when I go there. They live back in your country... well Ireland, actually. Are you sure I don't know you?"

"I'm positive we have not met before, *monsieur,*" she assured him.

He shrugged. "No matter. Here, I have some prints I took of the beautiful cathedral there — the Église de Nôtre-Dame. Do you know it?"

His words were a shock. She suddenly felt strange. "Yes... I do. It's... it's in the centre of the town."

Gilbert's gaze was again fixed on her. "Are you all right? You have gone a bit pale."

"I'm fine. Perhaps I could have a glass of water?"

"Of course." He headed for the kitchen.

In a whisper, Abigail told Caroline she thought she

might know the house he stayed at. Caroline started to ask her how that was possible when Gilbert arrived back.

"Here you are." Gilbert handed the water to Abigail. "As I was saying, I often go to the annual festival held there in Saintes-Maries. It has, how you say it, an importance… a meaning for me and my brother."

Caroline interrupted. "Oh yes? And why is that?"

"We go there to celebrate our saint. It is a very important festival for us." He did not elaborate.

They turned back to the pictures and Caroline said that she would like to take two of the larger framed prints of Avignon. Abigail wanted some of the unframed prints of the beaches and their dunes. They would be easier to take on the flight back without their frames. She said that she was still feeling a bit strange and could she use the bathroom.

"Of course." He looked concerned. "But you will have to use the one upstairs. I have had to put the dog in the bathroom downstairs to keep it quiet. You will find it when you turn to your left at the top of the stairs."

Caroline feigned uncertainty about her picture choices and returned to look again at the gallery, asking Gilbert about the buildings depicted and their architecture. She wanted to keep him occupied in Abigail's absence. He was more than happy to go into detail. She asked how he had got into photography in the first place. He explained that it had always been a hobby of his. By training, he was actually a civil engineer and had, for many years, worked for the Avignon municipality, looking after public buildings. This had included the churches and cathedrals of the area, which had also been an interest of his. He had decided to combine all of these interests by leaving his job, taking the plunge, and becoming a professional photographer. Having the farm had also helped. Despite her initial inclination Caroline found it difficult to dislike the man.

She asked him about the vineyard. He said his father had owned the farm and cultivated the vineyard, gradually building it up into a small but profitable business. "My brother lived here for a time and both of us helped my father when we could. When my father died, we both inherited the farm and it made sense for me to move here and give up my job with the municipality. My brother now works in the south, near Marseille, and we have someone who manages the *domaine*. It means that I can concentrate on my photography and Clement — the farm manager, looks after the wine and the olive trees."

They chatted until Abigail returned, apologising for having taken so long. "*Pas de problème*. We have been having a good conversation." He moved over to the table. As he did so, Caroline took the opportunity to glance at Abigail. She still looked pale, and Caroline felt a concern.

Whilst Gilbert carefully wrapped their purchases, he turned back. "If we have finished here, then I can show you our winery next door." Caroline looked at Abigail and she nodded. "You will try some of our wine. Also, the olive oil from our own trees here. It is very good."

*

Adam waited until everyone was inside the farmhouse. There was no sign of the dog or the old man they had met the day before. Confident that the coast was now clear, he got out of the back of the car and headed for the old barn. He squeezed through the half-open hanging door and looked around the gloomy interior. There was little of interest. Just thick cobwebs hanging from the corners and old farm equipment. Two wooden ladders were propped against one wall, surrounded by rusting farm implements. Discarded tyres lay in a pile at the rear of the building. He tripped over a small wooden bench in the gloom and an empty paint tin clattered to the ground. He froze for a moment. All remained quiet and he moved to an open barn next door. It contained a white van — a late-model Peugeot — and a motorbike. Both looked like they were in regular use. The van was unlocked. Adam opened the passenger door and felt around the seats, the side-pockets, and inside the glove compartment. It was stuffed with old maps, parking tickets, gloves, a comb and a cardboard box containing the photographer's business cards. The rear of the van yielded two fold-up tables and chairs.

There were another two, newer outbuildings on the other side of the farmhouse. Adam checked the coast was clear and crept across the gravel courtyard. He felt nervous and exposed. This was well outside his comfort zone. Reaching the first, and larger of the two buildings, he eased the door open. There was no sound and he slipped inside. The interior was pitch dark and a low hum came from somewhere. He felt around the wall by the door and found a light switch. Illuminated, the building revealed three large wooden wine vats. Beside them were stacked thirty or so cardboard boxes of wine. Leaning against the boxes was an old black bicycle with a wicker pannier. Metal shelving contained wine racks holding dozens of bottles. Adam picked up a bottle of red wine and looked at the label: *Domaine des Oliviers* was outlined in white against an olive-green background. It was the wine he had tasted a few years before.

The low drone he had heard came from the air-conditioning system. It was cool inside the building, though warmer than the chill of the outside and a sweet tang of fermentation filled the room. Two gleaming steel vats stood against the opposite wall. Adam headed for an old oak table in the centre of the room and opened the drawers. The first contained piles of wine bottle labels, a penknife and a couple of traditional wood and metal corkscrews. The middle drawer yielded two ring-binder folders: one black and the other red. The black file contained a record of wine sales. He flicked through the pages. Some entries included the names and, occasionally, the addresses of purchasers. Assuming that these details were retained for marketing purposes, he scanned through the entries. No names stood out but some of the sales were made to visitors from outside France. Probably holidaymakers who had come across Gilbert and his wines at one of the local markets.

The red folder contained orders. Most came from within France, but a few were for addresses overseas. Orders placed the previous year included the shipment of five cases of the Côte-du-Rhône to an address in Dublin. He put the folders back and, as he did so, he saw a fountain pen at the back of the drawer, a black Montblanc. He picked it up. It resembled one that Maryanne used. It was a gold-coated Meisterstück. She had been given one as a present years ago. It was a classic pen and not uncommon, but it was unusual to find one here. He weighed it in his hand, thinking, before replacing it where he had found it.

Adam pulled open the final drawer. It was empty, aside from a locked metal cash box, which felt light. It must contain papers or documents. He couldn't find a key in the drawer and so, replacing the box, he looked around for anything else worth investigating. A slightly dusty bookshelf above held a number of magazines and books, most devoted to viticulture and wine making. At one end was a pile of old flyers advertising town markets. He rifled through them and found brochures for a number of regional festivals. One, in particular, rang a bell: it was for a two-day event in the town of Saintes-Maries-de-la-Mer the previous May. Another promoted pilgrimages to 'Mary Magdalene's cave', the Holy Cave of Sainte-Baume. Photographs showed the cave set high up in the fortress-like rockface of the pale Massif-de-la-Sainte-Baume, near Marseille. In bold type, at the bottom of the brochure, was a warning that the climb to the holy cave was classed as strenuous. Adam smiled. Strenuous effort seemed to be a requirement for many forms of pilgrimage. Perhaps there was a direct correlation between the amount of effort required and the spirituality attained. As an afterthought, he folded the brochures for the cave and the religious festival and put them in his pocket.

There was no one around when he left the building. Up the uneven road that continued past the buildings was the *domaine's* vineyard, rows of low black vines glistening wetly in the sunlight.

The door to the smaller of the buildings was locked, so he walked around the side of the old farmhouse. As he turned the corner, a crow cawed loudly from above, startling him as it wheeled away over the trees. Recovering, he came across four wide stone steps leading down to a large wooden door. It was set below the level of the main house. Adam went down the uneven steps and tried the rusting iron door handle, but it would not budge. He peered through a small window that was partially covered by cobwebs. Inside were more wine barrels, standing on their side. This was the wine cellar. From deep inside the farmhouse came the muted sound of a dog barking. He looked at his watch. It had been almost an hour since they had arrived. He had better return to the car before the women emerged.

He was about to make his way across the gravel courtyard when the front door of the farmhouse opened and Caroline and Abigail emerged, followed by the photographer. They turned towards him, forcing him to duck back behind the corner of the farmhouse. He heard them enter the winery and the door closed. *Shit*, he thought, *I am really not good at this*.

*

Twenty minutes later, despite the women's protestations, Gilbert insisted that he carry the two cases of wine they had bought over to their car. They asked him to put the boxes in the boot, hoping that he would somehow not notice Adam crouched down in the back seat. Gilbert protested. They should put their pictures in the boot so they could lie flat and the wine should go on the back seat. Carrying the two cases he walked to the rear door and asked Abigail to open it for him. Bending his knees, he turned to place the cases on the back seat.

"Ah!" he exclaimed loudly. He straightened up from the car, his face creased with pain.

Abigail, eyes wide, blurted out, "I'm sorry. We can explain. We—"

"*Merde!* ... shit!" He massaged the small of his back. "I think I have... how you say it... a spasm in my back." He briefly massaged the small of his back and then turned to Abigail. "*Pardon, Madame.* I am sorry for my language... I interrupted you."

Before Abigail could answer Caroline called, "Abi, why don't you stay here at the car?" She closed the door. "I'll go back with Monsieur Gilbert to get the pictures from the house."

Abigail watched them retreat and cautiously looked into the rear of the car. She scanned the courtyard, the outbuildings and up the drive towards the vineyards. There was no sign of Adam. When Caroline returned carrying the pictures, Abigail opened the boot for her. The women looked at each other and Abigail shook her head.

"I don't know," Caroline shrugged, then started the car and pulled slowly away. They headed towards the gate. Jean Gilbert watched them go, a thoughtful expression on his face.

Chapter 9

Adam climbed into the back seat. "Thanks." He shivered as he closed the door. "It was bloody cold waiting for you. I just hoped you would realise where I was."

"We weren't sure." Caroline looked at him in the rear-view mirror. "And we were worried. We couldn't phone you with Gilbert looking on, but it felt like we were driving off, and just leaving you there. There was nothing else we could do, without it looking suspicious."

Adam looked at the boxes of wine beside him on the back seat. "I was around the side of the farmhouse. I saw you all come out of the house and go into the winery. I figured that if you bought some wine, he might help you carry it back to the car. I didn't want him to find me, to see me, so the only way was to get back to the road on foot and wait for you. I didn't think you would be so long, though." He shivered again.

"Good thinking. Thank God you did. That is exactly what happened. I don't know what we would've done if you weren't there."

"Luckily, it didn't come to that. Anyway, I'm here now. Did you manage to find out anything?"

"I think you should ask Abi. She might have found something." Caroline looked sideways. "She's been very quiet."

Adam looked more closely at Abigail. She was looking pale. "What happened? You look like you've seen a ghost."

Abigail took her time before replying. She needed to order her thoughts.

"It feels like I have. Mum's been there at the farmhouse,

I'm sure of it. I could feel her presence when I was upstairs. I just know that she's stayed there." She turned towards him. "I asked if I could use the bathroom. He said I could use the one upstairs. So, while Caroline kept him occupied, I took the opportunity to look around up there." She turned back to Caroline. "You know you said when we arrived that the place looked like it could do with a woman's touch? Well, upstairs was the same, apart from one room."

"OK," she said slowly. "So, what did you find?"

"There were four bedrooms, two of which were clearly used by Jean Gilbert and, I assume, his brother. Both the bedrooms were untidy — clothes, newspapers, receipts were everywhere, on the bed, the floor. In the one there was a half empty bottle of brandy, with unwashed glasses on one of the window ledges. The other bedroom was slightly tidier. A third bedroom was clearly just used for storage. I think it was originally used as a study. There was still a desk there but now it was piled full of things… camera equipment, books, magazines, and boxes and boxes of junk really. There was nothing really that stood out. And then I came to the last bedroom." She paused and looked back at Adam.

"Go on." His voice had softened.

"The bedroom was at the back of the house. When I opened the door. it immediately felt different. It had heavy shutters and I had to turn on the light on to see anything, but immediately I could feel her presence. I swear I even thought I could smell her perfume in the room." Abigail pressed her hands to her head. "Shit, I can feel a migraine coming on. It must be the stress of being there, at the farm." She grimaced in pain.

"Don't worry, Abi, we should be back home before

120

too long."

"Good. I think I am going to lie down. I need to close my eyes for a bit when we get back, if that's OK. But let me try to tell you what I found upstairs, before my headache gets too bad." She looked out at the passing countryside, as though to collect her thoughts.

"In comparison to the other bedrooms, this one was tidy. It looked like it was not being used at the moment, though. The bed was made, each thing was in its place. A bedside table had one of those old brass Tiffany-type lamps with a green and purple shade. It looked so feminine, and so out of place in the farmhouse. There were a couple of empty vases, as well as a dressing table with a mirror. It was the only room upstairs to have any pictures on the walls, even if they were only some of Gilbert's pictures.

"The room might have been a guest room but, unlike the other rooms, it also looked like a woman's room. Unfortunately, there was nothing personal anywhere. The dressing table drawers were empty. There were no photos. But then I remembered that there had been some framed photos of people on the mantelpiece in the first room I went into. So, I went back and, there, in one of the pictures, was a group shot with what looked like Mum, standing next to an older man. They were at the back of the group. The picture was a bit indistinct but... I swear it looked like her. Jean Gilbert was standing in front, next to someone I think I remember from years ago. There was one other woman in the picture, but I did not recognise her. I took a picture of the photo with my phone. Here, let me show you." She passed her phone over.

He turned away from the low sun that streamed into

the car. The colour photograph was of seven people, standing in a narrow street lined with shops. Half of the street was in shade. He enlarged the image with his fingers. Gilbert was the only one smiling, but the woman, standing on the side beside a man, was in the shadows and it was hard to determine her features. She seemed detached from the others. She was tall, as tall as most of the men. He could just make out in the shadows her long dark hair curling over her shoulders. It could be Maryanne. The way she held herself looked familiar, but he couldn't be sure. From the way everyone was dressed, the weather was clearly quite warm.

Adam turned his attention to the street itself, and the shops lining each side, whose signs were all in French. He passed the phone back to Abigail.

She peered at the image. "There's a shop selling beachwear. See here." She pointed.

"Yes, so there is. The town must be near the coast."

"I thought I recognised one of the men. I have a feeling that I remember him from when I was young in Dublin. He had a beard — a long, scraggly one." She brought the phone closer and squinted at the picture. "It's not the clearest of images, but it's possible that it might be the same man who came to stay with us in France. Remember, I told you about him. He used to visit the Dublin house when I was young. He doesn't have a beard in this picture. The hair is also shorter, but there's something familiar about him. He looks quite a bit older in this picture, but it was a long time ago." A sudden thought struck her. "I wonder if this was taken in the same town."

"It does have the look of a holiday town."

"There was another thing," Abigail looked at Caroline.

"Gilbert did say that, when he visits Saintes-Maries, he stays at a friend's house there."

"It's another possible link between the photographer and Maryanne!" Adam exclaimed. "When they met at the market in Uzès I thought at the time that they really seemed to hit it off. Now, I wonder…" his voice tailed off.

"There's one other thing. Gilbert kept on looking at me oddly. He thought he had met me somewhere before, which I guess is possible, although I have no memory of him."

"He did. I noticed that as well," Caroline interjected.

"Perhaps, though, I reminded him of someone."

Quiet descended as they mulled over what this all meant. Adam gazed unseeing at the acres of vines that flanked the winding road between Avignon and Uzès.

"You know, perhaps we should go back now and confront the photographer with this." He broke the silence. "Maryanne could still be there somewhere. Or we could force him to tell us where she is."

Caroline slowed the car. "Do you want me turn around and go back?"

Abigail shook her head. "Let's think about this. I understand how you feel, Adam, but I got the strong feeling that the room hadn't been occupied in some time. I know I said that I could sense that Mum had stayed there, but the room smelt musty, as if the shutters and windows hadn't been opened in a while. There was dust on the bedside table."

Caroline continued driving. "I agree. There was no suggestion there was anyone else in the farmhouse. Abi searched upstairs, and we saw most of the downstairs."

"But what about the picture?"

"It did look like Mum, although it's a pity my copy isn't clearer. Some of the group are also in shadow. I was tempted to take the original from the frame in the bedroom, but decided against it, conscious of how long I had been upstairs."

"OK. I was getting carried away." Adam grimaced. "It's so frustrating — I know she's around here somewhere. But I don't want to endanger her in any way."

"Don't worry, Adam. We all feel the same, but I think we need to be careful," Abigail cautioned.

"I don't think we would achieve anything by going back and confronting Jean," Caroline agreed. "He has already denied ever having met Maryanne. We know that's not true but if we all go back and directly challenge him, he would just continue to deny it. We might even make things worse for her, although I did get the sense from him that he is not the violent type. I found it hard to imagine that he would hurt Maryanne."

"OK. Let's leave it for now and think on what we do next." Adam started. "Oh, there was one other thing, though. I went into the winery. Did you notice the big table that sat in the middle of the room? It's obviously used for their wine tasting. Well, I looked through the drawers and found a pen — a Montblanc — very similar to the one that Maryanne used to use."

Abigail sat up. "Yes, I remember that pen. Mum loved it."

"Was there anything that would identify it as hers, any specific marks, or an engraving?" Caroline could be relied on to be practical.

He screwed up his eyes, thinking. "No, I don't think there was, unfortunately."

Abigail sighed. "So, I don't think we have anything

that could be considered conclusive. If we went to the police now, I suspect they would feel the same."

"I guess so, unfortunately. I know from my previous dealings with them, it will take more than what would be seen as a set of coincidences to convince the police to reopen the case. Everything we have is easily deniable by Gilbert and whoever else is involved. Besides, he would argue that he has committed no crime. We need more evidence. What about Gilbert's voice?" He looked at Abigail. "Did he sound like the man who spoke to you on the phone?"

She shook her head. "No, he didn't. Gilbert has quite a distinctive voice. It was definitely someone else on the phone."

Everyone lapsed into silence again. Adam resolved to remain positive. Despite Caroline's reservations, he felt as though they were slowly getting closer. The mystery of Maryanne's disappearance would surely unravel in time. He just needed to take hope from each small step.

*

Later that evening, Abigail woke with a start. Through the open shutter, she saw that it was now dark. There was little moon and the watery light from a street lamp shimmered dimly through the window. She had slept for longer than she intended, but her headache had eased. What had woken her so suddenly? Turning away, onto her back, she lay there for a short while, looking up at the ceiling, enjoying the feel of the pillows and the enveloping warmth of the bedroom.

Looking at her watch, she saw with surprise that it was now gone eight o'clock. Why hadn't Adam woken her earlier? Perhaps he had also decided to have a nap. He had looked exhausted. She roused herself and got up to investigate. Adam's door was wide open and she walked, barefoot, down the corridor and peered into the gloom. It was empty. The rest of the apartment was also dark. The scraping sound of a drawer being opened came from downstairs and a light beam flickered across the bottom of the stairwell. Abigail called out, "Adam, what on earth are you doing?"

The noise stopped and the light disappeared. "Adam, is that you?" Abigail switched on the hallway light. She waited, then took a step backwards, towards her bedroom door. There was a loud crash as something fell to the ground, followed by a muffled expletive and another thump as a chair was knocked over. Then came the sound of the patio door being wrenched open. Abigail froze. She should hide. Behind her was the door to the bathroom and she hurriedly locked herself inside.

Abigail sat, balancing on the edge of the bath, her heart pounding, for what seemed a lifetime. She waited for a noise of footsteps on the stairs. She tried to quiet her breathing. The door lock seemed sturdy. It would probably hold but she now felt trapped. She swore under her breath. She should have thought to grab her phone. It was still charging in the bedroom, by the bed. She glanced around the bathroom for anything she might use as a weapon.

Eventually, when the apartment had been silent for a while, Abigail turned the lock by degrees, then held the door open a few inches. She listened for any sign of movement. She carefully crept back to the bedroom to retrieve her phone before tiptoeing to the top of the stairs. In the dim light, she saw she saw the dining and kitchen area were in disarray. Books and papers were strewn across the tabletops. Abigail edged down the stairs. The kitchen drawers were half open, their contents spilling out onto the floor. A drawer to a sideboard at the foot of the steps lay upside down, maps and brochures scattered blindly across the floor. A blast of cold air came from the open patio door.

She turned on the kitchen and living room lights. The place had been thoroughly turned over. Cushions were everywhere. Books removed from the bookcase in the hallway had been thrown on the floor. The contents of her handbag had been tipped over one of the sofas. Abigail went through them and saw that her purse was missing. Thank goodness her passport was safe in the bedroom. Adam's empty backpack was on the floor, where pens, various pamphlets and a paperback novel lay in a heap.

Abigail locked the patio door, before retreating to the relative safety of the stairs. She sat down on the cold marble steps, legs shaking, and phoned Adam. "Where are you?" she gasped, when he eventually answered.

"Sorry, I'm in town, having a drink. I should've left you a message. Are you all right? You sound shaky. Has something happened?"

*

Adam reached the apartment in less than ten minutes, having run from the bar in the Place aux Herbes. Struggling to catch his breath, he knocked loudly on the patio door. Abigail let him in and he folded her in his arms, holding her tightly. "I'm sorry, I shouldn't have left you." He looked at the chaos in the apartment. "Good

God." He ran his hand through his dishevelled hair. "You haven't been hurt in any way?"

"No. I am fine. They left me alone, thank Christ. I just feel a bit scared." She felt weak.

"Come, sit down. You look pale. I feel awful leaving you."

"But look at what they have done." Abigail gestured at the upheaval. "What a complete bloody mess."

"The only thing that's important right now is that you're OK." Adam picked up a couple of cushions and put them back on the couch.

"I am. Just a bit shaken, I suppose. I was fast asleep upstairs, and I heard nothing." Tears welled and Abigail put her hands to her eyes.

She let herself be guided by Adam until she was sitting down. "Did you manage to phone the police?"

"Yes… yes, I did" she replied hesitantly. "They said they'd be here very soon, and that we should just wait for them — and touch as little as possible."

Adam stopped trying to tidy up. "Good. Did you manage to get a glimpse of any of them, by any chance?"

"I didn't. It was dark. I startled them when I called out from upstairs. I thought it was you downstairs. I was just so frightened when I realised it wasn't. I hid in the bathroom until I thought they'd gone. Why would they do this?"

"I don't know." Adam shook his head. "Let me get you a brandy. Stay there." He went through to the kitchen, where most of the drawers were half-open. He stepped over everything that had been thrown onto the floor. His laptop lay on the kitchen counter, with a notebook and guidebooks taken from his backpack. Also on the counter was his small pair of binoculars. The backpack was on the floor near the dining table. "You obviously interrupted them before they could take everything they wanted." He indicated the items piled on the worksurface. "Thank God, they at least left these."

Cushions, newspapers and table mats were strewn across the coffee table. Work papers Abigail had brought with her were scattered on the table and floor. She took a number of deep breaths and told Adam what had happened from the moment she had woken suddenly. "I must have registered some noise downstairs. Thank goodness. They must have thought the apartment was empty." The brandy had helped to calm her. "I'm just lucky they fled before they tried upstairs."

She wondered what the burglars had managed to steal, apart from her purse. What had they had been looking for? Her laptop, phone and camera had been upstairs with her in the bedroom.

"Do you know what they've taken? Have they got anything of yours?" Adam gazed around the room.

"Well, they've stolen my purse from my bag. I can't remember how much was in it, perhaps a couple of hundred euros. What else they have taken, I'm not sure, but not a lot. They obviously weren't interested in the work I had brought with me, and they left before they had a chance to come upstairs."

"I can't see anything obvious that's missing either. It looks like they were planning to take my laptop and a few other things before they were interrupted. It's funny. It doesn't look like a normal burglary though. It's as if…"

A flashing light heralded the arrival of a police vehicle outside. Adam let in two young police officers, a man and a woman. Apologising for his poor French, he described what had happened. After taking a statement from them both, and examining the scene, the officers asked Adam and Abigail to leave things as they were until the next morning, when a forensic specialist would be sent to check for fingerprints. They cautioned that, in their experience, they were unlikely to find any. The female police officer spoke the better English and did most of the talking. She asked Abigail whether she had seen any of the intruders and whether she had heard a vehicle outside. She said they would also check with the neighbours. After a couple of hours, the officers left, reassuring them there was little chance of the burglars returning.

When they had left, Adam wandered absently around the downstairs before pouring himself a brandy. All this seemed unreal. Someone had rifled through the kitchen cupboards — there were a couple of broken champagne flutes where the burglars had swept the glasses to one side. What on earth did they imagine they would find? He sighed and returned to the lounge where the Sonos wireless sound system was still sitting, untouched, on the sideboard. In a daze he sat down, nursing his brandy and stared, unseeing, at the mess surrounding them.

"I can't see that much has been taken. Well, nothing of any particular value. They didn't even bother taking the car keys. They're still where I left them on the sideboard. It doesn't add up. It's as if they were looking for something specific."

"I saw a torchlight." She looked around her. "It looks like they were searching for something. But what?"

"Well, it does look like they were planning on taking the laptop. And my notebook, which is odd. Luckily, I'd left my passport and money upstairs."

"If they were looking for something, it would have been only a matter of time before they came upstairs."

Abigail shivered. "Thank God I woke up, and they panicked when they heard me upstairs. I don't want to think of what might have happened if I was still asleep."

Adam felt numb at the thought of Abigail being hurt, or worse. He seemed incapable of protecting anyone close to him. "Don't even go there."

They sat, lost in their separate thoughts. "Let's see if the police manage to obtain fingerprints from the laptop and the door when they do come back tomorrow." In truth, he sounded more hopeful than he felt.

"Well, only if they weren't wearing gloves. If they were professionals, I'm sure they would be careful."

Adam frowned. "I should have locked the door to the patio when I went out," he admitted. "I was distracted when I left. A break-in was the last thing on my mind. I'm so sorry."

"Adam, don't worry. It's not your fault. You'd think it would be safe around here."

"I agree, it should be safe. This place is not an obvious target. I feel that there's a motive other than just a burglary."

"What do you mean?"

"I don't think it was just a random burglary. But we'll find out more from the police. I wonder if it could be connected to our search for Maryanne?" He shook his head. "Abi, it can't be, surely? No one, apart from you and Caroline, knows where I'm staying."

"Anything's possible," she replied. "Could you have been followed from town all the way back here the other day? If there was a connection to Mum's disappearance, perhaps someone is looking to see what you might know. Or could it be simply a warning? Either way, I have a feeling we're going to find out."

Chapter 10

"Do you feel a sense of betrayal by Mum? Do you feel let down?"

Adam considered this. "Yes. It's part of what I feel… and more so now than before." He paused. He should get this right for her. "But it's more complicated than just that. When she left me for someone else the first time, I certainly did. And, of course, I felt a huge sense of loss. That was partly due to my own insecurities. We were young." He shrugged. "I just thought she was wonderful."

"And now?"

"There are many emotions, some of which I still haven't reconciled. There's a sense of failure mixed in there, for sure. It's hard to put into words." He ran his hand through his hair. "I thought that she was dead somewhere. That she had died alone. As the days and weeks passed, there was nothing to give me any hope. My overriding feeling at that time was that I hadn't been able to protect her. I knew I needed to, and I should've done. In the end, I failed her."

"Oh, Adam." She shifted in the passenger seat to look at him and rested a hand on his arm.

They were driving to Sainte-Maries-de-la-Mer. Abigail was due to return to London in a few days and had suggested they drive down through the Camargue to the coastal town. It would give them the opportunity to spend time together before she returned to her work. The biting cold from the north had now all but disappeared, replaced by a more benign westerly breeze. It brought a warmth and promise of the spring to follow. Abigail said she would show Adam the house that she had stayed in with Maryanne, if she could remember where it was.

Adam, touched by her simple gesture, looked across at her, before turning back. "Of course, as time went on and there was no sign of her, I did start to think of other reasons for her disappearance, but really none made any sense."

He remembered the bleakness and hopelessness as he gazed through the windscreen, the road carving a path through the flat featureless landscape. They had followed the direction of the fast-flowing Rhône to Arles, along the D90, then turned off to follow the smaller road towards the coast. The countryside was becoming increasingly marshy. The wheat fields and small vineyards, interspersed with the occasional farming village, had given way to the stagnant *etangs* of the delta.

It felt like an ancient and different world, but Adam barely noticed. "I still don't know what to think. I thought that the postcard was a plea for help. That's why I am here, to find and rescue her — but now I am not so sure. Perhaps it was meant as a statement of some sort, or just an apology. If she really is alive, maybe I should come to terms with the idea that Maryanne intended to leave me all along. Perhaps that's why she phoned you, to get me to give up and go home."

His shoulders slumped with the weight of the past few years. He felt hollow. Perhaps it was the end of the journey and he had lost her. He glanced back. Abigail was sitting, silent, lost in her thoughts.

"I had known for a long time that your mother struggled. She found it hard to talk about certain things, things from her past. Even with me. But I have to say that, when she took her medication regularly, she was often fine, happy even. In the year or so before she vanished, she had seemed preoccupied, and more defensive about things." He couldn't help the sigh that escaped. "I tried to bring her out of herself, but sometimes it was difficult." Living with Maryanne had been, at times, like walking on eggshells. "I started believing that she might have done something to herself." He hesitated. "That's why I felt I should have looked after her better."

Abigail roused herself and looked across at Adam. "You shouldn't beat yourself up. I had similar thoughts. I found her difficult at times when I was growing up. Some of the things she used to do were unsettling and I never really got used to it. Even now I prefer order and reliability, rather than the chaos of my childhood." She gathered her hair behind her ears with a rueful smile. "I didn't really understand what was going on and it made me wary of her. But I loved her — she was all I had, really. I suppose I coped by doing my own thing when Mum became distracted. It taught me how to become self-sufficient."

She sat up and turned her gaze back to the countryside. They had just passed the turnoff to the ancient town of Aigues-Mortes. Either side of the narrowing road, as they continued southwards, the white horses, the *Camarguais,* roamed freely. The green of the marshland and rose-coloured salt flats stretched to the horizon, occasionally punctuated by reed-covered banks. Suddenly, she leaned forwards and pointed out, with unconcealed delight, the flamingos she remembered so vividly, shimmering pink across the wetlands in the morning sun. The seasons change quickly in the south of France.

A succession of small roundabouts indicated they were on the outskirts of Sainte-Maries. Abigail looked around her, brow furrowed. "You know, I believe I know where I am."

"OK."

"If you take the next turning on your right, before we get into the main town, I'm pretty certain we'll get to the house we stayed in."

Adam slowed the car. They were in a sleepy suburb of the town, with small, drab-looking houses each side of the quiet road.

"It still looks the same. There!" she exclaimed, "I'm sure that's the place. Pull over here."

Adam slowed and stopped alongside an unremarkable-looking two-storey grey and white cottage surrounded by a low wooden fence. Paint was peeling from the brown shutters. The car port to the side of the building was empty.

Abigail got out of the car and approached the wooden gate. "I'm sure this is the place. It looks more compact and run-down than I remember, but I was quite young when I stayed here. It doesn't look as though anyone's living there."

Adam studied the house as she tried the gate. It was padlocked. The place looked as though it had been empty for a while. A fallen branch from an apple tree lay forlornly on the grass. Weeds were growing between the paving stones. There was no one about and most of the other houses were shuttered. It had that air of desolation only an out-of-season holiday resort can convey.

They got back in the car, turned round and continued to the *centre-ville*, parking in the main square, with its view of the grey rolling sea, bounded by a low wall. There was just a scattering of vehicles, but at least one café was open. The imposing granite bell tower of the Église de Nôtre-Dame-de-la-Mer dominated the rooftops of the town. They headed towards it. A sea breeze blew in, carrying with it the briny tang of seaweed. High above the buildings, the gulls wheeled, offering their raucous welcome.

As the grey outline of the fortress-like church loomed closer, Adam shivered in spite of the spring warmth. There was something brutal about the building, which was out of proportion to the surrounding town — and the spiritual needs of its citizens. It filled the horizon and blocked the light in its efforts to subjugate all around it.

"I remember this street. We used to visit a supermarket here. Why don't we try some of the quainter side streets, away from the seafront? I'm starving. We might find a nice place for lunch before we go into the church."

The street they found themselves on was a main tourist shopping thoroughfare, with gift shops on each side of the road. An old lady laden with shopping bags weaved past them on an ancient black bicycle, muttering loudly to herself. Abigail glanced at Adam and, simultaneously, they both burst out laughing.

They turned down a side lane, too narrow for cars, where the Provençal scent of lavender, soaps and cosmetics wafted from the small shops specialising in regional produce. Others contained religious books and mementos. One displayed a large poster in its window showing a colourful crowd carrying a statue into the sea.

Around the next corner, as they passed a patisserie attracting a small lunchtime trade, Abigail stopped.

"This is the street. The one in the photo. Look, there's the shop the group were standing outside."

"Are you sure?"

She delved into her shoulder bag, found her phone and showed Adam. "See. The group were over there, looking this way. It's the same shop."

Adam looked over her shoulder. "You're right. Over there is the shop selling swimwear and sandals."

"So, they were here in Saintes-Maries. I can't believe it. Mum has been back here, in the past two years."

"Assuming, of course, that it is Maryanne in the photograph."

"I just know it is. But why was she here?"

"And why with these people?" Adam looked up and down the street as if expecting to see Maryanne at any moment.

*

"Somehow this town is associated with her disappearance." Abigail broke off from hungrily making her way through a *Quattro Stagioni* and looked at Adam. They had found a small pizzeria further down the street. "There's something going on, otherwise it would be too much of a coincidence. It's got to be something to do with the people who own the holiday cottage here or with the town itself... or, perhaps, the cathedral."

Adam had bought a guide to Saintes-Maries. "I thought this might be helpful." He opened it and read the first page. "This is interesting. Do you know how the place got its name?"

"Not really. I remember that its history goes back a long way — pretty much to biblical times — and, as I mentioned the other day, also involves Mary Magdalene."

Adam looked up. "Yes, that's broadly correct. The town is apparently named Saintes-Maries-de-la-Mer — the Saint Marys of the Sea — for three disciples, all called Mary: Mary Magdalene, Mary Jacobe and Mary

Salome. They were believed to be the first witnesses to Jesus's empty tomb after the resurrection and they were literally cast adrift from the Holy Land. They drifted in a boat, all the way across the length of the Mediterranean, before landing here."

"Yes, of course. I remember now. They were accompanied by a servant called Sara. I think she was originally from Egypt. She became the local saint that is celebrated each year in the town. I told you about her the other day."

He nodded his head. "Yes, yes, you did. The saint who was known as the Black Madonna." He picked up the book again. "It references these annual celebrations. It says that, in addition to the town being a popular beach destination, it's also known for its festivals, which are held each year in May and October, and date back to the Middle Ages." He read, "The May festival, in particular, draws a huge number of Roma people — not just from France, but from across Europe — to the town for a week." He looked up. "This must be the festival you witnessed when you and Maryanne were here."

"Yes. It was the part of the stay that I do remember vividly. I don't know if you know it, but the Romas originally came from northern India. From the Middle-Ages onwards they slowly migrated west across Europe."

"No, I didn't. I think I assumed they came from around Romania. I guess there is a lot of ignorance regarding them."

"There is, mixed together with a fair degree of racism. Anyway, they made the festival. It felt incredibly colourful and exciting. Well, to me certainly, as a young girl from Ireland. The Romas seemed to arrive well before the festival started and they camped everywhere

— in the streets, in the square, even on the beaches. For them, it is a real pilgrimage."

"It says here that the festival culminates when a large crowd carry statues of this Sara and the three Marys through the streets of the town to the beach, and then right into the sea. That was what was being shown in the poster we saw earlier."

"Adam, it was amazing to be part of. But it was also when Mum started getting ill." She looked pensive.

He looked up from the guide and regarded Abigail for a while before returning to finish his pizza. Putting his question to one side, he continued to read. "It says that the church was built between the 9th and the 12th centuries to be both a refuge and a fortress. I guess that explains its size. As for the saints, it says that someone 'discovered' the relics of two of them — Mary Jacobe and Mary Salome, in the church, six hundred years ago."

Abigail gathered up her phone and bag. "Well, let's go and take a look, then. It's not far from here. I've seen it before, but you will find it very interesting." Attracting the waiter's attention, they paid and left.

The immense church sat in the middle of a square fringed with restaurants, cafés and tourist shops. A woman selling religious trinkets and offerings accosted them as they walked towards it. The church's entrance was beneath a huge bell tower. Entering the cool of the interior, they found themselves in a high-ceilinged nave supported by stone columns. High above the altar was a casket adorned with a large silver cross. Adam pointed to it.

"That must be where the relics of the saints are stored. Excavations were apparently carried out in the 15th century and a small cave was discovered beyond the altar.

It had a door that led to an oratory where several human heads were found, arranged in the form of a cross, together with the bodies of two women. The bodies were later identified as Mary Salome and Mary Jacobe." He looked up and gave a wry smile. "It also says here that they gave off a sweet smell on their discovery."

"The statue of the saint — Sara — is kept downstairs in the crypt." Abigail pointed towards a narrow entrance. "I've been down there several times, but you must see it."

They waited patiently for an elderly man with a walking stick to climb the narrow stone steps. Reaching the top, he smiled his thanks, and they went down. Candles flickered in the small cave-like room, where the statue of Sara, dressed in a purple and gold gown and wearing a gold crown, perched on a black rock beside the altar. Black hair framed a mahogany-coloured face. In the flickering light, she looked strangely frail. Children's clothes, and trinkets, photographs and folded prayers were strewn around her. A pair of crutches leant against the wall. There was a sweet, musty smell about the crypt.

Adam consulted the guidebook again. "Sara has her own day next month. It is held the day before the one dedicated to the Marys."

"I first came down here with Mum. Originally, it was only the Romas permitted down here. Nowadays, I believe, it is open to everyone. When Mum and I visited, the crypt was completely packed with her followers and I remember how powerful the atmosphere was. If you are still here in France, and get the chance, you should come during the festival and see for yourself."

As they climbed the stairs, Abigail said that, as they were there, they should also go up onto the battlements. "It's really worth it. You can see for miles across the

Camargue." By now it was mid-afternoon, and the cloud had lifted. Paying their admission charge, they climbed the narrow winding staircase and emerged on the rooftop. They could feel the breeze that came directly off the sea.

"The view is spectacular," he had to admit, despite his usual twinge of vertigo. They walked the perimeter of the roof, taking in the panorama that encompassed the town's terracotta roof tops, the marshes, the dunes, the estuary and the azure of the Mediterranean beyond. Outlined on the distant horizon, a huge, heavily-laden, container vessel was made its slow progress to the port of Marseille. Above them sat the church's five bells in the gothic arches of the imposing granite tower. Abigail took her phone from her bag and took a picture of the two of them with the view in the background.

"We are really high up here." Adam edged his way to the low wall of the battlements and gingerly peered down into the square below. The faint sound of voices drifted from below. He saw figures in the queue waiting patiently to climb to the rooftop and he could make out the small groups of elderly women scurrying to converge on passing tourists, all trying to sell their wares. Among the tourists, his eyes were drawn to a stocky figure who seemed to be looking up, directly at him. With a jolt of recognition Adam realised he was gazing at the thug who had barged into him that freezing morning at the market.

"Look down there." Adam pointed. "See the man standing on his own. Looking right at us. It's the man I told you about when you first arrived. He's the guy that deliberately knocked into me." The man continued to stare at them. The old coat was not in evidence. Now he wore jeans with a light blue pullover and his slouch and unruly grey hair made him look shabby. He didn't move and calmy smoked a cigarette, seemingly unperturbed, as he looked upwards.

Abigail looked down to where Adam was pointing.

"He's definitely the guy who barged into me in Uzès. But I am sure I've also seen him before that. It was when Maryanne and I went to watch the Tour de France. At the time I just thought he was some homeless guy. It's not a coincidence that he's here now. He keeps on appearing and he's sending me a signal. Let's go. I need to sort this out."

He pointed at the man and shouted, "*Attendez*! Just wait there!" The man continued to calmly stare up at them. Adam grabbed Abigail's hand and they headed for the stairway where they descended the uneven steps as fast as was safe. They had been fortunate that they didn't have to squeeze past anyone going in the opposite direction up the narrow stairway. When they emerged in the square, the man had disappeared.

"Well, that was predictable." Adam hurried as fast as his knee allowed to the other side of the church, but, apart from the trinket sellers, there was no one there. He wasn't in the church, either. The man could have vanished down any one of the myriad of small side streets leading away from the square.

Shaken and dispirited, he returned to the other side of the square, where Abigail waited. He could feel the frustration building up inside of him. It was time to put a stop to all of this. On the spot where the man had stood moments ago, the remains of a discarded cigarette still smouldered and Adam angrily ground it out with his shoe. As he did so he felt the dull ache from his knee after the recent exertion. He grimaced in pain.

Abigail took his arm. "Whatever it is that he is trying

to do, and whatever his message is, please just let it go. Maybe you're right — that it is time to get on with your life. Perhaps it's time for both of us."

Chapter 11

Abigail absently picked up her phone. Four missed calls and two messages, all from Caroline. She had turned her phone to silent while she caught up on the work that had mounted up while she was away in France. Budget deadlines were fast approaching and research papers were strewn across her desk. As she switched the silent mode off, the phone rang and she jumped.

"Thank God. Finally. Where have you been?" Caroline was agitated.

"I'm so sorry. I was working. What's happened?"

"Adam's had an accident."

"Shit! Is he all right? Oh God, I'm sorry!" she exclaimed. "I should have got back to you sooner."

"Calm down. I'm at the hospital in Nîmes. I had to leave the ward to try you once more."

"Oh, Caroline, I'm so sorry. But what's happened? What sort of accident? Is he badly hurt?"

"We don't know what happened yet. His hire car was found on its side in a ditch early this morning. The accident happened on the road to Avignon, about five minutes before the turnoff to the motorway. I don't know how long he was in the car or what caused the accident. He was found by a farmer just after it got light this morning. It—"

"How is he? Christ. Is he conscious?"

"Yes. Abi, keep calm. I think he is going to be fine."

"Thank God," Abigail sighed with relief. "What on earth happened?"

"We're trying to piece it together. I'm here with Emile and Vivienne, some friends of his from a nearby village."

"Ah, I think Adam mentioned them to me. So how did the accident happen?"

"He seemed to have hit a tree on the side of the road before finally ending up in the ditch. The car was pretty smashed up, so it was a miracle that he wasn't more badly hurt. It took the *pompiers* some time to extract him from the car."

"Oh shit." Abigail sagged at her desk, imagining the awful scene.

"The doctors here are still assessing him," Caroline continued. "The good news is that he's conscious and stable, although a bit banged up. They'll do more tests, but they said he's has been very lucky. They don't believe there are internal injuries, but they want to make sure. We were only allowed to speak to him very briefly. He has now been sedated, but he asked me to let you know that he was OK. He even managed to smile. You know that smile of his."

"It does sound like he's been lucky. How did they know to contact you?"

"They found his phone wedged under one of the car seats. I guess they checked his recent calls. We must have been among the last people he spoke to." There was a silence.

"Caroline… are you still there?"

"I'm sorry. He gave me a ring yesterday morning. We were just chatting. We were going to meet up tomorrow for lunch," she said, her voice breaking.

"I should be there with you."

"Abi, there is nothing that can be done tonight. He's asleep. I will go back and check on him. Emile and Vivienne are going to come back to my place for a drink. The doctors here have our contact details. I've given them yours as well. In any event, they won't be doing any further tests on him now. Not until the morning. He had a bang on the head, probably from the windscreen, and I think they also want to give him an EEG just to rule out any brain damage."

"Shit. Shit. He's got to be all right!" she exclaimed, trying to convince herself.

"Calm down, Abi. He's a strong, fit guy. He will be OK. The doctors just need to rule things out."

"Thanks, Caroline. That helps a lot." After a short pause she asked, "Do they know how the accident happened? He's a good driver."

"They are still investigating it, but it looks like another vehicle was involved. There are skid marks on the road and, apparently, there's a dent on the one side of the car… as if he was hit from the side. The police think that another car came out from a side road and hit him."

Abigail went cold. "Are you… are you saying it might have been deliberate?" Her hand was shaking as she held the phone to her ear.

"No. Don't jump to any conclusions. The police simply don't know — it's too early to say. It could well be just an accident. And, of course, they haven't been able to interview Adam yet."

"Well, did anyone see anything?"

"I don't think so. No one has come forward. From what I have been told, a farmer was driving his tractor to his fields early this morning and spotted the car in the ditch. It was too early for much, if any, traffic on the roads. Anyway, the farmer stopped to investigate and saw Adam inside."

"Oh God, poor Adam. It's horrible to think he was just lying there."

"The ditch was quite deep and the car was on its side. The farmer tried to get to Adam but the doors were too smashed to open. Adam was still conscious and could communicate with him. He couldn't reach his phone but the farmer phoned the emergency services and waited beside the road for them to arrive."

"Shit, Adam could have been there in the ditch for hours."

"Abi, we don't really know much at the moment."

"I'll try and come back to France immediately. It will be tricky as I haven't been back long. But I'll try and clear it with work first thing. Hopefully, they'll be understanding. I will try to get a flight, perhaps tomorrow evening."

"Abi, listen to me. There's no need to panic. Adam's not in any danger. He is stable and he's being looked after very well here. Right now he's asleep. I'll be back here with him tomorrow. And I am sure that Emile and Vivienne will also look in on him. In any event, they'll run more tests tomorrow and then we will know the full picture. He has some bumps and bruises and has got to be hurting so they will also keep him on pain medication for a bit. Hopefully, he'll be able to leave hospital in a few days and he can come back and stay with me in Uzès until he goes back to the UK. I was due to come back the day after tomorrow to help out with Mum, but I'll delay my return until after Adam is out of hospital. Emile and Vivienne have said they'll help him around the house here."

"That's so kind of you all, but I need to do my bit as well."

"Look, I know that you are up to your eyeballs with your project. We'll speak tomorrow. I will give you an update when we know more. To put your mind at rest, I am sure will be able to speak to him yourself tomorrow. Then you can decide when to come back."

"Caroline, thank you for everything."

"No problem," she replied. "That's what good friends are for."

"I'll let you know my plans. Take care."

*

Abigail sat at her desk for a long while, staring at a computer screen. The words seemed to jumble and made no sense. She tried to concentrate, but her thoughts kept returning to Adam. They had shared a snatched goodbye at Montpellier airport as she hurried to make her flight. There had been a tacit understanding, and sadness, that their search for Maryanne was misplaced. They should now assume that she was indeed alive and now had a new life in France, one that did not include either her or Adam. Neither had heard anything further from her. She suspected that she found this easier to accept than Adam: she had lower expectations, and still retained some bitter memories. She wondered, though, whether Adam would be able to reconcile himself to this new reality. He told her he would probably stay in Uzès to the end of the month and would then return to London to get on with his life. She had hoped she could believe him. And now he was lying, injured and defenceless, in hospital. With an audible sigh, she forced herself to turn back to the monitor and her project proposal. There was nothing further she could do until the next day.

*

Waiting on the draughty Tube station platform, surrounded by other weary commuters, Abigail felt numb and more alone than she had for some time. The south of France suddenly felt a world away. Later, she emerged from her station into a light London drizzle and walked the short distance to the red-brick Victorian semi, whose top floor she shared with a friend. As she opened the door to the apartment, she realised that she had completely forgotten to buy food from the small supermarket in the High Street.

"Damn!" she exclaimed. She couldn't be bothered to walk all the way back. She didn't have much of an appetite, anyway, after the news about Adam. It felt as if a dark cloud had descended, and with it the unsettling feeling that what had happened was not an unfortunate accident.

She found a note on the fridge from her flatmate, saying that she was out, but they needed more wine, which was underlined. Abigail sighed. The bloody wine would just have to wait. She was tired, but, before she could think of any early night, there were a couple of things she needed to do first.

She sat down wearily with her laptop at the small kitchen table to see how her work schedule might allow her to return to France. Ever since her return, and after their shared understanding, a concern had still nagged at her. Adam's accident had reinforced the feeling.

Later that evening, she stretched out her arms behind her and put her laptop to one side. She had gone through her diary and had reprioritised her busy schedule as best she could, and there was a glimmer of a way forward. She was stiff when she got up to make a fresh cup of coffee. She rummaged in the cupboard above and found a couple of biscuits. When she sat down on the sofa, she opened the photo album she had left on the coffee table.

On her return, she had pulled out all the old albums that Maryanne had compiled, with some help from herself, whilst they were in Dublin. Along with the old photo albums was the odd dog-eared and frayed school exercise book. She had been a sporadic diary keeper. She was struck by how little they really told her about herself. The inadequate and random attempt to document her childhood reflected the lack of continuity she had felt in her life.

There were days, sometimes even weeks, with no entries at all, except a tick to show that the day was completed. She had kept these diaries since childhood but there was little mention of friends, other than Magda. Perhaps it was because very few friends, aside from Magda, ever came to the house. Was this rather a symptom of the detachment she had felt from her childhood? Eventually the diaries seemed to peter out at about the time they had moved to London. She sighed. Perhaps that was why she wasn't good with relationships.

She opened the first of the photo albums and searched for the picture she wanted. It was a colour photo that had faded to shades of light brown. She could just about make out the figures in the picture. It had been taken in the back garden of the old house in Dublin by her mother and it showed her grandmother surrounded by three men. Abigail must have been eleven or twelve at the time. The group were posing, all holding drinks. The man on the right clutched a bottle of Guinness. They stood in the shade of a gnarled apple tree that she fondly remembered climbing when she was young.

Abigail recognised two of them. They were regular

visitors to her grandmother's house. The man standing closest to her grandmother stood out, not just because of his height or unkempt beard, but also because of the malign look about him. She had been frightened of him. By contrast, the rest of the group were smiling. Abigail compared the picture to the one on her phone. The taller man no longer had a beard but, despite the fuzzy image, he did look like the man who had stayed with them in Dublin: the same man who arrived at the Saintes-Maries cottage all those years ago.

There were no more pictures of them. Could she remember his name? She had not seen him since her childhood. Her mother had not mentioned him either. She knew that he had not owned a home in Dublin, which was why he had stayed with them. Hadn't her mother said that he was part of a small religious order? She recalled another distant, jarring, memory. The phrase 'Dog of God' had come to mind. She'd once asked Maryanne if he had called himself that because he looked fierce?

With a start, she suddenly remembered something else. Something much more recent. When they had visited Gilbert's *domaine* the first time, Caroline had returned to the car chuckling about what the old man at the gate had called the fierce dog — '*Chien de Dieu*'. Was it just a strange coincidence? She sat back. A numbing fear ran through her.

Abigail looked at her watch. It was now 9.30. Was it too late to call Magda? Probably. She couldn't remember the last time that she had spoken to her. Magda's mother was an aspiring artist and part of the same crowd of Dublin artists as her grandmother. Most times she visited she would bring Magda with her and the two girls would happily take themselves off to her bedroom. Occasionally, if they had some money, they would disappear off to the corner shop at the end of the street to buy sweets. Abigail's grandmother was more friendly with Magda's mother than Maryanne, despite the two being closer in age. Abigail never knew why.

Magda lived in Bristol now, but Abi was sure her mother was still in Dublin. Abigail dialled the number. The phone rang for a while, then went to voicemail. She didn't leave a message. It was too complex. It was better that she try again in the morning.

It was late-morning before she was able to phone Magda. Meanwhile, she'd managed to have a conversation with Adam, before he was taken off for more tests. He had been at pains to assure her that he was fine, just a bit bruised. He did sound like the old Adam. He had been very lucky — a car had come from nowhere, at some speed, and there had been no way of avoiding the collision. All he remembered of the accident was that it was a green vehicle, and large. It had hit him on the passenger side.

"Did the vehicle stop?"

"I don't know. I don't think so. I ended up almost upside down in a ditch beside the road and it was some time before anyone came to my aid."

"Christ. And no sign of the other vehicle?"

"When I was freed from the car by the firemen, there was no sign of another vehicle, other than broken glass on the road — and skid marks."

"And no-one reported it? Apart from the farmer who found you?"

"No. I don't believe that anyone did."

"So, was it a hit and run?"

"I guess so," Adam replied patiently. "The police took photographs and they are coming here later to interview me. I was lucky. The car only just missed the trees along the road before going into the ditch."

"I wonder if there are any witnesses?"

"That's the odd thing Abi. It was early in the morning — it had only just got light — and there was no other traffic around. I don't know how the other driver couldn't have seen my car. He just pulled out straight into me. It was a completely clear road."

"I'm so sorry, Adam. I'm just firing off all these questions at you. I suppose it's thrown me," she admitted.

"I know. I was really shaken as well. But I feel better today."

"What were you doing driving at that time of the morning?"

"Ah, that's a bit of a long story. Look, I am just about to be taken off for further tests here. I'll explain when we next speak. Hopefully, I'll also have a clearer idea of when I might get out of here."

When the call to Adam ended, she immediately dialled Magda's number. The phone rang for a while and, as she was about to end the call, her old friend came on the line. "Hi Abi. Gosh, we haven't spoken in ages. It's great to hear from you. How are you?"

"I'm fine. Magda, I have to apologise for not being in touch more over the last year. Somehow, events seemed to have got in the way of everything recently. And how are you?"

Magda filled her in. She was working in a Bristol estate agency before deciding whether to go back to Dublin or to go travelling, possibly to Australia, with her new boyfriend. It was a while before Abigail had the chance to explain why she was phoning. "You remember how, when you used to come round to my Grandma's house, there were always other people there?"

"I remember the big old house." She laughed. "It was exciting coming to your place. There was always something interesting going on."

"Do you remember any of the people who were around at that time? I know they were friends of Gran's, but your mother also knew them well. I'm thinking of one, in particular, a man who used to stay there sometimes. He was tall, with long hair, and odd staring eyes. He was French and younger than Gran."

"I think I do. I remember the accent. He always wore the same dark coat, even in summer, and he had a beard."

"Yes, that's the one."

"He was around quite a lot at your place. I remember that I didn't much like him."

"Nor me. Your mum knew him quite well. Do you think she would mind talking to me about him?"

Abigail wrote down the number.

*

That night, Abigail phoned Adam to let him know she'd booked a flight for Saturday. The meeting with her boss had gone better than she expected. He had been sympathetic to her need to help look after Adam, and had agreed that she could return for two weeks. She would need to complete her immediate project proposal by Friday midday and also to be readily contactable during her time away. Adam was touched by her concern but said he would be fine with Caroline. Abigail was having none of it, telling him that she had already booked her flight for the Saturday afternoon: he would just have to put up with her. He told her that he also had good news:

the tests had shown no major injury, just bruising and a few scars. He would be leaving the hospital in Nîmes the following day. Vivienne would take him back to Caroline's. Before she left the office, she had taken the opportunity to phone Caroline. She had insisted that Abigail stay with her. They could share the duties of looking after the patient until Caroline returned to the UK. These would largely consist of convincing him to rest. He was bruised and shaken and would need time to recuperate.

Abigail laughed. "We'll have our work cut out with that. That is not his way, as you know well."

On her way home, Abigail had bought a couple of bottles of red wine and she now poured herself a glass. Events of the past days had raised questions that she needed to address before returning to France. She had no alternative. Straightening her back, she scraped her long hair away from her face and twisted it tightly between her fingers. It was what she did when she felt apprehensive. She felt a dull foreboding as she dialled the number for Magda's mother.

An hour later and she had the beginnings of an answer to the question that had begun forming in her mind. Whether it was relevant, only time would tell. The implications left her numb and she sat with her still half-full glass of wine for some time, staring blankly out of the darkened window. How was she going to explain this to Adam — and not sound like her mother? Adam was more down-to-earth: would he think this was all too far-fetched? Probably, but she needed to do more research. That, and her now crammed work schedule, meant she would get little sleep over the next few nights.

Magda's mother Siobhan had been surprised to hear from Abigail. Her request to speak to Siobhan about her childhood in Dublin was initially met with silence. Abigail initially thought she had lost the connection, but then there was a sigh. Magda's mother said she owed Abigail an apology. She should have said something a long time ago. She admitted she had tried to distance herself from the house following the death of Abigail's grandmother. Abigail said she had not understood at the time why her daughter had stopped visiting. Siobhan repeated that she was so sorry: part of the reason she had stepped back was because she didn't want to see Maryanne. "Please go on," Abigail encouraged.

Siobhan replied that Maryanne had become wrapped up with the few 'zealots' that made up a vociferous subset of the regulars to the Dublin house. She felt they exerted an influence over Maryanne. At the time many of the artists had drifted away and Siobhan had found it hard to find a common ground with those that remained. Eventually she just stopped visiting. Maryanne had not seemed to notice.

"I found it hard to understand why Magda suddenly stopped coming round."

"I'm so sorry for that. It's hard to explain my feelings at the time — and hard to talk now about your mother. I feel I let both of you down. You needed proper friends and support at that time."

"Magda didn't know why you stopped coming. I am not sure she knows why now. I thought it was something I had done."

"I should have done better by you both," she admitted.

She had heard about Maryanne's disappearance from Magda. It must have been hard for Abigail.

"That's really why I am phoning. I have some questions about the people you had concerns with — well, one in particular."

There was another sigh. "Go ahead. I think I know who you're referring to. I remember him clearly."

"He was about your age. Tall, I think. But it was his eyes, though, that you would particularly remember — there was an intensity about them."

"If it's the person I'm thinking of, he was French or Belgian. I think he was called Andrew." There was a brief pause as she tried to remember. "No. That's not right. Perhaps it was Andre... or Anton. Anton Girard, something like that. Yes, he was tall. Tall and hairy. And also thin. I would describe him as austere." She laughed. "You're right about the eyes. He seemed to stare right through you. He said he was a priest, but he reminded me of Rasputin. I know he unsettled others in the house."

"Siobhan, did this priest ever refer to himself by anything other than his name? Or did others give him a nickname which described him or his behaviour?"

"There was something. I think he was occasionally called 'the inquisitor' by others. It was probably his manner. I think he quite liked the term."

"I know this sounds odd, but did you ever hear him called 'God's dog'? Or something quite similar?"

"I don't know. I just can't remember. I wasn't there that often and, when he was around, I tried to avoid him. He spoke good English. I think he went to the Dominican College in Dublin, which was why he was there in the first place." She hesitated. "Despite his religion, I felt at the time that he had a strange obsession with your mother. I was never sure whether she was fully aware of it."

"I… I don't really know. Perhaps not then."

Siobhan said, gently, "Why are you asking? Now, after so many years?"

There was a long silence. "Do you know what happened to him?"

Chapter 12

Abigail slowly put the phone down, numb with shock. Adam was in real danger. Still reeling from what Siobhan had told her, she reached for her laptop. She had to find out as much as she could about the Dominicans, and fast. The man she had asked about had apparently suffered from a serious mental illness in his youth and, when he recovered, he moved to Dublin to study.

A year or so after he had qualified, he returned to France to work within the church, somewhere near Marseille. He had some sort of disagreement with the church leaders, resulting in his suspension. Following that, he had a further breakdown, ending up in hospital. On his recovery, he rejoined a branch of the order, returning only occasionally to Dublin. Siobhan described him as a loner, someone who never really fitted in anywhere. After her grandmother's death, he had disappeared.

Abigail sat on her bed, back against the wall, and stretched. She took a last sip of wine and began tapping on her laptop, searching for anything she could find on the Dominican Order. She had been baptised and raised a Catholic. In Dublin she had attended mass regularly with her mother and grandmother. She remembered she enjoyed the singing, though Maryanne had the better voice, sandwiched in a pew between the women. As she grew older, she felt less need for the ceremony or the sense of belonging it had provided during her early years. Maryanne never forced her to go to church and spirituality was rarely discussed. It was as if her mother was trying to distance Abigail from aspects of her own life. Perhaps Maryanne had been trying to shield her.

The Dominicans, founded by Saint Dominic in Toulouse in the 13th century, were very much a mystery to her. The order was founded originally to broaden the base of the Catholic Church. This was to be done by getting out and preaching amongst the population, initially across the south of France. At the same time, they actively sought to oppose conflicting beliefs — those that were seen as inconsistent with their medieval doctrines. These conflicting beliefs they labelled as heresy. She remembered from somewhere that, well into the 20th century, the Catholic Church had still defined Protestants as heretics.

Abigail jerked awake, as she felt her eyelids close. It was getting late and she needed to continue her search through the web. She got up stiffly and went through to the kitchen. She wondered if she should risk one more glass of red wine, but then decided on a cup of jasmine tea.

Settling herself once again in front of her laptop, she plumped up the pillows supporting her back and resumed her education. She had heard of the Dominicans, of course, when she was younger but really knew very little about them beyond their connection to Catholicism.

As the order grew, both in strength and influence, it became known as the Order of Preachers or the Black Friars, due to the black coats that were often worn. It quickly developed a reputation for the enthusiastic manner in which they dealt with heretics. The Cathars, an early religious movement from the Languedoc area of southern France, fell squarely into this category and were particularly singled out for persecution. They rejected the

Catholic Church's teachings and practised a simple form of Christianity which denounced ostentatious wealth. They also believed in the existence of a direct bloodline going back over the centuries to a union between Jesus and Mary Magdalene. These beliefs brought them into direct conflict with the full power of the Catholic Church and, as a result, they were subjected to a particularly brutal repression.

Abigail had known none of this. She had heard of the Cathars, and their romantic castles built high on mountain tops across a corner of southern France. She had not realised the extent to which they had been hounded by the established church. Feeling more awake, she sipped her rapidly cooling tea and continued reading.

The Catholic Church's efforts to halt the spread of Catharism was to become known as the Albigensian Crusade. The Dominicans sent out inquisitors across Europe and they quickly gained a notorious reputation for the way they pursued their prey and then extracted confessions. As a result, they were sometimes referred to as 'Chien du Dieu'. She felt her breathing stop momentarily. This couldn't be a coincidence. A grim reality was starting to form in her mind.

She shivered but continued to read. She saw that the use of torture by the order was commonplace. Those found guilty were typically sentenced to death by burning at the stake, the preferred method of execution. Their effectiveness meant that the order became integral to inquisitions, which lasted for the next five hundred years across Europe. She had certainly heard of the Spanish Inquisition; she didn't know of their antisemitic ideology to drive Jews from Spain. Nor its practice of genocide, which brought to mind Germany under the Nazis. She thought back to the priest from her childhood. Could he really be part of this? She felt the hairs on her arm stand up.

She found descriptions of the various devices of repression used by the order over the past six hundred years to force confessions from suspected heretics. These methods were still widely used by many countries.

Abigail shivered again and wrapped her dressing gown around her more tightly. She was tired and cold, and she closed the laptop and leant back against the pillows.

*

Over the next few days, Abigail's unease grew. She needed to share her concerns with Adam when she returned to France. Before that, it was almost a relief to concentrate on work. Working late into each night, she managed to complete her project proposal by its Friday deadline. She also spoke to Caroline. Adam was now back in Uzès, at Caroline's house. The phone was passed to him.

"The hospital has been wonderful — the doctors and all the nurses," he enthused. He had been picked up by Vivienne and had managed to hobble his way to the hospital car park on crutches, and, he assured Abigail, he would be walking unaided within the week.

She laughed. "Why does that not surprise me? OK. Let's see. Don't forget, though, that you'll soon have two bossy women to deal with."

"I suspect it will be three for a time. Vivienne won't even allow me to retrieve my stuff from the apartment. She is going there later to pack and tidy up for me. She is treating me like an invalid!" He sounded astonished.

"I wonder why?" Abigail answered, continuing to laugh. "It sounds like Caroline and Vivienne have become good friends."

"They have. I'm very grateful to them both. Abi, before you ring off there's something else I need to tell you. I haven't mentioned this to Caroline, and I debated whether to wait to tell you."

Her interest was piqued. "Go on, Adam."

"I should explain what I was doing driving at that time of the morning."

"Go on." She hadn't forgotten the unanswered question.

"I got a call from Jean Gilbert, the photographer, the night before. It was quite short. I didn't recognise the voice, but he identified himself, reminding me I had visited his display at the market in Uzès. He said he knew that I was Maryanne's husband, and that I was looking for her. He sounded different, more contrite. He told me Maryanne was alive. He had last seen her about six months ago and knew that she was still around, somewhere in Provence. He said he was calling because he was concerned about her wellbeing. He felt it was right to tell me… and he wanted to meet with me."

Abigail exhaled sharply. She had been holding her breath.

"Are you all right?" he asked, concern clear in his voice.

"Sorry. Just taken aback. Yes, carry on."

"He wouldn't say anything more other than he needed to meet up with me. He said it was urgent."

"And did you?"

"Well, we agreed to meet up at a motorway service station, on the way to Orange. He insisted we met early, at six in the morning, because he was on his way to a local market. I was to come on my own and not to tell anyone about the meeting." Adam coughed a couple of times and then resumed. "Sorry. I was on my way to the meeting when the accident happened."

"Christ." There was a lot to take in.

"Thank God you were back home. If you had still been here and had come with me you could have been severely injured. The impact was mainly to the passenger side of the car."

There was a silence for a moment, eventually prompting Adam to ask, "Are you still there?"

"Yes."

"I had wondered whether he knew who you were, and that you were with me. It was one of the things I was going to ask him when we met up."

"No, I am sure he didn't know who I was, but he seemed to think we had met before."

"I wonder…"

"Have you heard from him again? Surely, he must have wondered why you didn't turn up for the meeting?"

"I had a few missed calls while I was in the hospital. Gilbert's phone number was withheld when he phoned me, so I don't know if any of them were from him. Since then, nothing. It's very frustrating, Abi. There's nothing I can do at the moment to contact him."

"Let's leave all that to next week, when I'm there with you."

"OK," he acquiesced. "I don't know what to make of it all. The other odd thing is that I don't ever remember giving him my phone number."

"We'll work out a plan. And we know where he lives. Have the police got back to you yet about the accident?"

"No, not yet. They've asked that I come into the police station in Uzès next week to make a further statement. Perhaps you should come with me. It's the same place I visited when I first reported your mother's disappearance. I wonder if they will remember?"

"Adam, do you think it's possible that your accident was linked to the call from Gilbert?"

"What do you mean?"

"Is there a chance that you were being set up? That the accident was planned?"

"I just don't know."

*

Now, sitting in the departure lounge of North Terminal at Gatwick, she looked out of the window onto the white and orange livery of her easyJet plane. It was early afternoon and a grey, damp drizzle had descended over the airport. The lounge for the Montpellier flight was barely half full, with a mixture of French and British travellers. There were spare seats to each side of her. A young girl, sitting next to her father, tried to engage her by smiling coyly at her through splayed fingers. Abigail smiled back at the little girl but felt strangely dissociated from events around her, even as the competing loudspeakers announced their boarding information.

Chapter 13

Arriving into the bright sunshine of Montpellier, she collected her bag from the luggage carousel and emerged into the main Arrivals concourse. Scanning the exit signs for directions to the hire cars, she was taken aback as a pregnant red-haired woman detached herself from the small waiting crowd and, hesitantly, approached her. She certainly hadn't been expecting anyone to be there to meet her.

"Hello, I am sorry to surprise you. You are Abigail… Adam's daughter?"

"Step-daughter. Yes, I am," she replied. "And you are…?"

"I am so sorry. I am Vivienne, a friend of Adam."

"Ah… I know who you are. Of course."

Vivienne smiled broadly in recognition. "Yes, we have become friends with Adam. And don't worry — he knows that I am here greeting you." She explained that her husband had dropped her off on his way to visit a factory on the outskirts of Montpellier. She hadn't wanted Abigail to arrive in France on her own. She then announced that she would travel back to Uzès with her, and Emile would pick her up from Caroline's house later.

"That is so kind of you," Abigail replied uncertainly as they walked together across the road towards the hire car offices. "It is lovely to finally meet you." She suspected, though, that there might be an ulterior motive for the unexpected meeting.

Despite the initial surprise, Abigail found that she immediately liked Vivienne. The woman was only a few years older and there was an appealing warmth about her.

She was a good four or five inches shorter than herself, and she possessed that recognisable French look, and style. Whilst Abigail sorted out her hire-car arrangements Vivienne waited outside in the sun with the bags. Soon they were negotiating the succession of roundabouts that the French favour for the periphery of their towns.

"It is about an hour, before we get to the Uzès turn-off," Vivienne explained, finally sitting back in her seat. "So, we can now relax for a while." It was lucky for Abigail that Vivienne's English was good or else any meaningful conversation would have been difficult. She glanced at her passenger and Abigail knew what was to come.

"Whilst we are on our own, I thought it might be a good opportunity to talk to you about Adam."

"Please go on," she replied.

"Both Emile and I have some concerns about him, about his safety. We know about your mother, and Adam is still determined to find out what happened to her, but we fear that he doesn't understand what he is getting involved in."

"As her daughter, I also need to know what happened to her."

"Of course. It will be very important to you also. I understand. But we know some of these people. They don't see the world like us, like normal people do."

"Vivienne, which people are you referring to?"

"Sorry. I am not making myself clear. Adam said he thinks your mother has got mixed up with some strange people, down here in the south. He thinks that Jean Gilbert, the photographer who sells his pictures at the local markets, is perhaps part of the group. These people are not as they seem. They keep to themselves and believe in different things to you and me."

"Actually, I've met Jean Gilbert. At his farm. I bought some of his pictures. He seemed normal to me, really quite gentle. I didn't get the feeling he could be dangerous to other people."

"He is not so much the problem," she agreed. "Emile knows him a bit and thinks he is fine. It is more his brother and the people that he spends time with. They are not people to get on the wrong side of."

"It's funny that you say that. Adam thinks he has been followed ever since he arrived here. We were in Saintes-Maries, in the Camargue, and we believe we were followed there. It was very creepy. Adam thought that the person following us was the man who pushed him over at the market in Uzès."

"That was when I first met him! It had just happened!" Vivienne exclaimed.

"Do you think all these things are linked?"

"It's possible. We think that these people are trying to frighten Adam off, but, of course, we are concerned for you both. You might also get hurt if you continue to help him."

"I agree, but I believe that Adam is in the most danger. It's complicated and I'll try to explain it to you sometime. I've a feeling that I will be OK. That's really why I am back here."

There was a long silence whilst Vivienne looked thoughtfully out of the window. Eventually Abigail broke the silence and asked, "Do you know why Adam was driving so early in the morning last week… when he had his accident? Has he explained where he was going to?"

"Yes. He told us at the hospital that he was going to meet Jean somewhere on the autoroute. I think it was something to do with your mother. Jean had some information about her."

"Yes, that is what Adam told me. Do you think Jean Gilbert might have deliberately caused the accident?"

"I don't really know. You mean… was he was waiting by the roadside for Adam to come along?"

"I don't know what I am thinking. I am just not sure that the accident was a coincidence. There can't have been many cars around that time of the morning."

"You are right. Where the accident happened is a quiet road. I will show you. And it would have been still quite dark. The only people around at that time would be farmers, perhaps a few going early to the market."

"Have the police any more information? Have they managed to track down the driver?"

"Hah. Don't get your hopes up. You are expecting too much from our police. Once they know no one was seriously injured, they will probably turn their attention to other things." She shook her head. "They assume it will become a matter for the insurance companies."

"They've asked to interview Adam again next week. I'll go with him. It will give me a chance to see what efforts they are putting into the investigation."

"Well, good luck with that!" Vivienne laughed.

Just before they reached the outskirts of Remoulins, she asked Abigail to slow the car and park on the side of the road, nearby a roadside stall which was selling fresh strawberries. "This is where the accident happened," she explained. "The police believe the other vehicle came out of that road opposite." She pointed to a nearby junction. "As you can see, Adam would have had no time to respond."

Abigail could see what the Frenchwoman meant. The

side road was a minor road, little more than a dirt track, and was screened from oncoming traffic by tall pine trees and a hedgerow. There would have been little time for a driver to react to a car emerging from the side road. They both got out of the car.

"See the ditch up ahead? The one that runs alongside the road. That is where Adam's car ended up." Abigail saw how deep the ditch was. "In some ways, the ditch being there was fortunate. He could easily have gone into the trees instead. He only just missed taking out the empty fruit stall."

The roadside was still littered with broken glass and pieces of fibreglass. Part of a shattered side-mirror lay on its side. Abigail picked it up and looked around. A small strip of police tape fluttered from a nearby branch. Beyond the ditch and the trees, the ground fell away sharply towards a field of brush and scrub. She wondered how long the car might have lain hidden if the farmer had not been observant. She could see just how lucky Adam had been.

They drove on in thoughtful silence towards Uzès, and Caroline's house. As they drove up the narrow driveway, parking under the trees beside Caroline's car, Caroline emerged from the kitchen door.

"Welcome." She gave Abigail a huge hug. "Come in, both of you. The patient is waiting for you downstairs."

Vivienne apologised and said she couldn't stay. Emile was on his way to pick her up. She needed to help him pack the van for the market in Bessan the next day. "We have a new range of ceramics we are just starting to sell. But, if you have time tomorrow, please come and visit us. It's a lovely market."

"I would love to. And thank you for meeting me at the

airport. It was very thoughtful."

Adam was sitting upright on the edge of the living room couch, crutches by his side. He smiled warmly as the women entered and struggled to get to his feet. Abigail and Caroline simultaneously told him to not get up and to sit back down, before laughing at each other. Despite preparing herself, Abigail was still shocked by his appearance. He had a black eye and dark purple bruising to his face and arms. She gingerly bent over and gave him a light hug before kissing his forehead. "I've seen you looking better," she had to admit.

"That's not the first time you have said that to me over the past few weeks. I could develop a complex."

"Well then, please try and stay out of any more trouble."

"It looks a lot worse than it is. I really only need one of these crutches." He smiled crookedly. "Soon I'll be able to get around perfectly normally."

Caroline left them, saying she had to make a quick call. Abigail fixed Adam with her gaze. "So, how are you actually doing?"

"Really, I am all right. And all the better for you being here. It's mainly bruising. Nothing was broken. It could have been a lot worse. Thanks so much for making the effort to come over. You've been wonderful."

"I didn't really mean physically, but mentally: it must have been quite a shock."

"Ah." Adam's grin was rueful. "It's OK. I think I am quite resilient. It has been a bad patch though. However, I've been thinking about what we discussed — I've had too many unfortunate things happen for them to be unrelated. Someone has been watching me closely, and it has to be related to Maryanne."

"I agree. And I'm worried for your safety." Her face creased in a frown. "There's a few things I need to tell you. Things I've found out. Let's talk later when we are on our own."

*

Adam put the phone down on the kitchen counter very carefully and reached for his cup of coffee. It was stone cold. *Shit*, he thought. *Now what am I going to tell Abigail? How would she react to this?* At least she was here with him in France, and he could talk face-to-face with her.

Abigail and Caroline were at the Sunday market in Bessan, on the way to Pézenas. They had left the house early, having promised to visit Vivienne and Emile's stall and give them a hand. He knew they had then planned to have lunch with them there in the town once they had finished packing up for the day. He had told them not to worry about him, he would be fine. That was before the phone call.

It was a fine day outside and he needed to do something. He would go for a short walk. It would still be a few hours before the women returned. Walking was an important part of his rehabilitation, for both his body and his mind, and he managed to go further each time. Being out in the fresh air would help him to think over what had just happened, to try to make some sense of it.

The previous evening, Caroline had told them both that she had to return to the UK in the next few days to look after her mother. Now that Abigail had arrived, she could leave Adam in safe hands. She might be away for a couple of months and would try to come back for the odd weekend. Caroline insisted that Adam and Caroline stay on at the house for as long as they needed. She was just sorry that she would not be around to help them both.

Grateful as he had been for Caroline's help, Adam knew that, going forwards, all responsibility for action lay with Abigail and himself. It would be better this way.

As he walked along the country road that wandered past the property, he noticed that the season had changed further. It had softened and there was a gentle warm breeze. Gone were the biting mistral winds of early spring and the woodland and water meadows were coming alive. The dirt road was uneven, and Adam had to tread with care to avoid stumbling over stones and potholes. He was trying to walk as much as possible using only the one crutch and it was slow going. To his right, the fields ran down to a meandering river. The few homes that he had passed had long driveways that hid the buildings from the road. The only evidence of life was the barking of dogs in the distance. Eventually, the road emerged from the trees and wound down towards an open area of fields, planted with sunflowers and with vines. The early season growth of the vines was now evident. Adam found a fallen log at the roadside and sat down, with the morning sun on his back. He stretched out his leg and took out his phone. There had been no calls, since the one he had taken two hours ago. The caller's number had been withheld. He put the phone back in his pocket. His search for Maryanne had taken him along this route, expecting to see her around each corner. It felt as though he had come almost full circle from that fateful summer over two years ago.

*

"The photographer — Jean Gilbert — phoned me again while you were out." Abigail and Caroline had just returned. It was now late-afternoon.

"Christ. What did he want now? Abigail rolled her eyes. "To check whether you were still alive?"

"Yes, something like that. He said that he knew that I'd been involved in an accident on my way to meet him. When I didn't show up, he had made enquiries. He even knew I'd been taken to hospital in Nîmes."

At that moment, Caroline emerged from the kitchen, carrying a tray of cups. "Well, that's very nice of him, particularly after he'd just tried to kill you," she interjected. "Did he ask how you were? Was he disappointed that you are recovering?"

"He said that he was very sorry to hear about what happened. He wanted me to know that it was not him that had driven into me. He even tried to phone me an hour after we were due to meet, and obviously received no reply."

"And did you believe him?" Caroline persisted.

"Oh, I don't know, Caroline." There was a pause. "Actually, yes. Yes, I did. It was something in his tone. He sounded sincere... different to how he has come across before. He went on to say, however, that inadvertently he might have been the cause of the accident."

"I'm very confused," admitted Abigail.

"It goes back to the reason why he wanted to meet with me in the first place. The meeting was about Maryanne." He looked up. Both women looked at each other. Neither said anything.

"When he first contacted me, he said he was concerned that she was in some danger. He refused to be more specific. I asked him how he knew this, and why I should believe him. He said he would only tell me more when we met in person."

"And that was why you were on the road so early in the morning?" Abigail added.

"Yes, it was." He remembered something. "Damn it, I again forgot to ask how he had my number."

"Do you think he got it from Maryanne?" Caroline suggested, handing him a cup of tea.

"I don't know. I guess so. Anyway, that's when he apologised, when he said that he might have been the cause of the crash." He took a sip. "There was another thing. He sounded... concerned. He said he thought I might also be in some danger." He looked across and caught the two women looking at each other again.

Caroline asked, "So, what did he mean when he said he might have been the cause of your crash? Is he now admitting that it was him?"

Adam sighed. "No, he is not saying that."

It was Abigail's turn. "So, you believe him, Adam?"

"Yes, I do. Because he told me who he thought it was."

"OK," she said tentatively, thinking that she knew what was coming.

"He said it could have been caused by his brother who, it seems, knew Maryanne when she was living in Dublin. He didn't give his brother's name. He asked me not to go to the police and said that if I did, he would deny everything. Also, if his brother heard I'd gone to the police, it would only place Maryanne in even more danger."

Abigail nodded. "So, what made him believe it was his brother?"

"He said he had confronted his brother the night

before he was due to meet me. He told his brother that what was happening was not right. He was concerned about Maryanne's safety and felt that it was the correct thing to warn me. He said he had contacted me and was going to meet me the following morning."

"How did his brother react?"

"Very badly. He flew into a rage, forbidding him to speak to me. He told Jean to stay out of it. He shouted at him, telling him he would not allow it. The evening ended with the brother rushing out, hurling threats before he drove off."

"Did he say, by any chance, what the car was?" Caroline asked.

"It was an old Land Rover."

"Did he, by any chance, say what colour it was?"

"I think he said it was green."

Caroline jerked upright, spilling her tea. "Shit, the car that crashed into you was green!" She mopped at the tea with a tissue.

"Gilbert said that he had no idea that his brother would try to hurt me. He heard on the local news that a large green vehicle was spotted and may have been involved, and it made him suspicious. The police haven't identified it or found the driver yet."

"Don't hold your breath." Caroline got up to draw the curtains. By now, the day was starting to turn to night and she turned on a couple of table lamps in the lounge, throwing long shadows on the walls.

"Gilbert said he saw a large dent on the left front of the Land Rover when his brother came home. And the left headlight was broken. When he asked his brother about it, he said he had run into a sheep on the road. He was still in a state and refused to talk about it further. He left the *domaine* an hour later and Gilbert has not seen him since."

"We should go to the police," Abigail urged. "This is important. They will be able to check out the vehicle."

"No, Abi. He begged me not to. His brother is not in a good mental state and he's scared of what he might do if the police were involved." Adam ran his hand over his face. "He as much admitted he didn't really know what his brother might be capable of."

Abigail remembered the bruise under Gilbert's eye when they visited the *domaine*. It had looked recent.

"Gilbert said he thought it likely Maryanne was being held somewhere against her will. Christ... I just feel so helpless, so powerless to help her," he finished.

"I know." Abigail's brow furrowed. "So do I. What do we do now?"

"Well, the police are out for the moment. Anyway, if we go to them, he will just deny our conversation ever happened. He asked to be given a bit of time and he would try to help me. His brother has had these episodes in the past. They seem to be getting worse, but Jean said they do respond with treatment. He believes his brother now needs urgent hospitalisation."

Abigail clenched her fists. "And what are we meant to do in the meantime? We can't just wait."

"No, we can't," he agreed. "Gilbert says he has an idea of where Maryanne may be being held. He believes it can't be too far away, as his brother seems to be able to get to wherever it is and back again quite easily, so it has got to be somewhere here in the south."

"OK, well that is something, I guess." Abigail unclenched her fists, but she was still taut with anxiety.

"Gilbert promised he would keep trying to contact his

brother. If his brother doesn't return in the next couple of days, he said we should meet in town and he would tell me everything he knows. That is, if I agree not to go to the police with this."

"Unfortunately, I am going to have to leave all this to you guys. I will be back in the UK by then," Caroline reminded them both. "I've got to go and help Mum." She looked at Adam. "Are you going to be all right?"

"Yes, thank you." He smiled. "I'll have Abi with me." He turned to her.

"Does Gilbert know I am here with you?"

"I don't know. He has not mentioned you, although he did say for me to come to the meeting on my own."

Abigail had a sudden thought. "Do you think that Mum is back in Saintes-Maries? That she is being held in that house there? That's not too far away."

"I don't think so. I asked him that. It is the only place I know. But the house looked completely deserted when we saw it."

"And what did he say?"

"He said that it was unlikely. He thought that it was more likely to be around Marseille. It's where his brother has worked over the last few years. And he has connections across the area through the church."

The lamps in the lounge flickered just as the stillness of the night was splintered by a piercing scream. The sound of an animal in extreme pain. It came from the bottom of the garden. The high-pitched screech lasted for a few seconds. They froze momentarily, but the cry was followed by silence.

Caroline was the first to move. She ran out of the house, followed by Abigail who had picked up a torch on the way. They made their way carefully towards the bottom of the garden where the cars were parked. The night sky was cloudless and stars shone brightly through the trees. The temperature had fallen quickly with the clear sky and Abigail shivered. As they made their way forward, they could make out a shape, at head height, hanging from a tree. Something quite large, swinging slowly. Abigail pointed the torch at it and let out a scream.

"What is it?" asked an out-of-breath Adam, now arriving with the aid of his crutch.

The torch beam played over the object. A large cat, a rope twisted tightly around its neck, swung from a short branch of the tree. Its head hung at a strange angle, its tongue lolling out of its open mouth, fixed in a terrified grimace. Blood oozed from the white chest where a narrow hunting knife had been plunged into its heart.

Leaning on his crutch Adam reached up to untie the knot of the rope and lowered the poor animal to the ground. The knife pinned a bloodstained note to the lifeless body. Adam bent down awkwardly and felt the animal's body. It was still warm: the blood continued to ooze from the wound. He pulled out the knife, flinching as a spurt of blood sprayed his arms and clothing. He detached the blood-spattered note from the cat's matted fur. By torchlight they could just make out the crudely scrawled words — '*Reste Loin ELLE MOURRA*'. Caroline backed away from the scene in horror, while Adam and Abigail could only stare bleakly at one another.

Adam finally broke the silence. "Whoever did this must still be nearby." Everything was still. There was no movement. An owl shrieked in the trees high above, breaking the silence. Adam hobbled towards the bottom of the driveway, looking for any sign of movement. Before he reached the road, he caught the distant sound of a car being started. He stood for a moment, then returned to where the two women still stared in horror at the prone body.

Abigail looked up. "Anything?"

"I thought I heard a car in the distance. I guess the person who did this has gone."

Abigail played the light over the cat. "It looks like its neck has been broken. Whoever did this is a sadist." There was no collar on the animal. "It could be feral, or it could be someone's pet."

Adam bent down again and picked up the blood-soaked note. "Do you know what this says?" He turned to Caroline. She was still standing alone in the darkness and stepped forward to look again at the blood-soaked message.

"It means 'Stay Away. SHE WILL DIE'," she said, her voice breaking. "Christ."

Adam's face was ashen. Still clutching the note by its edge, he asked, "Are you sure it doesn't say '*Or*...she will die'?"

"No. It doesn't. Oh, Adam, I'm just so sorry."

Chapter 14

The meeting with Jean Gilbert took little more than an hour, but its impact would last for a very long time. The two men arranged to meet late afternoon, just two days after the phone call. Adam had asked Abigail not to come as he still feared that she might put herself at risk, but she was having none of it. She told him she had as much at stake as he did.

Caroline had left the previous evening, with Abigail taking her to the airport in Montpellier. Both women were still in a state of shock from the gruesome killing. "I have reported it to the police so they may come round to speak to you. I have left the note in the storeroom on a shelf so they may wish to take it with them. But don't hold your breath. This is the countryside, and strange things happen here."

The three of them had met at a small bar tucked away in the shadows down a quiet alleyway which ran from Place aux Herbes through to the main road encircling the old town. All around, shop shutters were being pulled down. Gilbert was sitting in the corner at the far end. He eyed Adam's crutch, then his eyes widened in recognition as saw Abigail behind Adam.

"I know you. You bought some pictures from me a few weeks ago. You came to the studio with another Englishwoman."

"Yes, you are right," she replied, keeping her distance. "I'm Abigail. I'm Maryanne's daughter."

He was still for a moment. "I thought I recognised you when I first saw you. I can indeed see the likeness to your mother. I..." He seemed dazed for a moment. Recovering himself he said, "Please sit, both of you," indicating the seats around the table. "Can I get you something — *un café,* or perhaps something stronger?"

They opted for coffees. Gilbert ordered, then turned back to Abigail, his mind still on her revelation. "So, was it just a coincidence that you arrived at my farmhouse?"

"No, I'm afraid it wasn't. We believed you might be mixed up in my mother's disappearance."

Gilbert shrugged. "OK. I understand why. But let me tell you all that I know. I can only hope that it helps you."

He said his brother, who was three years older than him, had protected him from their overbearing, often violent, father. Their mother had died when Jean was three. He explained that the father had struggled to cope with single parenthood. He was a simple man of the soil, ill-equipped to deal with children. His frustrations, fuelled by pastis and the local brandy, frequently spilled over with the two boys, particularly Jean, often suffering drunken beatings. His brother had tried to shield him, often physically inserting himself between the two. This took a terrible toll on both boys. They had been brought up as Catholics and, as his brother grew older, he became more inward looking and began to seek out answers to the situation they were in through spirituality. By the time their father died of liver failure, his brother had come to see religion as both a protective blanket and an escape. By his late teens, when his first breakdown occurred, he had become increasingly withdrawn. He recovered but retained a preoccupation with religion. At this time he joined an order of the church called the Dominicans. They were very good to him and they sponsored his studies in Ireland. Of course, the family could not have afforded this, but I think they saw something, something special in him. These studies then led to his subsequent admittance to the priesthood.

"That was when he first met Maryanne — in Dublin?" Adam asked.

"Yes. He was friends with her mother. They had met at church. Both belonged to a discussion group. She was kind to him and invited him to stay at her house between terms at the college and sometimes when he returned from France. It was an innocent friendship, but he became obsessed with her daughter, your mother, Maryanne." He fixed his gaze on Abigail. "When he returned to our farm from Ireland, he would speak only of her. I thought he had fallen in love. He showed me pictures of her. She was, after all a very beautiful woman. But, over time, I now believe his interest is...." He searched for the right words. "It seems something else... something disturbing and problematic." Gilbert's coffee had by now gone cold, but he took a sip.

Behind them, the bar was filling with customers, but Adam and Abigail were focused entirely on the photographer. "Please go on." Adam shifted his chair to allow people to squeeze past to get to the bar counter.

"I think, at this time, my brother was not well again. I remember the one time he came home and his eyes were vacant, he seemed to be in another world. He told me that he had met Mary Magdalene, our patron saint. He was serious. I assumed he had had some form of religious... how do you say it? Visit... vision? But then he said no. She was real. He could speak to her, he could touch her. I believe it was Maryanne he was referring to."

"But why? How?" Adam leant towards Jean.

"He was obsessed. Perhaps it was the long red hair, like yours." Jean turned towards Abigail. "Perhaps it was that she was spiritual. I don't really know. But you must please understand, it was very real to him. I tried to talk to him, but he would have none of it. He said it was *un miracle* and I would not understand. I tried to get him help but he refused. I had not seen him like this before."

"I do remember him," Abigail replied quietly. "I found him strange. I'm sorry. I was a child at the time, and I was nervous of him."

"I am sorry for you. Your life might have been very different if my brother had not come into it. I believe—"

"What's your brother's name?" she asked suddenly.

"It is Anton… Anton Gilbert."

Abigail said nothing.

"What happened next, Jean?" Adam needed to hear more.

"Eventually, of course, he was forced to have treatment. He was ill. When he left Ireland for the last time, he returned to France, to Marseille. They, the Dominican Order, took him back in and looked after him. Have you, perhaps, heard of the Dominicans?"

"Oh yes." Abigail's response was vehement. Startled, Adam looked at her, a question forming.

Before Adam could ask anything, Jean continued. "He continued his work for a couple of years, but his behaviour became more erratic, and more alarming. He was transferred to a smaller town. He moved to Arles and that was where he started to believe that he was really a misunderstood artist — very similar to Vincent van Gogh. Did you know that Van Gogh also lived in Arles?"

Abigail nodded.

Jean sighed. "Anton had taken up painting as a boy. He was quite good. He had rediscovered his interest whilst he was in Ireland." His gaze turned to Abigail. "I think it was your grandmother who encouraged him to take it up again. But he was only an amateur. You could not really sell his work, although we did try with some of his better pictures at the markets. Anyway, whatever the cause, the church became so concerned about his behaviour that they had him admitted to hospital — the same hospital that Van Gogh had been admitted to more than a hundred years earlier. He was there for almost six months."

"What was he was treated for?" Abigail asked. She remembered Magda's mother saying that the priest had had a breakdown after he had returned to France and had been hospitalised.

Adam looked quizzically at Abigail.

Gilbert ran his hand across his brow. "Well… he was in a bad way to start with, almost completely unresponsive. He hardly recognised me when I visited. The doctors wouldn't give me any information at the beginning. They said he needed to stabilise. Eventually, the doctors said that he was being treated for schizophrenia. I didn't know what that was, and I was quite frightened. Once he had improved, the doctors told me it could be managed quite well with medication and I must make sure he took his tablets when he came out of hospital. I tried my best. When he was released, he spent some time on the farm. Then, almost with no warning, he went back into the order. I think he felt protected there — they look after their own. I saw him every few weeks and he seemed much better. He was calmer than he had been in a long while. He said he was taking his medication regularly. About three years ago, he was transferred to a place called Sainte-Baume, down in Provence. Most of the time he stayed at a local hostel nearby."

"Where does Maryanne fit into all of this?" Adam was impatient to move the conversation on.

"I apologise. I will get there. When Anton moved to Sainte-Baume, he would occasionally come back for a few days during the week. I began to suspect that he was not taking his medication regularly. He was jumpy and not able to concentrate. When I questioned him, he would get cross, and become agitated. During one of these visits, he mentioned that a friend of his was coming to stay. That she would be staying for a while. It was Maryanne."

"How long ago was this?" asked Abigail.

"She arrived about three years ago. It was summer, really hot, and I remember that it was strange that she had no luggage with her. Just a shoulder bag. When she arrived with Anton, she looked distressed. She had been crying. However, I did recognise her."

"From the market the day before?" Adam asked quietly. His eyes hadn't left Jean's face.

"Yes." He didn't meet Adam's gaze. "Although, when I first saw her, I felt I might have met her many years before."

"So, what actually happened when we came to your stall that Saturday? Was it all just a coincidence?"

"No, it wasn't. She had asked to meet me before she came to stay. She wanted to understand that I would not mind. When Anton—"

Adam felt as if a cold fist had squeezed his heart. "I just find this so hard to believe."

"As I said, I am very sorry. When Anton told me Maryanne was coming to stay for a while at the *domaine*, I objected. I said we were busy enough on the farm, and at the markets, without looking after someone else. I was firm, but Anton pleaded with me to meet her. He said that it was urgent, that she needed help. There was nowhere else that she could go. In the end I agreed to meet with her at my stall in Uzès. She was very interested in my pictures. We talked for a bit and I eventually told her that she could stay for a short while. Possibly that was a mistake."

"Christ." Adam shook his head. "I had no idea."

"I didn't understand it either, but she convinced me that it was for the best." He shrugged. "She seemed desperate. I was worried about my brother, and I thought I might help in some way."

"When I asked you at the market whether you remembered Maryanne you bloody denied everything!" He was angry. "You even became aggressive towards me. Do you remember that?"

"I do and I am very sorry," Jean repeated. "I didn't know what to do. And I was scared. Anton had warned me that you were back. That you were looking for Maryanne. He said that you would cause trouble for us."

"For you, or for Maryanne?"

"Well, for my brother and myself. By then, she had left the farmhouse some time before. Anton made me promise not to mention anything about Maryanne. He said you would go straight to the police. That he would get into trouble and lose his job."

"So, where is she now?" Adam demanded.

"Please, I will come onto that. I promise I will tell you everything."

Abigail interceded more calmly. "What happened when my mother arrived at your place?"

"She thanked me, and then she just went up to the room we had prepared and slept for almost a week. She looked exhausted."

Abigail took Adam's hand. "Did she say anything about what she was doing there… and why?"

"*Non.* All she said was that she was going through a difficult time. She kept very much to herself, sleeping most of the time. Anton had to return to his church soon after she arrived, and I just left her alone. She looked awful when she arrived. She could hardly talk, and I did not want to push her. Anton told me that she was an old friend, from Ireland, and that she needed help. She needed somewhere calm for a while, and he would come back for her. The way he talked, I assumed that she was connected to the church."

Adam felt shaken. He wasn't sure whether to believe what Gilbert had said. He had to look away. His gaze fell on a couple sitting at an adjourning table, talking companionably, enjoying their drinks and his eyes misted.

"Did you eventually speak to her?" he asked, when he could look back.

"Not really. She hardly left the room for the first week. Mostly, she kept to herself when she did leave her room. Later, before she went away, she would sometimes help around the farm. She tidied up the winery and would also take some of the orders and prepare them for shipping. She made her own meals and she would read a lot. Of course, I was often away at a market."

"Did she ever explain what she was doing there? You must have thought it odd? What did she say to you earlier at the market?"

"Well, I really only knew her as an old friend of Anton, coming to stay—"

"Surely you must have wondered why she was there?"

Adam interrupted with frustration, running his hands through his hair. "Did she say why she needed to get away from me so urgently?"

Jean shook his head. "No, I am sorry, *monsieur*. She did not say anything."

More to himself, Adam said, "I honestly had no idea she was thinking of leaving. I just wish we could have talked about it."

Abigail put her hand on Adam's. "You couldn't have known. It wasn't your fault."

He smiled at Abigail, grateful for her words of comfort. His hand shook as he put his coffee cup carefully back on the saucer. "How did she seem when she arrived at your farm, emotionally I mean?"

Jean gazed beyond them, as though weighing up what he should disclose. Eventually, he said, "She seemed sad but relieved, if you can understand that. She looked exhausted. When I did try to talk to her, she was closed, very much on edge. She did not invite any conversation during that time."

"And later on?" Adam asked.

"She didn't talk about you. In fact, she refused to talk about anything in her past. She seemed very fragile." He shrugged. "She talked about getting away from things. I noticed that she prayed in her room a lot. Perhaps that helped her. She talked more to Anton when he visited. Gradually, she seemed to relax more and open up a bit, but she would only talk about the future. It was as if she had no past."

Adam had to ask where Anton slept when he visited the *domaine*.

Jean hesitated before replying. "Mostly he slept in his own room, but sometimes he did sleep in her room. I am sorry."

Adam's stomach churned and he felt sick. His world was slowly slipping away. He was surprised that he could still feel this way, despite all that had happened.

"Was she locked inside the house?"

Jean raised his eyebrows. "No. No. Of course, she was free to come and go. All the time. She was Anton's friend. Sometimes she came with me into Saint-Rémy for the market and the shops. Sometimes she would take herself off by train to Avignon. I do not imprison people." He sounded indignant.

Attempting to calm things, Abigail asked, "How long did Mum stay with you there at the farm?"

"About seven or eight months. It was early spring, the next year, that she moved out. I don't know where she went when she left. I didn't ask."

"Did you see her again?" Abigail persisted.

He thought for a moment. "Two months, three months, after she moved out, we met up for the day by the coast with some friends. We met in Saintes-Maries. You know the town!" he exclaimed. "You told me you had stayed there when you were a child."

"That explains the photo," Abigail said, half to herself. "And how was my mother when you saw her?"

"She seemed calmer, more at peace, I think," he replied, thinking back. "We only spoke a little but when I asked her what she was going to do, she said she wanted to enter a retreat."

"Do you have any idea where?"

"Anton would often stay in a *hostellerie* in Sainte-Baume. Maryanne said she liked the place. I think she went there."

"And since then?" Adam had recovered his composure.

"As far as I know, *monsieur*, she has been living mainly there, in the *hostellerie,* over the past year or so. Well, until—"

Adam interrupted. "Has something now happened to her?"

Shaking his head Jean said that he had no real idea. He had had little contact with Maryanne over the past year apart from her brief visits with his brother. "I saw her from time to time with Anton. She was happy there until recently. I think she and Anton are not getting along well."

"Do you know why she contacted me, out of the blue, six months ago?"

Jean started. "So that is why you suddenly appeared back in Uzès."

"Yes. I was looking for you. You were the only person I could think of. I had to do something, to start somewhere."

Jean looked at Adam with sudden sympathy. "I understand."

"Did you tell your brother that I was here looking for Maryanne?"

"Yes, I did. He was staying at the farmhouse for a couple of days when you came to see me at the market. I didn't recognise you, of course, but then you told me about your wife and then showed me those photographs. What could I do?"

Adam could only shrug.

"Anton said that Maryanne did not wish to see you, and that you were a trouble-maker. You would only cause trouble for everyone. He said that keeping quiet was the only way to protect Maryanne, to maintain her peace."

Abigail leant towards Jean. "You said that she had

been happy at this *hostellerie* until recently. Has she now moved somewhere else?"

"That is the problem. I don't know. She seems to have disappeared."

"What do you mean?" Abigail and Adam echoed the question simultaneously.

"I mean she has gone. She left the *hostellerie*. It is part of the priory run by the Benedictines. They contacted me a month ago. to ask if I knew where she was. She must have given my address and phone number as a contact. They said that she had just disappeared and asked if I knew where she was."

"How is this possible?" asked Adam.

I am sorry. I don't know. She left owing a couple of months' rent and had left behind some of her clothes. The sister who phoned said they are all baffled. Maryanne was well liked there. She often helped them out in the gardens and on their reception desk. She seemed happy."

"Surely they asked your brother where she was?" Abigail asked.

"They did, but he told them he had no idea. He said he hadn't seen her for a while, and that she might have returned to the UK."

"Shit!" Adam swore in frustration. "And what has Anton told you about her disappearance?"

"Not much. He says that he doesn't know, but I believe he knows something. But he refuses to talk about her."

"So, to be very clear, Maryanne left this *hostellerie* a month ago and no-one has seen her since. And your brother claims not to know anything?" Adam sounded doubtful.

"That is right."

"Why then, was he so determined that I should not meet up with you?"

Jean could only shrug. "I don't know what else to say. I have told you everything I know."

"I need to go there and look around." With an increasing frustration Adam's voice rose. "I am still her husband. I need to speak to your brother."

Jean was startled. "That is not a good idea. As I said, Anton is not well and he will react badly. He will be violent." He turned to Abigail. "Please get him to understand it is not a good idea. It will not end well."

"We can't just do nothing. Mum is out there somewhere, and she needs our help. Is there anywhere else that we could look for Maryanne?"

Jean thought for a moment. "I think both Saintes-Maries or Arles are unlikely. Marseille could be a possibility, but it is such a big city. I wouldn't know where to start to look for her, or for Anton." Jean looked away, his brow furrowed. "There is somewhere else. It's a bit crazy but have you heard of the Holy Cave? Mary Magdalene's cave? It is above the village of Sainte-Baume. People who stay at the *hostellerie* there often come to make a pilgrimage to the cave." He looked at them both. "Do you know the history of the place? Have you heard of Mary Magdalene's cave?"

Adam and Abigail looked to each other.

"You should look it up. It's set halfway up a high cliff, the Massif-de-la-Sainte-Baume. It is where Mary Magdalene lived for thirty years and preached to her followers. Maryanne would know it well. She probably has climbed it as a personal pilgrimage."

Adam recalled the brochure he had found at the farmhouse. It had shown a high, grey, rocky cliff emerging above a canopy of trees. He would look for the brochure later.

"The cave is considered one of the holiest places in all of France. It is huge and inside there is a shrine to the saint. Services are held there regularly. Beside the entrance to the cave is an ancient priory that houses the Dominican priests who live there throughout the year. The Dominican Order have looked after the sanctuary for hundreds of years."

"But why do you think Maryanne might be there?" Adam persisted.

"It is so remote. It is cut off from normal civilisation. Anton worked as one of the guardians of the holy site. He would sometimes stay there for months."

"I get the feeling that there's something else you're not saying." Abigail fixed Jean with her gaze. "What is it?"

"Well, it is the connection with Mary Magdalene. Anton started to believe that she was... how do you say it? .....An incarnation of the saint. It is possible that this has started again. It is why I needed to speak to you. To warn you—"

"Jesus!" Adam sat up. "You're genuinely worried. You really feel that he might do something awful to her."

He turned to Abigail. "Oh, God, Abi. That note on the dead cat." He recounted to Jean the incident at Caroline's house a few nights earlier. "Could that have been Anton? Does this sound like something he could do?"

Jean stared at the floor of the café. He sat that way for quite a while. Finally, replying softly, he said, "I am sorry. In his present condition... yes, it is possible." He looked grey and tired.

"There's something else, isn't there?" Abigail said,

with a deepening sense of dread.

"Yes," he whispered. "The last time I saw him he was not making much sense." He paused again before summoning the words. "He kept on mixing up the names of the saint and Maryanne. He claimed Mary Magdalene was talking to him from beyond the grave. Her voice was in his head all the time."

Chapter 15

The trip would take a few hours. They left early, before the rush hour had commenced. Abigail remained watchful for vehicles pulling out from the half-concealed side roads leading to tiny hamlets. Passing the sign for Pont du Gard, they continued towards the motorway taking them south to Marseille and the Côte d'Azur beyond. Before they reached the motorway, they passed a number of roadside stalls. Wooden kiosks were already selling bundles of freshly picked green and white asparagus. The verges and the fields beyond were gaily patterned with swathes of red, with the arrival of the first poppies of the season.

It wasn't long before they passed the scene of Adam's accident. He was grateful to be a passenger for this trip. Traces of the accident still remained, though he hardly seemed to notice. The May sunshine had seemed to brighten his mood and he sat back and took the opportunity to explain what he had gleaned from his recent research.

On his lap was a black notebook and inside were a couple of pamphlets. He opened one. "This is one of the brochures I found at Jean's *domaine*. It describes the retreat of Sainte-Baume. I think this must be the place where Maryanne was staying. Why else would Jean have it at his home? The place calls itself a *hostellerie*, which I assume means a hostel and it is located at the foot of the Sainte-Baume mountains. It seems to be past the town of Saint-Maximin, which is just off the main motorway to Nice. I must have driven past the mountains many times without particularly noticing them." He was silent for a moment, thinking. "We should start at this *hostellerie* and take it from there."

"Do you think these Benedictine Sisters who run the place will talk to us?" Abigail asked, looking quickly at him.

He shrugged. "I really don't know. I hope so. She's your mother, and I am married to her. Surely, they must understand."

Abigail chuckled. "Mum might still owe them money due to her sudden departure. If so, they might well choose to be cooperative. Did you find out much about the town there?"

"A bit. Sainte-Baume itself is just a small village, high in the hills above Saint-Maximin. I found a bit on the history of the area and I made some background notes. It all makes a good story and, you never know, some of it might be relevant."

Abigail looked sideways. "Well, we have a long trip." Adam was already opening his notebook. "Go on. I think anything will be helpful."

"From what I managed to find, in one way or another, everything seems to come back to the mythology surrounding the saint Mary Magdalene," he mused. He tucked the brochures down the side of the seat and looked through his notepad. "The town of Saint-Maximin that we will go through was completely transformed in the 13th century by the discovery, by Charles II of France, of an intact shrine containing a sarcophagus. The sarcophagus contained an inscription that it was the true burial site of Mary Magdalene. It rapidly became the focus of a cult of the saint and Charles founded a large Gothic cathedral on the site of the tomb — now known as the Basilica Sainte-Marie-Madeleine."

She quickly glanced back to Adam. "How did she end up there? The mountains and the town must be quite a way from where we were on the Camargue coast."

"You're right. It's a long way from Saintes-Maries. However, tradition has it that, after she made landfall there, she then travelled on to Marseille to preach to the local population and to convert them to Christianity. After spending some time in Marseille, she decided on a life of solitude. So, she then retired to the nearby Sainte-Baume mountains — to a cave there — where she remained for thirty years, teaching to her disciples."

"That is one hell of a story. Imagine thirty years in a cave, two thousand years ago." Abigail was lost in thought before asking, "How on earth could anyone live like that? What would she have found to eat?"

Adam could only shake his head. "I am guessing that her diet was mostly plant-based, foraged from the forest. In those days I suspect people were more adaptable, through necessity, than we are today. They ate what they found around them. In Mary Magdalene's case, her diet might well have been supplemented by fish and meat brought by her followers."

"There must also have been a water source somewhere close by the cave," Abigail added. "Otherwise, how would anyone survive?"

"That's a good point. There must be a river or stream nearby."

"So, she spent thirty years in this cave. How then did she end up in this town many miles below?"

Adam turned back to his notes. "Ah… It seems she then had a dream of her impending death and commenced what must have been an arduous final journey down from the mountain, in order to see the Bishop for this region of southern France. He had come all the way from Aix and was waiting for her arrival in the town. On her death, he laid her body to rest in an alabaster tomb. He was later to become a saint — Saint Maximin — and the town duly became known by the same name."

Abigail regarded Adam. He looked to be returning to his old self. He seemed to be regaining a sense of purpose. She smiled at him, before concentrating back on the road. "I wonder…" She paused, then asked, "Has there ever been any actual proof that this tomb did contain the body of Mary?"

He shook his head. "From what I could determine, I don't think there has been categorical proof. I am not sure how you would obtain anything definitive. However, genetic testing of hair found in the sarcophagus did confirm it was from a woman, possibly of Jewish ancestry. At some stage, over the ensuing centuries, the head of the woman became separated from the rest of the body. The skull ended up on display in the cathedral in Saint-Maximin. Subsequent testing of the skull also confirmed it to be that of a woman, and moreover dated it to the 1st century."

"OK. That is intriguing, and it does provide support to the story."

"Whatever the proof, the cult of Mary Magdalene is very much alive in the town," he continued. "She is commemorated during a week-long festival. It culminates in a procession bearing the skull through the streets of the town. It all sounds just a little bit gruesome."

The motorway divided as they neared the outskirts of Marseille. They had been travelling for almost two hours. Taking the Toulon and Nice fork, there was now a Mediterranean feel to the towns and countryside as they continued their journey eastwards. Adam turned his attention away from the passing countryside and continued reading from his notes. "The tradition of early Christians —the Cathars — who populated this area of France, across Provence and deep into Languedoc, had the belief that Mary Magdalene was the wife or the mistress of Jesus. This belief was later shared with the Knights Templar. It was claimed that a child, or children, had originated from this union. Furthermore, they believed that a direct and unbroken bloodline continued thereafter. At the time, it was believed that this lineage was traceable through the first millennia to William the Conqueror. There are those that currently believe that it has continued, unbroken, through Europe for the next thousand years. All the way to modern times."

Despite the mildness of the day, Abigail suddenly shivered. "And is there any proof of this?" she asked, glancing sideways.

He shrugged. "Who really knows? We've all got to be related to someone thousands of years ago. I did a bit of research on the internet. It is recorded somewhere that King Louis XI of France proclaimed that Mary Magdalene was the source of the French royal line. Charlemagne, who ruled Hapsburg, made a similar claim. You'll remember the well-known book that asserted the existence of a so-called 'royal' bloodline. I found quite a lot of references to the same thing, from very different sources. Did you know, for example, that there is the belief in both Japanese and Kashmiri folklore that descendants of Jesus are presently alive in Europe?"

"Yes, I do remember the book." She stared ahead, looking pensive.

"Apparently, the Catholic Church has made repeated

attempts to eradicate this royal bloodline. They were almost wiped out in the Catholic Church's crusade against the Cathars — known as the Albigensian Crusade — in southern France. Only a remnant of this royal lineage was left as a result."

"As it so happens, I read up on the Albingensian Crusade very recently." Seeing Adam look quizzically at her, she sighed and said, "It's a long story. It's associated and I will explain it to you later. But I read that, as part of the crusade, the Dominican Order was tasked with this — with the elimination of this bloodline, this royal lineage."

"Yes. The Pope also determined that even a belief in the existence of a royal bloodline was heretical, and the Dominicans were just the people to call on to deal with it."

"But why? Why was this seen as a threat?"

Adam could only shrug. "It's the old story: just as the Cathars' broader views on Christianity were deemed to be heretical, belief in the bloodline, and indeed the actual existence of a bloodline, was seen as a threat to the fundamental beliefs of Christianity and, as such, the continuing power, and accumulated wealth, of the established order. In France, the established order was, of course, the Catholic Church."

"And you mentioned the Knights Templar? How do they fit into this?"

"Ah, yes. Sorry, I got a bit sidetracked." He paged through his notes again, eventually finding the right page. "Originally, the Templars were just a military order. They were founded as a Holy mission to ensure the safety of Christian pilgrims making their journey through the Holy Land."

"And the name 'Templar'. Where did that come from?"

"I believe it was because their base was the Temple Mount in Jerusalem. And, they protected the ancient scriptures and scrolls stored in the Temple of Solomon library there. When the Holy Land was invaded by Muslim forces in the 12th century, support for the Templar Order gradually faded. However, what is forgotten is that they still remained a significant and influential business organisation, rather like a modern-day international conglomerate. They maintained a widespread presence through Christian Europe through Templar Houses, which managed a large network of local properties and businesses, including, importantly, Templar banks. The order was not subject to local government which, in effect, made it a 'state-within-a-state'. The Templars kept a standing army which was able to pass freely through borders. As you can imagine this led to heightened tensions within some countries in Europe. In France, Philip IV, already deep in debt to the Templars from his war against England, decided to take action against them. He saw it as a way of freeing himself from his significant debts. So—" He looked up from his notebook and asked, "Too much information?"

"No. Not at all," she replied, smiling. "It's still interesting. I had forgotten most of this from school."

"OK. Bear with me just a bit longer. It will give some background and might help us understand what we are dealing with."

"Carry on. I am listening."

"All right. Hopefully, you will see just where this is going. In 1307, Philip decided that he needed to act against the Templars. He ordered scores of Templars across France to be simultaneously arrested. Not only were they deemed to be heretics, they were also accused of various offences — fraud, idolatry, indecent behaviour, homosexuality were among many of the charges. Dominican inquisitors were called in, of course, and many Templars were forced to 'confess' to their charges. Under pressure from Philip, Pope Clement issued an edict instructing monarchs across Europe to arrest Templars. Their assets were all seized. As a result, the Templar Order was dissolved. Just as the Cathars had done, the remaining Templars fled and in the same direction — west towards Spain — to escape the persecution.

"And this is where it gets interesting. The Cathars passed on their belief about Mary Magdalene and the existence of a continuous royal lineage to the Templars. She became the special saint of the Templars. It is a large component of their heritage to the present day."

The turnoff from the motorway was signposted and Adam pointed to the massive grey cathedral clearly visible in the middle of a small town. "There it is. That's Saint-Maximin, where Mary Magdalene was supposedly buried." The sheer size of the cathedral was out of proportion to the town, dwarfing the surrounding buildings.

As they slowed to turn, Adam added, "Interestingly, there is significant Templar influence across London. Living there, you will know the area around the Inns of Court and, of course, you know Temple Tube station. Temple Church is just down from Fleet Street. It was built by the Templars as their UK headquarters, and the location of their initiation ceremonies."

She nodded her head. "I do. I know it pretty well. Well, the Inns of Court, at least. When I have needed some quiet time, I've often taken a stroll through the gardens there, and then along the river. It makes for a wonderful Sunday afternoon."

Taking the turnoff at a roundabout marked La Sainte-Baume, they bypassed the town and passed through a number of small villages before the road started climbing steeply. Suddenly, they saw ahead the stark grey-white cliffs of the distant Sainte-Baume mountain range, rising high from above the trees. The road narrowed as it climbed. Consulting the satnav, Abigail reassured herself that they were still on the right road.

Navigating the steep climb and the hairpin bends took her attention, until she was able to ask, "This royal bloodline." She looked sideways. "From what Jean said, do you think that this belief in a bloodline all the way from Jesus and Mary Magdalene might form part of Anton's illness?"

"I really haven't a clue what's going on in his mind, but, yes, this could be all part of his obsession," he said, closing his notebook.

Abigail remained quiet.

Shaking his head, Adam continued, "All of this is so difficult to conceptualise."

By now, they had stopped climbing and emerged on top of a plateau. Beyond the plateau stood the Sainte-Baume massif. Adam asked Abigail to stop on the side of the road. She pulled off on the gravel and turned off the engine.

"Look. Look up there. See, halfway up the cliffs, you can just see a building. It looks as if it is built into the rock." Abigail peered through the windscreen, following the direction that he was pointing.

"Yes, I can see it. That must be where the cave is. Christ, how does anyone get up to it?"

"Apparently, there are steps cut into the actual mountainside. But first, let's find this hostel or *hostellerie*."

"All right." She started up the car again. They terrain was now flat, dotted with trees and brush. Ahead, they saw what looked like a camping area. "Any idea where this place might be?" she asked.

"I'm guessing that it is likely to be near the small town of Sainte-Baume. We are about to come into it and I'm sure there will be signs."

It wasn't long before they saw a series of buildings each side of the road. The first was a tourist shop, the *Espace Tourisme et Découverte*. Beside it was the Boutique du Pèlerin, which provided the commercial opportunity. The building looked new with its cream-coloured walls and bright olive green shutters. It was open and looked inviting. The large parking area next to the building contained a dozen or so cars, as well as two tourist buses. Opposite the tourist office stood what looked like a large priory surrounded by high walls. Grey and austere, it stood in silent contrast to the building opposite.

"I think we've found it," Adam said, looking about. There was nothing obvious to indicate what the building was. Just a high wall, with an ancient wooden gate and two large bricked-up windows. It looked more a prison than a religious retreat. Adam pointed to an area in front of the wall. "Pull in there and we will go in and investigate." He felt very uncertain of what they were about to find out.

As they got out of the car, two nuns, dressed in white and black habits, emerged from the wooden door. Adam was about to ask them where they could find the hostel when Abigail nudged him, pointing to an unequivocal sign saying 'Silence'. He nodded and they carried on walking. They passed an ancient bell, high up and suspended between two curved granite stones, resembling elephant tusks. Then, beyond a rounded turret, was an entrance, the door ajar, and a small sign for *Hostellerie Sainte-Baume*. Above the door was a narrow window in the shape of a cross. Above the window was an ancient stone figure of a priest, looking out on the world.

They entered the old building. To the left was a small reception area with a young woman in everyday clothes sitting, talking quietly to a tall middle-aged man. She seemed to be explaining boarding arrangements and meal options on offer. This would take some time, so they decided to look around the hall.

A notice explained that the *hostellerie* was not a hotel, but rather a religious house that was run by Dominican priests. It was, however, open to everyone and the notice explained that it catered for family groups, as well as hikers to the area. Simple accommodation was available and meals were prepared on site, using only fresh produce. It provided conference facilities for up to two hundred and fifty people. The *hostellerie* offered prayer in their chapel, either as part of their regular church services, or alone. Abigail was impressed.

Another notice further on described the *hostellerie* as situated at the foot of the mountainous Massif de la Sainte-Baume, about an hour's drive from either Marseille or Toulon. It was in walking distance of the grotto of Saint Mary Magdalene 'placed between heaven and earth in the heart of the Massif's mountainside'. The *hostellerie* itself was open throughout the year and currently run by the Benedictine Sisters of the Sacred Heart of Montmartre. They welcomed pilgrims 'bringing their needs before Saint Mary Magdalene', as well as tourists and hikers in search of peace and tranquillity.

Adam wondered which of these categories Maryanne had belonged to during her stay.

Further along was a small exhibition on the chapel. It was dedicated to the saint and displayed vivid canvas paintings depicting the life of Mary Magdalene. One showed Mary preaching to the fishermen of Marseille, another showed Saint Maximin meeting her in the town. Most poignant was one showing Mary at the entrance to her cave, looking out over the Provençal countryside.

They called back at reception. The woman was now busy checking the man in, so they carried on along the corridor. They read that the origins of the priory and the hostel lay with Mary Magdalene, whose life in the cave at Sainte-Baume and her subsequent death, marked it as a place of pilgrimage from very early on. In the 5th century, hermits and monks coming from Marseille had withdrawn themselves to the solitude and wilds of Sainte-Baume for a dedicated life of prayer. These hermits and monks subsequently became Benedictines. Hundreds of years later, with the discovery of the remains of Mary Magdalene nearby, there was a revival of interest in pilgrimages. Then in 1295, under the instruction of Pope Boniface VIII, the Dominicans replaced the Benedictines in Sainte-Baume.

Following the French Revolution, the cave, and the ancient priory next to the cave, were looted. With the help of the inhabitants of the nearby town of Plan d'Aups, the white marble statue of the Virgin and relics of the saint were rescued from the cave and hidden in the village church. Important documents held in the priory by the cave were also brought down and secured. The relics and the statue were eventually returned to the cave in 1816. The buildings around the cave were also restored and Dominican monks, together with their priceless books and documents, returned permanently to their home on the mountainside.

Chapter 16

"*Bonjour*. And how may I help you?". The hostel's receptionist had appeared quietly behind them. Abigail jumped. She had been on edge since they found the cat and there was something oppressive about this place.

"I am sorry. I have startled you." The young woman spoke English with a slight German accent. "How can I help you?"

Adam smiled at her. "We're looking for information on someone who has stayed here recently. Her name is Maryanne."

"I am sorry *monsieur*, but I am not permitted to give details of other customers. I cannot help you with this." She retreated behind the counter and sat down.

Abigail stepped in. The receptionist was about her age. "You don't understand. The woman who stayed here is my mother. We've been looking for her for some time. Can you please just check on your computer to see if you had a woman staying here for a long time, and who left recently. I will give you all her details?"

The receptionist hesitated. "This is very unusual. We do not normally provide details of those who stay with us. People here are very careful about their privacy. They come here for the quiet and to contemplate. You understand what I mean?"

Abigail nodded, but said that surely these were special circumstances.

"They come to get away from the world and we respect that. What if she does not want to be disturbed?" There was a short pause as she weighed up Abigail, then she turned to her computer screen. "She is your mother, you say?"

"Yes. I will give you all her details. We're only asking you to check your past records."

"I have a photograph if you would like it," Adam interrupted, reaching into his pocket.

"No. That is not necessary. When did she come here?" She pressed some keys on the computer and turned back to Abigail.

"I'm sorry, but we don't have precise dates. She arrived sometime in the last year, but she did stay up until last month. We believe she left in a hurry."

The receptionist shrugged and scrolled through the booking system. After a few minutes she said, "Are you sure she left in the last month?"

"Yes." Adam and Abigail answered together.

The receptionist sighed and looked up at them. "I am sorry. We have no one of that name staying here in the last year. Perhaps somewhere else?" she offered. "A lot of people come here to make a pilgrimage up to the cave. Not all stay here at the *hostellerie*. There are some guest houses in the village and hotels in Saint-Maximin and also Saint-Zacharie."

Abigail looked at Adam and shook her head. "No, I don't think so. I am certain she stayed here. Can you please check again?"

She sighed and resumed her search. After a while, she said, "Are you sure that is the name? We have one single room that was occupied since last year, for more than ten months, and the person did leave three weeks ago."

Abigail grabbed Adam's arm. "That must have been her. The timing is right."

"It is not the name you gave me. But it is a woman who stayed. I cannot give you the name that she registered with. It is not allowed."

"What about her passport details?" Adam asked.

The receptionist stopped and looked up from her computer. She regarded Adam sternly. "*Monsieur*, we do not require to see passports here at *Hostellerie La Sainte-Baume*."

"I am sorry," he replied. "We understand. Perhaps you saw this woman. Let me show you the photograph. Perhaps you may remember."

"I am sorry. Unfortunately, I was not working here at the time that she left. I cannot help you." With finality, she turned away from her computer.

Abigail smiled at the receptionist. "We really appreciate your help. Is there someone here who might remember this woman? Who might recognise her from a photograph? After all, she stayed here for quite a while."

The receptionist looked at her watch. "They, the sisters, are all at prayer now. When they finish, I can ask Sister Bertranda — she helps with the bookings and does the accounts for the *hostellerie*. She may know."

"That would be very helpful," said Abigail. "What time might she be free?"

"Prayers will end at two o'clock, so perhaps two-thirty or three o'clock? You can have lunch in the restaurant next to the monastery, or you are welcome to walk around the grounds while you wait. If you do go into the grounds, we just ask that you keep quiet. We provide a silent retreat and, even outside, many of our guests prefer silence."

"Will there be time to walk up to the cave afterwards?"

She smiled at Adam and shook her head. "It will not be possible. The grotto closes at five o'clock and you would not be able to get there in time. You will have to come back in the morning."

Adam and Abigail looked at each other. They had packed two small cases just in case they needed to stay nearby. Adam asked if she had rooms available for the night. She did and they booked, saying they would be back for two-thirty.

"Would you like the evening meal as well?" the receptionist asked. Confirming that they would, they left the *hostellerie* by the front entrance.

As they headed for the small restaurant next door, Abigail shivered, despite the early afternoon sun. "I'm really not sure about staying here for the night. I just hope we have made the right decision."

*

Sister Bertranda looked to be in her eighties and was about five feet tall, but her presence filled the shadowed room, where light squeezed through a high narrow window. She sat behind an ancient wooden desk piled with papers, well-thumbed books and journals. In spite of the disarray, there was a sense of tranquillity.

"Now, how can I help you two?" An Irish lilt coloured her commanding voice, but Adam and Abigail were transfixed by her wispy bright yellow hair.

She must have misinterpreted their looks of astonishment. "Now don't you worry your heads. I know it looks like chaos in here but…" She smiled and gestured to the desk and disorganised bookcase. "Everything has its place here and I know exactly where to find things."

They smiled and Adam cleared his throat. "We explained to your kind receptionist that we're looking for someone who has stayed here recently."

"And who would that be, pray?"

They explained how Maryanne had been missing for three years and they had been told she had stayed at the *hostellerie* for the past months.

"Ingrid has already told you that no one of that name has stayed here. I am not sure what else I can tell you." She held her arms out as if in supplication.

"Please hear us out, Sister," Abigail pleaded. "We understand a woman has been staying here: someone who only left recently. Perhaps my mother stayed here under another name. Is that possible?"

"Well now, my child, we have to assume that if someone was staying here under an assumed name, they had a reason to do that. We do not question people's reasons. We assume they come to the *hostellerie* for solitude and personal reflection, and, of course, for pilgrimage. All our customers have a right to their own privacy and we do not disclose to anyone, not even family, who is staying with us or why."

Abigail's eyes welled up. It all suddenly felt hopeless. "Can we at least show you a photograph. Can you at least say whether you have seen my mother? Please?"

Adam placed the picture in front of the woman. She turned on an ancient anglepoise desk lamp and hunted through the scattered papers on her desk until she found a battered pair of tortoiseshell glasses. She examined the photograph of Maryanne, then put it down, removed the glasses and sighed. "I am sorry, I don't know what you expect me to say."

"Please just tell us if you recognise her. Is this the woman who has been staying here?" Adam's muscles clenched with frustration.

With a shrug the Sister replied "I cannot say anything.

I am not permitted to say... anything, but I will seek further guidance on this matter. What I will say is that I am very sorry for your loss." She took off her glasses and smiled across to them. In the lamplight her hair had taken on a neon tinge. It was hard not to stare.

"I understand that you are enjoying our hospitality here at the *hostellerie* tonight. I hope you will find our facilities adequate. I will consult with our brother later this evening on this and will see you before you leave tomorrow. Will you be going up to the Holy Grotto?"

Recovering, Abigail replied, "Thank you, Sister. We both appreciate your efforts on this. Yes, we will be making a... a pilgrimage there tomorrow."

With that, the interview seemed to have concluded, and the sister stood and wished them a good evening. "Please use our chapel should you wish," she urged. "You will find it peaceful." As a final gesture, she added, in a friendlier manner, "I am very sorry that you are so troubled, and I was not able to ease your pain."

Their rooms were furnished simply but they were surprisingly comfortable. Certainly not what Abigail was expecting. Her room was a good size, with a bed in one corner and a comfortable chair situated beside the large window overlooking the gardens. The single bed was covered by a thin blue and white striped bedspread and above it, a small wooden cross was prominently positioned. A white plastic reading light was fixed to the wood panelling to one side of the bed. A picture of Mary Magdalene in her cave decorated one wall. Turning on the light in the bathroom, she saw it contained an old-fashioned shower surrounded by multi-coloured tiles and a basic, functional, porcelain basin. *Not too bad*, thought Abigail. Its brightness allayed some of the fears that had been mounting. It was still hard for her to understand why her mother had chosen to live here. In spite of her spiritual leanings, she had still enjoyed the good things in life. *What had she been doing here in this hostel, in the middle of nowhere?*

They had agreed to meet up in an hour and explore the *hostellerie* and attached priory, starting outside with the garden. Abigail had thought that she would need the time to calm down from the frustration of earlier. She needed to compose herself, and to try to better understand what had been going through the mind of her mother.

Adam was standing by the unattended Reception desk, looking through various English-version booklets, when Abigail emerged.

"How are you feeling?" he asked, a look of concern across his tired-looking features.

"Actually, not too bad. I visited the chapel. It was so peaceful and it helped me to understand why Mum might have chosen such a place to take herself away from the world for a while."

"Good. All I managed was a quick nap. I don't know why I feel so tired. Anyway, tell me about it."

"It was strange. You know, I'm not particularly religious, but I found the chapel strangely calming. It was peaceful in a way I can only describe as spiritual. It's a lovely place and there are the wonderful frescos of Mary Magdalene — both in Marseille and also here, on the plain at Sainte-Baume, with the mountains in the background. I started to have some understanding of how Mum might have spent her time. I had a strong feeling that she was often there, in that chapel. You should go. You might feel better for it."

The extensive grounds of the monastery were to the

rear of the building. Walking slowly around, they found an area laid mainly to lawn, trees providing shade for a number of benches facing fields fringed by a dense forest. The Sainte-Baume massif loomed in the distance.

"I read one of the exhibits earlier all about the legend of the fierce dragon of La Sainte-Baume," she said, pointing out towards the mountain range. "The legend explains their strange shape."

Adam looked out towards the jagged mountains in the east. "All right. Let's hear about the dragon."

"Long ago there was a dragon that hated the beauty of this place. So, with its evil power, the dragon created a series of storms which completely changed the landscape. I translated it from the French, so I might have got some of the details wrong," she apologised. "One day, one of the gods saw this and unleashed a fierce lightning strike. It hit the dragon directly in the heart and it died. The landscape then returned to its former beauty. However, after its death, the dragon's body remained and it became the mountain you see directly in front of you. See up there," she said, pointing, "the head of the dragon formed what became known as the Saint-Cassien Heights. The body is stretched out across those peaks and the dragon's long tail is wrapped around the valley down here. The wound in his heart caused by the lightning strike then became the cave of La Sainte-Baume."

Adam listened and then looked around. "It's certainly a dramatic view. I can think of worse places to spend eternity," he said, indicating the nearby cemetery. It was situated to the one side of the buildings, in a quiet area, with neat lines of graves, each marked with a simple wooden cross. At the end of one of the lines, a fresh mound was still waiting for its cross. The cemetery looked out over the mountains in the far distance. There was an air of simplicity and finality about the peaceful place. Walking on, they came across two inner courtyards within the jumble of interconnected buildings, only one of which they were allowed to access. The smaller of the courtyards, surrounded by buildings and a high wall, was marked as private, presumably for the personal use of the monks and nuns. The other was for use by visitors and prominent signs advocated silent contemplation. A small cottage garden vegetable patch took up the one corner. As they walked back, they saw a statue of Mary Magdalene on top of the chapel, looking serenely out across the plain towards her eventual sanctuary.

When they returned to the *hostellerie,* they asked the directions to the dining room. It was at the rear of the building. At the end of a long, dimly-lit passageway, they entered what was a surprisingly large and light room, with a dozen tables. Those that were laid were covered by mustard-yellow tablecloths. That evening, only four tables were occupied and they joined another couple at their table. The couple were in their sixties and from the USA. They explained that they were on a pilgrimage, having already spent a few days in both Avignon and Marseille.

"This is something we have always dreamt of doing. I still cannot believe that we are here... here in the south of France," the woman explained in a nasally American accent. "We have been planning this trip for years." They were staying for two days and would make the climb to the cave the next day. "We can't wait. It's going to be tough, but it will definitely be the highlight of our trip." Adam and Abigail could see that the American couple were curious about their relationship, so they explained that Adam was married to Abigail's mother.

The meal was pleasant and the company light-hearted. The food proved as fresh and wholesome as had been advertised. They were both surprised to be offered wine with their meal and a clay pitcher duly arrived for the table, enough for one glass of red wine for each of them. Later, Adam said goodnight to Abigail and went in search of the chapel that she had recommended. On his way, he passed a reddish stone statue of Mary Magdalene holding a vase, surrounded by votive offerings of flickering candles and fresh flowers.

The chapel was empty. It was larger than expected, with at least twenty rows of seats, with a central tiled aisle leading towards the altar. The wooden benches and chairs were highly polished. Adam took a seat halfway down. Abigail was right. It was cool and surprisingly tranquil. He felt the cloak of weariness that had weighed on him shift as he sat there for what seemed a long time. Eventually, stirring himself, he looked around, as if the chapel might give clues to where his wife now was. The altar stood in the centre, at the end of the chapel, under a domed cupola. Fresh flowers had been placed to each side. The cupola was decorated with a fading fresco of Mary Magdalene ascending, accompanied by angels. A large white cloth provided a backdrop to the altar. The cloth was decorated with faint, concentric, circles on the outside with, in the middle of the draping, a thick dark circle was bisected top and bottom. Adam had his phone with him and took a quick photo of the drape. He would research the unusual design when he got the chance.

That night, as he lay in his narrow bed, with the bedside light on and his eyes closed, Adam, too, felt Maryanne's presence. It wasn't just that she had stayed here but a feeling that she was close by. He hadn't felt this way since she had disappeared. He had spent so long with his doubts; battling the feeling that she had completely disappeared from his life, and the belief that there was little chance of her return. Despite his weariness, he felt a sudden lift as if something was going to happen — and soon — and a resolution that he would continue his search for her. He lay there for a long while, staring up at the ceiling. Finally, he turned off the light. As the darkness enveloped the room, he sensed that the *hostellerie* was unnaturally quiet. It was as if time had stopped in that moment.

Chapter 17

The next morning was overcast with a low mist. It was unusually humid, and a storm felt imminent. Despite this, they set off from the *hostellerie* for their long walk up to the cave. All the guidebooks advised that the route to the cliff involved a strenuous climb through the forest and was not for everyone. They were not sure what to expect. To start with, it was just a gentle walk along a signposted path beside a large, ploughed field, towards the distant forest. Ahead were a couple of hikers making the trek. The climb remained gentle, as they skirted the forest edge, until they entered what they took to be the national park.

Abigail, mindful of Adam's injured leg, urged him to stop and rest. She worried how he would cope when they reached the serious climbing. Adam, though, was determined to carry on, fuelled in part by their earlier frustration.

*

The morning had not got off to a good start. After a simple breakfast of coffee and a croissant in the restaurant they had been summoned to Sister Bertranda's office. They had sat, waiting for her to lift her head from an old accounting magazine she was reading. She took her time and Adam and Abigail looked at each other. When she finally lifted her head and acknowledged them, she apologised. It wasn't the fact that she had kept them waiting that prompted the apology, though.

"I'm sorry but, unfortunately, I am not able to help

you in your search. I spoke to the brother, as I promised I would last night, and he confirmed what I already knew. We undertake to respect the wishes of all our pilgrims, and we do not disclose the personal circumstances to others."

"Surely you must be able to at least tell us whether or not my mother has stayed here?" Abigail leant forward towards the sister who shook her head.

"And what about this 'other' woman who had been staying here? The woman who only left a few weeks ago?"

Sister Bertranda hesitated. "I have checked the records. She is not the woman you seek, unfortunately."

It was obvious she was lying. "Could you give us her name and a phone number so we can check she is not my mother?" Abigail's voice rose as her frustration increased.

"Please calm yourself, *madame*. I am not able to give you that information. As I said yesterday, we do not divulge private details of our guests."

"So, we are unable to ascertain whether what you are saying is true," Abigail said with dismay.

"That is correct," the old woman replied, looking levelly at her.

Adam put a calming hand on Abigail's arm. "Sister Bertranda, you gave us the clear impression yesterday afternoon that you would provide us with a satisfactory answer on whether the woman who stayed with you for a long period was the woman we are seeking. We even showed you her photograph. Our request yesterday was simple. That's why we stayed here overnight and why we are here this morning. We've been very patient, and we expect you to respect our need, and not to try to fob us off with vague and insincere platitudes." His voice was level. Abigail looked sideways at him. He had seemed different at breakfast. The Adam of the past weeks had changed — there seemed a newfound resolve.

The sister looked steadily at Adam and took her time before replying. "I am very sorry, sir, that I am not able to provide you with the information you were hoping for. But I do thank you for being so patient." Her tone bristled with barely concealed anger.

Abigail had one final try. "Please Sister. Can you at least say whether she stayed here? I don't see how that would be divulging any confidences."

"I cannot say any more. Good day to you both." The meeting was over.

Abigail and Adam stood. Adam made to leave then stopped and turned towards Sister Bertranda. She had replaced her glasses and returned to her reading. A strange calmness washed over him. In an even voice he said "Madam, I know that Maryanne, my wife and Abigail's mother, has stayed here. I know you are aware of this. Your platitudes, your frankly aggressive refusal to assist us, and what amount to downright lies, are not what we would expect from a woman of the cloth. You represent your church. As such, your behaviour shows it to be an empty vessel, lacking in a basic humanity. Good day to you as well."

The sister raised her head. "Get out. Leave now." Her voice was now a whisper.

*

A large board at the entrance to the national park and forest welcomed them to the route of the Grotte de Sainte

Marie-Madeleine. It was where 'according to tradition the first witness of the resurrection of Christ lived,' and also where 'men come to admire creation and seek the peace of God'. The Dominican Order had been guardians of the sanctuary since the end of the 13th century and visitors were asked to respect their life and traditions and to observe silence once up there. Next to the sign was a bench. They stopped and sat for a while. Adam had bought a guidebook of La Sainte-Baume and he took it from his rucksack and passed it to Abigail. The ancient forest that they were about to enter was unique in Provence. She read that 'to reach the Mary Magdalene cave, the visitor or pilgrim has to climb up through a strange and somewhat troubling forest. The bright Provençal sunshine does not penetrate this thick forest which has developed on the north facing slope under the shelter of the high cliffs'. Apparently, some of the yew trees in the forest were more than a thousand years old. It concluded that 'the atmosphere is dark and silent'.

Abigail added, "I read somewhere that the Druids consider the yew the tree of death." She shivered involuntarily. In truth, it had suddenly become noticeably cooler than a few minutes before and a wind had sprung up, as if from nowhere. Apart from yew trees, there were also oaks and lindens, their branches fresh with new leaves, moving with the breeze.

"It doesn't sound welcoming, that's for sure. It feels spooky, even in the daylight."

"Yes, not a place to get lost in," agreed Abigail. "But we feel that Maryanne is not far away. This search has included Mary Magdalene almost from the outset. What better place to look than where she was meant to have lived?"

"I think you're right. After our meeting, I am sure the priests are hiding something. They know something… something important. I can feel it."

"And it could be up there… in the cave," she pointed, although the high granite cliff was now hidden by the thick vegetation.

He stood, looking resolute. "Fine, let's get this climb out of the way."

The dirt pathway wound its way through the dense forest until it gave way to worn cobblestones. Around them, the forest closed in. As they rounded a bend, they came across an ancient stone shrine, inset with a carving of Jesus on the cross, with Mary Magdalene kneeling at his feet. A sudden stillness descended. The forest was quiet and all bird song had vanished. The earlier breeze had died, bringing the return of an oppressive humidity.

They heard it before they felt it. A distant rumbling that they first took for thunder. The sky, glimpsed through the canopy of overhanging branches, had darkened. The sound built, as if a huge heavy truck was rumbling down the forest slope towards them. Then the tremors began, a slow and gentle rolling, before the ground itself started to shake. Adam felt that he might slip over on the shiny cobblestones, so he sat down heavily on a rock, holding onto it with both hands. Abigail stayed upright, though the shaking grew more violent and persistent. The rumbling became louder, then it suddenly stopped. It had probably lasted for no more than half-a-minute, but it had seemed an age.

"What the hell was that?" Abigail's face was ashen. The unearthly quiet was broken by the sounds of the birds through the forest. Abigail sat down next to Adam and clutched his arm. "Was that an earthquake?"

"I don't think so. Just an earth tremor, but we should wait here for a while before we go on," he replied. "There might be more."

"Shouldn't we get down to the bottom, or at least out in the clearing away from the trees? I am not normally superstitious, but do you think that that was some sort of omen?" She looked skywards. "Perhaps something is telling us that we shouldn't be making the climb?"

He smiled. "Perhaps it's the dragon, coming back to life."

Abigail gave him a playful slap on the shoulder. "Make fun of me if you want."

"Let's give it a couple of moments. This area of Provence is prone to earthquakes and tremors." He looked up and down the path. "I can't see any damage. There aren't any cracks in the ground as far as I can make out. No trees seemed to have fallen across the path. Let's wait. If nothing else happens in the next five minutes we should be fine to carry on."

"OK," she agreed. "But shit, that was scary. Well, I found it scary. I have never experienced anything like that."

"If you don't want to continue, just say. We can come back in a couple of days if you prefer?"

"No," she said resolutely. "We're here. If nothing else happens, we continue." She did not wish to consider spending another night in the *hostellerie*.

After a while, they stood and looked around. Continuing, the forest path soon became steep and Adam began to struggle. He had to stop every five minutes to catch his breath. He had begun to regret his vanity and wished he had a walking stick.

"I apologise. What with the recent injuries from the

bloody crash, I'm just not as fit as I used to be."

"Don't worry, old man," she said with tenderness. "Between the two of us, we'll get there. There's no rush. We have all day."

It was twenty minutes before they came across anyone — two fit-looking French women — walking back down the hill. They asked if Adam and Abigail had felt the earth tremor. The women seemed completely unconcerned, as if the ground shaking was an everyday occurrence.

A fountain, clear water flowing through a curved iron pipe and cascading into a stone basin, beckoned beside the path. Above was an inscription for '*La Source de Nans*'. The cool mountain water tasted wonderful, and they stopped to recover and take in a view of the plain below.

"We don't know how far we are from the cave but I wonder if this was not the source of its water supply." Abigail gazed up the steep track. "How on earth did Mary Magdalene know there was even a cave in these mountains?"

"Well, the cave has been around for millions of years. It has probably been known to those who lived around this area for thousands of years and, in all likelihood, been home to many generations of prehistoric man, well before Mary Magdalene came along."

"I guess so. Amazing to think that." She dipped her hand in the water and drank some more. "But how did she make it up here? There were probably no paths. We drove the fifteen kilometres up the mountain from Saint-Maximin. It must have taken her bloody weeks to get up here. They must have been so fit in those days."

Adam looked around. "Two thousand years ago, there were probably only hunter or animal tracks through the forest." He thought about that, and then added, "And what would she have lived on up here? Presumably, things she could forage in the forest."

They continued on, now making slow progress. The path was steep and the forest seemed impenetrable.

"It's strange but I can feel the spirit of Mum within the forest, as if she is guiding us onwards."

There was still no sign of the cliff face or the start of the stone steps built to help pilgrims climb up to the grotto. Some Dutch hikers with serious-looking metal walking sticks caught them up. They were concerned about the tremor and said they intended to spend as little time as possible in the grotto before making their way off the mountain. They left Abigail and Adam behind with a wave of their sticks.

What did you make of the *hostellerie*?" Adam asked.

Abigail bit her lip and thought about the question for a while. "I found it unsettling. I didn't like the place. Apart from the chapel, which was surprisingly peaceful. The rest of the place felt claustrophobic. It felt like a place that had secrets."

"Precisely. It felt like the place to go if you wanted to hide away from the world. Perhaps that was what Maryanne was looking for."

Abigail looked at Adam, a question forming.

Before she could respond, Adam added, "I should have asked about Anton. They must have known him or known of him."

She shook her head. "I very much doubt we would have got anything out of Sister Bertranda about him."

"I know that there is a monastery built next to the cave which houses the priests who live up there. I wonder if that is where we will find Anton?"

Abigail raised her eyebrows and turned to Adam

again. "If Anton is there, will we even recognise him?"

"Well, if he was one of the men I met with Maryanne at the Tour de France, I think I would."

"And, if he hasn't changed too much from the man I remember, then I'll know him," she said with a grim certainty.

"Well, we might find out shortly. You said that the order has a chequered history. They're not people we really want to come up against."

"No, they're not. They're powerful and most people would do well to keep their distance from them. Their history shows a lack of basic humanity. They seemed to enjoy the hurt and humiliation they inflicted on others."

"And yet now they now present a very different face to the world."

"Isn't that most religions, though?" Abigail made a wry face.

"Probably," he shrugged, agreeing. "They have tried hard to sanitise their past. I'm guessing you will find little in their records which reference their role in the Inquisitions. That will all have been rewritten."

The last part of the climb was the hardest, forcing Adam to concentrate on putting one foot in front of the other to keep going. They knew they were approaching the cave when they came across a wooden sign beside the path requesting that silence be now observed. Adam was reminded that kings, popes and saints had trodden this path over the centuries.

Around a sweeping corner, they had a first glimpse of the massive grey cliff face ahead. A tree was angled across the pathway, and they saw a collection of outbuildings huddled at the base of the cliff. High above the buildings they could see the overhang of the monastery. Two sturdy ropes, presumably a rudimentary pulley system, connected the monastery to the buildings far below. This would allow the priests to haul up their provisions. As they neared the base of the cliff, a sign finally welcomed them to Grotte de Sainte Marie-Madeleine.

To the left were the start of the hundred and fifty stone steps which would lead them to the cave. From below, it was hard to imagine how pilgrims had managed to scramble up the sheer rock face before their construction. Now, the worn steps were testament to the sheer volume of pilgrims to make the climb to one of the oldest religious sites in the western world.

As they commenced this final climb, they were met by the same Dutch couple who had passed them earlier on the climb. This time, though, Adam and Abigail did not merit a second glance as, eyes only on the final step, the pair hurried down and headed towards the path into the forest.

"When we get to the top, we're probably going to need to access areas that the public aren't allowed into. We can't just shout out Maryanne's name. We need to come up with a plan," Adam whispered.

Abigail frowned. "How can we ask questions if we have to be silent up there?" she whispered back. "We need to find a way to get into the monastery itself."

"You are probably right. Let's have a look around first before we make that decision."

As they commenced their walk up the stairway to the cave, it felt that there was something very final about the climb. Water trickled through the lichen and moss that clung to the cliff face. The stairs offered them a panorama of the valley and the mountains beyond. The *hostellerie* lay far below them. At the top was a stone entrance complete with a faded coat of arms.

The double wooden lattice doors were open. At the entrance, a sign provided a brief history and welcomed all visitors to the sanctuary of Sainte-Baume. Beyond was a cave providing a reconstruction of the Crucifixion scene. Turning right, they ascended the last few stairs and, there in front of them, stood the monastery, and courtyard, balancing on the cliff edge. The monastery was partly built into the cliff and was attached to the cave by an early stone edifice with a heavy door below, and three open arched windows above. The final few stairs led to a vista across Provence. They stopped in front of a bronze statue and briefly marvelled at the view. Its beauty only served to highlight the sense of isolation from the world beyond. A cool breeze tugged at their clothes.

"Surely Mum isn't here," Abigail murmured softly, feeling the aloneness.

A low stone building stood opposite the monastery. The two doorways of the non-descript building were framed by trees either side. One of the doors was wedged open. The monastery door itself was firmly shut, as were the two windows, and the two windows above. Inset into a small alcove above the door, much like that of the *hostellerie*, was the figure of a Dominican priest, dressed in his black cape.

They walked across to the entrance to the grotto. There were no priests in evidence and the whole place was deserted, apart from a middle-aged couple studying a plaque on the monastery wall.

Mary Magdalene's cave was huge. It was some sixty metres deep and seemingly could accommodate up to a thousand people. Abigail shivered at the chill inside the dark quiet cave. The floor was inlaid with red, white and black tiles, echoing the colours on the stone walls, colours associated with the Knights Templar. In the middle was an imposing white altar, with a flight of stairs leading up to it. The altar rose to the roof of the cave. Behind it stood a statue of Jesus on the cross with Mary Magdalene crouched at his feet. The altar was covered by a white cloth and three white candles burning in the gloom. In front of the altar, rows of seats and benches were placed, enough seating for at least two hundred people. The cave was silent and empty.

There were a number of large nooks and crannies off to the left. In one, perched high on a rock, was a white marble statue of a woman holding a baby. All around were scattered offerings of flowers, letters and cards. Numerous candles had been lit. Beyond the statue was a locked wooden door set into the stone of the cave wall.

They walked up the stairs to the altar. Behind was a reliquary containing bone fragments of the saint. A single lightbulb glowed, illuminating a glass container holding the ancient relics. They retraced their steps with care to avoid slipping on the worn stairway. At the bottom, they stopped and took in the ornate stained-glass windows, each depicting well-known biblical scenes, set into the front wall, allowing light to filter into the grotto.

"According to the guide, if you look carefully, you can see a number of odd details in the windows, including masonic symbols and the letters J and M, connected by a line," Abigail whispered to Adam. "See there," she continued, pointing towards a window. "There's another one. It shows Mary in a traditional pose at the foot of the cross. However, what is really odd in this representation is the absence of Jesus above."

In the shadows, to the right of the altar, stone steps led

down to a lower chamber of the cave. Adam nudged Abigail. "That looks like it might go down to a crypt. We need to have a look." They went down a set of worn marble stairs to a darkened interior. Flickering candles cast strange shadows across the ceiling and walls. There was a strong musty smell accompanied by the sound of dripping water. There was movement to one side, as a tall figure drifted away into the gloom.

Following the movement, a white alabaster statue shone out from the dark. As they stepped forwards, they saw it was the figure of Mary Magdalene, emerging from a recess in the corner. The statue was seated, dressed serenely in a long flowing robe. As they got closer, they saw it was lit by dozens of flickering candles.

"I wonder if this was where Mary Magdalene lived?" Abigail looked around. "If so, I can understand why. It looks like the most sheltered part of the cave."

"It's very dark down here. But, look. Over there." In the gloom, they saw a natural stone basin full of water, pooling from the water dripping through an ancient fissure in the black rocks of the cave ceiling high above. "This is clearly the source of her water."

They made their way towards the other end of the lower cave, nearest to the entrance and to the monastery above. There was no sign of the two visitors, nor of the shadowy figure they had seen earlier. As they approached the cave wall, they saw a metal door with a grille, recessed into the sheer rock face.

"Could the figure we saw earlier have gone through this door?" Adam pressed his face against the grille, but it was too dark to see anything. "It looks like it might lead all the way through to the priory. Let's check it out. There must be someone we can ask."

"I saw a doorbell next to the entrance. Come on. Let's give it a go." Abigail headed for the marble stairs and the exit to the cave.

Chapter 18

The yellowed ivory button would not move. Adam tried it again with more force. The third time he used the heel of his hand and they were eventually rewarded with what they thought was a faint chime from within the depths of the building. Adam tried pushing the bell once more. The faint chime from within again went unanswered. There was no sound beyond that of the birds behind, wheeling in the wind that funnelled up the cliff face. He tried a final time, without a response. Abigail and Adam stood looking at each other.

"I wonder where they all are? It sounds pretty deserted in there. I have my doubts that Maryanne is here."

"I don't know." Abigail tensed and glanced around them. "I have this feeling though, that we're being watched."

"Well, there must be priests around somewhere. The chapel in the cave looked like it had been set up for a service. Did you notice the schedule of services down at the entrance gate?"

"I didn't take in the detail but I think they hold daily services, so there must be someone around."

"Well, where are they?"

They looked around. The wooden door set in the old two-storey structure which connected the priory to the grotto was firmly closed. Above the door, the open gallery that ran through to the upper level of the cave was dark and deserted. Across the square was the gift shop. It was flat-roofed and single-storey. A yellow and blue sign outside declared it was *Ouvert*. It was the first positive indication of life. Next door, the entrance was adorned by a picture of three monks, a sign signifying that it was the *Abri du Pèlerin*: the Pilgrim's Shelter. The door was half-open, revealing a black-and-white tiled hallway. A large iron-barred window with darkened glass revealed there to be a further room to the right of the entrance.

"Let's try the gift shop first," suggested Abigail.

"I agree. There surely must be someone there."

The gift shop was sparsely filled and gloomy. A few posters, postcards and books on La Sainte-Baume and Mary Magdalene were on display. Not all looked brand new. There was also a small collection of books on the flora and fauna of the surrounding national park. A cabinet held a few touristy items, including pens, commemorative spoons and penknives. A young man stood beside the counter and seemed startled by the arrival of potential customers. Abigail asked where everyone was but the man could only shrug and explain that he spoke no English. It was not worth pursuing and, after a cursory look around, they left.

The entrance on the right, though, looked more promising. The room they entered was, however, empty. It was larger than the gift shop and, with two windows opening onto a spectacular view of the forest below, was clearly set up as a visitor area for rest and contemplation. To one side of the room was a long table, with long wooden benches on either side. Other wooden chairs were scattered around. They sat and rested their legs for a while, hoping in vain that someone from the priory might join them.

Returning to the corridor, there was one area still to try. The heavy door was ajar, so they pushed it open and entered. A greyish light barely penetrated from the outside and the dusty window did little to illuminate the narrow room. It was simply furnished, with a desk and three chairs, placed along the one wall. A couple of steel cabinets at the end suggested it was used as an office or storeroom. Beyond the cabinets was a narrow corridor. They looked for a light switch and as they did so, the heavy entrance door swung shut with a loud clang and the room was pitched into semi-darkness.

Abigail jumped and knocked over one of the chairs. "Ouch."

"What happened?"

"Just this bloody chair I bumped into." She gingerly touched the graze on her leg.

Careful to avoid the dark furniture, Adam went over to the door and tried the handle. It was jammed shut. The metal handle would not move.

"Did the wind blow it shut?" Abigail's voice shook.

"I don't think so. The door's too heavy. I think we've just been shut in." He went to the window and tried to wipe away some of the grime with his hand. It was deeply ingrained and his efforts made little difference. Hazy outlines were all that was visible outside. He tried the door again, then banged on it, shouting, "Hey! Hey!" There was no response. He put his ear to the door and listened. No sound. He tried pounding the door with both fists.

Abigail placed her hand on his arm. "Stop, Adam. You're going to hurt yourself. Let's look around to see what we're dealing with."

"OK." He was now breathing heavily. When he recovered, he resumed his search for a light switch and eventually found one by a cabinet. He flipped the dusty switch but nothing happened. He continued to feel his way into the narrow corridor, past the steel cabinets, and tried the walls for another switch. Eventually finding one he tried it, again without success.

"There's no power to this room. Or, it's been switched off."

"What now?" Abigail slumped into a chair.

"We're going to have to wait for someone to come along. This isn't an accident. Someone knows we are here."

Abigail took out her mobile phone. "Damn. Nothing. There's no signal here."

"I'm not surprised. We're miles from anywhere, and anyway we're surrounded by solid rock." Adam tried the door again, then used the torch on his phone to survey the room. Dust lay on the empty shelves and cobwebs filled the corners. It was not a room in current use. Turning the beam to the ceiling, he saw the lightbulbs had been removed from the two sockets. In the narrow back room another empty light socket dangled forlornly above a small table covered by a thick layer of dust. At the far end was a door. It was locked. He gave up and rejoined Abigail, who was staring at her useless phone.

"Nothing. I'm sorry. There's no one to help us."

The afternoon was slipping away. Soon they would be in total darkness.

"Someone will come for us, eventually," Adam sounded more hopeful than he felt. "Whoever it is, they won't just leave us here."

"I know. Ever since we got to Sainte-Baume I've felt as though we're being watched — both whilst we were at the *hostellerie*, and also when we climbed through that spooky forest. I've had the same feeling up here."

*

It was a long time before they heard a scrape, then a rattle, outside the door and a key being inserted. The door edged open to reveal a tall, slightly stooped figure, holding an oil lamp. As he entered the lamp swung, casting long shadows that danced around the walls. Adam and Abigail jumped to their feet.

"What the fuck is going on?" Adam took a step towards the man.

The tall figure was dressed in a long black cassock, his face obscured by a hood. He lifted the lamp. "Stop. Sit back down, both of you," he commanded. He spoke good English, with just a trace of a French accent. "I apologise for the inconvenience of the long wait. It was necessary to wait until all the visitors had left."

"Why? What do you mean?" Abigail tried to make out the man's features, but his face was still in shadow.

"We have closed the grotto. The gate at the entrance is locked." He walked further into the room and part of his face was visible in the lamp light.

Abigail started. "I know you."

"I think you do." He pushed the hood back to reveal more of his face. In the dark the priest's eyes seemed to shine.

"I knew you when I was young, in Dublin. You used to visit our house."

"Indeed I did." A strange smile now played across his face.

"You knew Maryanne... my mother. What have you done with her?"

"A good question. It is one I will answer for you later." He held the lamp up so that he could see both Abigail and Adam clearly. "I know you have both spent much time looking for her. I've been following your progress with interest."

"I recognise your voice now," Abigail answered. "You're the person who phoned me in England. It was you who put Mum on the phone."

"It was necessary," he agreed. "We knew you would come to us eventually, but we needed to speed things up. This man," he nodded towards Adam, "needed some assistance. But now I must congratulate you. You have been getting much closer. You have been doing just what we hoped you would do."

"I don't know what you are talking about." The priest looked at Adam, then dismissed him. His attention was now solely on Abigail.

"And now you are finally here. I should formally welcome you." There was little warmth in his voice. "For now, you both stay with us here at the cave." There was a pause. "Unfortunately, you cannot escape."

"I also know you," Adam interrupted. "I recognise you from that day of the Tour de France, three years ago. You spent some time speaking to Maryanne." The priest turned and studied Adam with sudden interest.

"You have a good memory."

"You, and your friends, have been following me for the last few months. Your name is Anton, isn't it?"

"Very good," the priest replied, with a half-sneer. "You have met my brother, then."

"He tried to explain to us what was going on. He is concerned for your mental health."

Anton laughed harshly. "I am sure he is. He always looks out for me."

Abigail interrupted. "He tried to explain to us what was going on. That is why we are here."

"I know. Please do not underestimate me." His focus

settled back on her. "I knew that, with some little encouragement, you would get around to look for me up here. Far better this way, than us having to bring you to the cave ourselves."

Adam and Abigail looked at each other, understanding slowly dawning. Adam stood and took a step forward, towards the monk.

"Stop!" Anton withdrew his hand from a fold in the depths of the cassock to reveal a large handgun which he pointed at Adam's chest. With a lop-sided smile he said, "Believe me, it might be old but it still works. So please, sit down again." Adam hesitated.

"Do not think you can escape from here. It is not possible." He placed the lamp on the edge of the wooden table. "There is no way down from here, other than over the cliff. And, I assure you, you would not wish to do that."

"But you can't just hold us prisoner here." Abigail flinched at the sight of the gun.

"You will find I can. And don't think of trying to get past me. There is no other way down from here."

"You've no reason to keep us in here. We have our rights. What would your fellow priests say about this?" Her voice rose.

"My colleagues will help to keep you safe and secure," he smirked. "Believe me, we are good at looking after people. There are four of us up here, and we are all of the same mind. We have been planning for this for a long time. Now we are finally ready for you."

His eyes glowed with a fierceness born of malice or madness. As Anton stood over them, she had no doubt about the danger they were in.

His eyes settled on the mobile phone, still clutched in

her lap. "That is useless up here. There is no signal. We have just the one old landline in the priory, as our communication needs are very limited."

"Can we at least have some water?" Adam tried to shift the priest's unsettling attention away from Abigail. "We've been in here for hours. Perhaps also something to eat."

"Someone will bring you something. We have our Rosary and Evening Prayer shortly. I will be back later to explain what we intend to do with you."

"What about Maryanne, my mother? Can I at least see her?"

"Of course." He smiled. "But you will have to wait. When I return, I will explain the plans that we have for you. I am afraid they will be different for each of you." He turned to Adam. "You are irrelevant to our needs. However," he said, focusing back on Abigail, "you are very special. But I am sure you are aware of that."

Inside Abigail, a cold fear was mounting but her gaze gave nothing away.

"This is a very important moment for which we have been waiting for a long, long time," the priest continued. "The earth tremor earlier was a sign for us that you were on your way, and we should be prepared. We will be offering our thanks in prayer later."

"What are you talking about? This all makes no sense at all." Adam was baffled.

Without replying, the priest turned, and, leaving the lamp still burning on the table, left. They heard the key being turned in the lock and there was then silence.

"I'm scared." Abigail's voice was low. "What did he mean by all of that?"

"I've no idea." Adam shook his head. "I don't believe

he is sane, though. He seems consumed by hatred. Did you see his eyes?"

She shivered. "Yes. I remember that look of his from before. It always scared me. Now he just seems... worse."

"This all makes no sense," he said, shaking his head. "He said something, just before he left." Adam looked into her eyes. "He said that they had been waiting for you for a long time. That you knew you were special—"

Abigail shook her head. "I don't know—"

"Is there something I should know?" he asked quietly.

"No. No. No. I don't know what's in his mind. He is confusing me with someone else."

"I'm sorry. This is all madness. I'm so sorry I dragged you into this."

"You didn't. It was my decision to visit you after that phone call. She's my mother," she said simply.

They sat in silence for a time, each lost in their own thoughts. Eventually, Adam asked, "What do you think? Do you think that Maryanne is here, that perhaps she is close?"

"I feel that she is here."

"I wonder if she knows that we're also here?"

"I don't know. I just... I just don't know what to believe." Tears rolled down her face. "This isn't right."

Adam leant across and put his arms around her. "Don't worry. We're going to get out of this. One insane man is not going to intimidate us. And, one way or another, we're going to find Maryanne... soon. It's been a long road."

Abigail wiped away her tears with the back of her hand and extricated herself from his reassuring hug. "Thank you. You're right. I'm being stupid. This is all completely ridiculous. The man is mad and is living in his own strange universe. People around him must see that." She smiled. "It will be just a bad dream."

They did not have to wait long before they heard the key in the lock again and the door slowly swung open. A shorter, older, man, wearing the black cassock and hood of the Dominicans, entered. He carried a plastic bottle of water, half a loaf of coarse bread and some cheese. He put these on the table next to the lamp.

"Are you letting us go now?" Adam searched the priest's blank expression. The man also looked familiar, but with the hood, he could not be sure. The man stood silently by the door. "Do you speak English?" Abigail repeated the questions in halting French, but the priest did not respond. At least he was less threatening than Anton. Adam sized up the new priest. Could he rush him at the door and try to flee with Abigail?

She read his mind and shook her head. "Let's wait. I'm sure they have an explanation for this," she said quietly. "And I need to see my mother." She tried to sound more positive than she felt.

The silent priest took a seat by the door to ensure they did not try to leave.

Adam sat back and offered Abigail the plastic bottle of lukewarm water. He broke off some bread and took a piece of cheese. "OK. We wait. But I'm not spending the night in here."

It was almost nine o'clock, and the room was getting cooler, when the door opened again. The short priest moved away towards the back of the room as the tall figure of Anton appeared through the door, holding a gun.

He pointed to Abigail with the barrel of the gun. "We

will take you to your mother now."

"Hang on!" exclaimed Adam. "You don't need a gun. Put it away and we will come with you."

Anton ignored Adam as though he were not there. He motioned with the gun for Abigail to leave the room.

"Where is she? Why can't she come here?" There was a tremor in her voice.

"She is close. She is waiting across the courtyard for you, in a quiet room in the priory."

"What about me?" Adam challenged Anton. "Maryanne's my wife. I have every right to see her. Rather, we will go together."

The priest's attention was solely on Abigail. It was though he had not heard Adam. He repeated his request. Finally, Anton stopped and turned to him, his piercing eyes boring into Adam. "That will not be possible."

"We both go together," Abigail took Adam's hand.

Anton's contemptuous stare remained on Adam. "You do not understand. The girl we want. You are nothing. You are completely irrelevant to our purpose, and you will remain here. Understand?" The other priest had been standing silently at the back of the room. Now he stepped forward from the shadows. His face had changed. There was a determined set to his jaw as he positioned himself next to the seated pair. Anton stood over Adam and prodded him hard in the face with the steel gun barrel, drawing blood from Adam's cheek. The man looked as though he enjoyed inflicting hurt. "You, my friend, have caused us too many problems." Adam flinched from the pain.

"Stop that." Abigail's tone carried a resolve she did not feel. "We will both see my mother together. And then we will leave… together."

Anton stepped away from Adam, although he kept the gun pointing directly at him. "You are making a big mistake. In time we will explain, and then you will finally understand."

Abigail pleaded with him. "We care very little about your explanation. We just want to see my mother. I am her daughter."

Anton sighed, before helping himself to a piece of cheese. "You will both have the opportunity, but the girl goes first. You!" he gestured at Adam. "You will go later to visit your wife. We will not interfere and afterwards you will be free to go. If your wish is to leave tonight, we will allow you to go. We do not recommend this, but we will give you a torch to help you on your way down. Or you can stay until dawn, when it starts to get light. The choice will be yours."

"Why can't we just go together to see my mother? After all, we arrived here together."

Anton hesitated before replying. "Unfortunately, the ancient rules of the priory do not permit more than one outside person to enter at any one time. Maryanne has particularly asked to see you." He turned to Adam. "She has not said she wishes to see you. We will have to ask her if she even wants to."

"And what about Mum?" Abigail asked. "Will she also be allowed to leave with us if she wishes?"

"She is one of us now. I would be very surprised if she now wants to leave here."

Despite his earlier doubts, Adam challenged, "I don't believe you. You are holding her against her will. I know my wife."

In return he was met with a contemptuous sneer. "You have never understood your wife." He turned back to

Abigail. "Come. I will take you to her. You," he waved the gun at Adam, "will remain here until we come back for you."

Abigail stood and looked back uncertainly at Adam and walked to the door. Adam remained seated. Anton ushered Abigail into the corridor and the door closed. As Adam turned back from the door, he heard a movement immediately behind him and felt a crushing blow to his head before he lost consciousness.

Chapter 19

Anton escorted Abigail across the darkened courtyard. The priory door was now ajar, providing a sliver of light to guide them across the cobbles. He shoved her in the back.

"Carry on," he grunted, as they climbed the stone stairs and entered the old building. She was nervous but excited at the prospect of seeing her mother after so long. It was the end of a tortuous journey. Would Maryanne be the same person she remembered from their good days together? Above all, though, she still wanted to be a daughter who made her mother proud.

They entered a long, dimly lit corridor, flanked with solid-looking closed doors. It was lit by oil lamps that had been converted to electricity in a rudimentary way. Bare wires snaked around the walls and ceiling, and the scent of decay filled her nostrils. Everything was old and dated. The corridor seemed to stretch back a fair distance. Wooden crosses adorned the walls. Eventually they came to an open doorway to her right, leading into what seemed to be a kitchen. An old-fashioned brick bread oven was built into the stone of the wall. To its left stood a long wooden counter on which were stacked a number of plastic-wrapped crates. She remembered the old-fashioned rope pulley system at the foot of the cliff. Ahead was a narrow stone staircase that must lead to the bedrooms. Was that where Maryanne was living? Abigail hesitated at the foot of the stairs but Anton ordered her to continue to the end of the corridor. The stone and brickwork here was much older and, at the end, were a pair of doors with heavy bolts on the outside. Abigail hesitated. This didn't feel right. She turned to face Anton.

"Where is my mother?" She stepped back from the door. "I am not going any further until you tell me what is going on."

"She is inside." He gave his lop-sided grin. "She is waiting for you."

"What?" she exclaimed. "She knows I'm here?" She felt on the brink of tears. "But why is she locked in, then? What have you done to her?"

"She has not been well. You will see for yourself." Anton pulled back the sturdy bolt and opened the door. He pushed Abigail inside and switched on a small lamp on the floor. Inside was a single bed, with a small bedside cabinet. A table and two chairs sat against the far wall, under a small, barred, window. In the corner stood a small wooden cupboard.

"So where is my mother?" Abigail demanded.

"I am afraid she is not here right at the moment. I will explain everything to you in due course. For now, you need to make yourself comfortable. You will be here for a while. There is a bathroom through there." He pointed to a small door in the corner. "We will also bring you some food soon."

Abigail felt very frightened. And alone. "It feels like you're imprisoning me."

"Not at all. You are our guest, just like your mother. Please understand that this is a very holy, and private, place. Visitors are not permitted to roam freely inside the priory. We will not keep you long and you will be comfortable and private here. I would suggest you get some sleep."

"When do I get to see her?"

"It is late, but you will see her soon, that I promise

you. Then the two of you can finally be together. It is what she would also want. You will see."

"How is she?" Abigail persisted, feeling very alone. She felt she needed to keep the priest talking.

He made as if to leave, and then paused. He turned and stared at her. His penetrating gaze seemed to bore into her soul. Eventually, he sighed. "You will see. She has been unwell for a long time, but she is getting better. She is peaceful."

"And what about Adam?" she persisted.

"He is not important to us and we cannot keep him here. We will shortly let him go. Or he can wait until first light tomorrow. That will be his choice."

"But he has every right to see Mum as well. He has been searching for her for months. She will want to see him, I know she will."

Unperturbed, the priest merely gave her a cold look.

"This is not right. Bring him here and we will wait together."

Anton merely shrugged and turned again to leave. "We will be back soon." The door clanged shut behind him and she heard the scrape of the bolt being drawn.

She was locked in — again. Abigail forced herself to remain positive, turning to examine the room. She picked up the well-thumbed Bible on the bedside cabinet, flicked through it then put it down again with a sigh. She felt so weary. She opened the door of the small cupboard in the corner. Inside, women's clothes hung on a rail. Startled, she examined them. Were these her mother's clothes? Some of them looked familiar, they were the right size and the labels showed they were from British high street stores. So, where was her mother? Could she be at prayer or was she somewhere else in the priory? Was she in one of the bedrooms upstairs or might she even be next door? Abigail struggled to make sense of what was happening. What would be going through Adam's mind?

She sat on the bed and put her head in her hands. She wasn't sure whether she was more worried for Maryanne or Adam. Eventually, she forced herself to her feet and went to examine the small bathroom in the corner.

It was tiny and seemed to be built into the rock of the cave itself. There was no bath but there was a toilet and a chipped porcelain basin and a basic shower, without a curtain. A wooden chair was in the corner by the basin. Again, there was a small, barred, window high up. It was too dark to see whether she could see anything through it. A half-used tube of toothpaste, a toothbrush and a small white bar of soap of the type found in hotels sat beside the sink. A well-worn white towel was folded on the chair beside. Abigail returned to the bed and leant back, resting her head against the single, hard, pillow. There was nothing for it but to wait for Maryanne, or for dawn, whichever came first. She closed her eyes.

Her dreams were of her childhood. She was walking with her mother through the Wicklow mountains outside of Dublin. A warm breeze drifted through the overhanging branches of the tall oak trees in Rathmichael Wood and the cries of the gulls came from above as they ventured further inland from Dublin Bay. They came upon the granite Fassaroe Cross, which marks the entrance to the church, its face engraved with a crucifixion scene. Maryanne was keen to enter the cool of the old church, but Abigail became frightened and refused to enter. They then continued on to the summit of the hill where she now smelt the foxgloves and the hedgerows as they walked on in the sunlight.

Eventually they found themselves in a grassy clearing before the ruins of Puck's Castle, guarded by tall conifers that stood sentry. This time they entered the confines of the high stone walls, and it became dark. Maryanne led her through an arch. They came to an old wooden door which her mother opened. Inside it was pitch dark. Abigail felt for her mother. As she did so the door slammed shut behind her and she realised she was on her own. She called out loudly, time and again, but Maryanne did not respond. She was gone, leaving Abigail in her terror as the room and the darkness closed in.

She awoke in a panic. Her heart raced. It took a while to bring her breathing under control. Realisation returned that she was locked in a strange room in the priory. Abigail sat up at the sound of a brief rap on the door and the bolt being drawn back. The monk who had brought them the cheese and water earlier carried a tray bearing a jug of water, a bowl of oatmeal porridge and half a baguette. He put it on the table in the corner and indicated that she should eat. Abigail looked at her watch. It was early morning. Surely, she had been asleep for just a moment. She still felt tired.

"Where is my mother?"

The implacable monk said nothing and left.

She was hungry, so she sat uncomfortably at the small table and stared out of the still dark window while she ate. How often had her mother sat on this same wooden chair, looking out? The thought brought some small comfort. She poured some water from the pottery jug. It was cold, with a mineral tang. The porridge was at least hot. Absently breaking off a piece of baguette, she thought about the coming hours. How could she prepare herself for meeting her mother after such a long time?

She looked down at her mud-streaked jeans. She looked a fright. What would her mother make of her unkempt appearance? She knew in her heart that she should also prepare to be disappointed. Adam was the one person who had never let her down. She was comforted by the thought he should be safely down the mountain by now, no doubt waiting for her at the *hostellerie.* All she could do now was to wait.

It was still early morning, so she settled herself back on the narrow bed. Sleep was out of the question. She lay there, waiting for events to unfold. Lying on her back she noticed that, in the dim light cast by the light beside the bed, a large black spider had made its way across the ceiling. It had now stopped in its stealthy journey directly above her, as if considering its new companion. She watched it in return. Gradually she felt her eyelids become heavy and before she knew it, she was asleep.

The funereal tolling of bells penetrated her dreams and roused her to consciousness with a sudden realisation that they were real. She opened her eyes and looked at her watch. It was now the afternoon. She had slept for nine hours. Where were the monks and why they hadn't they come to take her to her mother? Aside from the slow peals of the bells, there were no other sounds from inside the priory. Abigail reached for her phone. There was still no signal and she now she only had limited battery life remaining. The charger, along with their two small suitcases, had been left behind in the hire car. She turned the phone off. It was of no use up here anyway.

Abigail took a lukewarm shower and towelled herself dry, wrapping the threadbare towel tightly around her long hair. When she emerged from the bathroom, a small strong-smelling cup of coffee, a fresh croissant, no doubt baked in the kitchen only ten yards away, and a bowl of chicken stew awaited her. Perhaps it was the aroma of the food, or the shower she just had, but Abigail felt suddenly buoyed. Surely they would not keep her waiting much longer?

The mood did not last long. As darkness drew in, she gave in to the inevitable and lay back down on the bed. Despite all the sleep that she'd had, she fell back into another restless night of troubled sleep.

The first rays of dawn woke her to the full realisation of her forced incarceration. She sat up and listened for any sound. Half an hour passed before the mournful bells started again. Then the door bolt was drawn once more and Anton entered. He looked tired. His hood was pushed back from his face and, as he lifted his head to regard her, she saw that a large plaster covered what looked like a cut above his eyebrow. The cheek below the eye was bruised and discoloured.

"Why have I been kept for so long?"

When he didn't reply, she pointed at his face. "What's happened to you?"

The priest regarded her with a look of open dislike.

"Where is Adam?" she demanded.

"He is gone," he replied simply.

"He wouldn't have left without seeing Mum. That is absurd. He would've wanted to see me as well, before he would ever think of leaving." Her shoulders fell. Her earlier positivity had fast evaporated. "What have you done with him?"

"He chose to leave early this morning." Anton's penetrating gaze unsettled her.

"I don't believe you. And where's my mother?" Her voice rose "I want to see her now. Then I want to leave as well. I won't stay here any longer."

His lop-sided grin briefly played across his otherwise emotionless features. "Sadly, leaving here is not an option for you. At least not at the moment. But you will meet your mother, I can promise you that."

"You cannot keep me here against my will. I demand to speak to the other priests to let them know what you are trying to do to me."

Anton laughed. "First, please call us friars. Dominican priests are called friars. Second, all my brothers know why you are here. They are in full agreement about the present — and about the future. The eyes of the order are on you. This day will be remembered." His eyes glistened with fervour.

Abigail felt very scared under his intense scrutiny. Her hands had started shaking and the room felt as if it were tilting. "I don't know what you are talking about, but it does not make any sense." She stumbled over the words. Realising she needed to keep some control of events she got up carefully from the bed and tried to walk as purposively as she could past Anton to the unlocked door. Before she reached the handle, he grasped her shoulder and she was spun violently across the room, crashing into the wall in the corner. She lost her balance and her head hit the stone wall as she slid to the floor, blood streaming from her nose. Abigail felt herself black out as she huddled in the corner, arms clasped around her head.

*

She wasn't sure how long she had lain there unconscious. When she came to, the towel that had wrapped her long hair was lying beside her. She lay, crumpled, as she slowly tried to regain her senses. Her shoulder and arm throbbed. She pressed the towel gently to her bleeding nose, trying to stem the flow of blood. Abigail lay on her side, her face muffled by the towel, until she felt the nausea recede. She could still feel Anton's presence in the room. It took an effort to sit up, still holding the towel to her face, blood seeping down her chin. Through tears of pain and surprise, she saw Anton was sitting on the bed regarding her with a look of disdain and disgust at the blood still flowing over her mouth and down her chin. He had enjoyed hurting her and she suspected he would relish another opportunity to punish her.

"Why? You are meant to be a good man."

His laughter was hollow, devoid of any warmth or humour.

"Surely all of you priests are men of God?" she persisted.

"Friars. We are called friars." He shouted in a flash of anger, banging his hand against the metal bedframe. "You will find out our divine purpose very soon. We are here to make sure that the most sacred vow of our order is carried out. We have been very patient and have waited for a long time."

Abigail shrank. "What are you going to do?"

It took a while for his rage to subside. Eventually he replied "We have a very special Mass tomorrow. We have much to consider and much to give thanks for. After that things will become clearer for you. In the meantime, you have to wait, in here." He made for the door. "You will not be disappointed, I assure you."

Abigail remained huddled against the cold stone wall in the corner until she felt stronger. She used the walls to slowly raise herself to a standing position before she took a tentative step. She had stopped bleeding but her shoulder and arm were still painful. She felt dizzy and she waited until her head cleared before she took another step across the room. Her progress was slow but when she reached the bed, she lowered herself onto the edge. She let herself relax and examined and tested out her arm. It wasn't broken, although it was heavily bruised. She carefully rolled onto her side, to protect the shoulder and arm. She lay that way for some time until she felt able to think more clearly. Drying her tears with the back of her hand she tried to make some sense of what the monk or friar had told her. Adam would not willingly have left her here. Did her mother know she was a prisoner here? Surely, she would not condone her daughter being treated this way. She slowly realised that Anton was in control of all their destinies.

*

The morning brought an opaque light that filtered through the dust of the narrow window above the small desk. How long would it be before morning Mass ended, and Anton would return with her mother? What had Maryanne ever seen in him? What had been the allure? Perhaps his unsettling intensity or his complete indifference to the norm had appealed to her. There was a cruelty to the man. These were things that she would put to her mother. She sighed. She had to be prepared for what Maryanne might tell her and she suspected that she might not like it.

After about an hour, Abigail got up slowly and made her unsteady way to the bathroom. She didn't want Maryanne to see her like this, so she tried to wash away the caked blood in the shower. Luckily, her clothes were not too stained. She baulked at wearing any of her mother's clothes. Her nose didn't seem to be broken but the bruising on the side of her face would remain for some time. Looking at herself in the faded mirror above the basin, she hardly recognised the woman who stared back at her. She dabbed at her face with the corner of the damp towel. Returning to the bedroom, she sat at the table under the window and waited.

It was mid-morning when Anton returned, his head was covered by the black hood of the order. He was alone. "I am going to take you to your mother, soon." He seemed different, more relaxed than he had been earlier. He sat on the bed and surveyed the room, before turning back to her. "How are you feeling?"

"You are kidding, right?" There was a dull ache on the side of her face.

He looked confused, as if he had forgotten his earlier assault on her. "Sorry, I don't—"

Abigail snapped, "I'm all right... although I've been better."

The priest seemed oblivious to her tone. "Good. Good." Her response seemed to please him. He was more willing to talk, to engage with her, as if he needed to validate himself. "It is good that you have cleaned yourself up," he remarked absently.

It would have been better not to respond, but Abigail couldn't stop the sarcastic laugh that escaped. "How very good of you to even notice."

It was wasted anyway. He didn't notice the sarcasm. Instead, he got up from the bed and wandered over to look into the bathroom, before sitting back down on the bed. He looked at his watch. "It is almost time before I take you to your mother. Any questions before we go?"

She had many and needed urgent answers. "You said something yesterday, that the earth tremor was a warning. What did you mean? What was it a warning of?"

"It was the sign from above that you were here. That you were on your way to your destiny and that we should be ready for your arrival. We will be very soon."

This made no sense. "You have me confused with someone else," she stated flatly. Deciding to persist, she challenged, "Tell me then, why you think I'm special."

Anton looked surprised, then all expression left his face. "You know who you are. You are your mother's daughter, so you know exactly what that means."

She stared at him blankly.

"That woman — your mother — had no right to give you life. But she did. Unfortunately for you, you cannot be allowed to do the same. Do you understand this?" His eyes blazed. "You cannot be allowed to continue. It is the end."

Abigail could only shake her head. "I don't know what you are talking about."

"Well, let me tell you." He sneered. "Your mother was told by us that she should never conceive. It was unthinkable. We... I tried everything to stop it."

"Why?" she asked, shocked. "Does she have some dangerous disease? I am sure I would know."

He ignored her. "We thought she understood why she was different. Why she had to end it, but she was stubborn and refused to listen."

He finally noticed the look of horror on her face. "Ah, you didn't know any of this. Your mother should have told you."

She shivered and went white. "You're not well." Her

voice was a whisper.

He continued in a monotone. "You should never have existed. This has caused us many problems for so long. This will be the end. It is for the greater good. You will come to see that." He nodded in acknowledgement of this statement. The black hood fell forward, almost hiding his face.

The priest was undeniably mad. "You don't like women much, do you? I'm guessing that the whole lot of you hate women."

"Of course, we despise women. Our hatred goes back a long time."

She had a sudden insight. "But you have your own personal reasons for hating women, don't you?"

The priest looked at her as if seeing her for the first time. "I have never seen much in them at all. They are insignificant to a higher purpose. They are only there to be used."

"When did you start feeling that way? Something awful must have happened in your life."

"I have felt it my whole life. My mother left my father to bring up two young sons. She hated all of us — my father, Jean, me. Women personify evil and it was a blessed relief when she left. History tells us that they have only ever been the cause of trouble by leading men into temptation." He looked at his watch again. "This was the reason I went into church, and why I decided to join the order."

"What happened to your mother? Did you ever see her again?"

Anton did not answer immediately. Eventually he said "She moved away to Normandy — to a small village outside Cherbourg. I managed to find out where she was."

"And…"

He just grinned. Before he could continue the bells started up again, slow and methodical. This time she knew the mournful toll was for her.

"Come." He rose. "The time has come."

Chapter 20

Adam opened his eyes and groaned. He lay on the floor of the storeroom, an upturned chair on top of him. It was still dark and there was a sweet musty smell. Blood had pooled and congealed where he lay. He touched his head and felt a warm stickiness behind his ear. His head ached so he lay still for a while, trying to recover his senses, then he pushed away the chair and sat up. His head swam, a wave of nausea gripped him, and he vomited. He heard something scamper hurriedly across the floor. Little light filtered into the room and he felt disoriented. Where was he and why had he been lying on a dusty floor? It took a huge effort to even begin to recollect the events of earlier. His memory returned in snatches, only to ebb and fade into the distance. He had a flashback to the dead cat swinging eerily from the tree branch and of the horror of lying, unable to move, in his upturned car after the crash. Then the punishing climb up the mountain and the ground shaking from the tremor came back to him. He was looking for Maryanne. She was nearby. A snatched vision of the cool and darkness of the cave inserted itself in his mind. *Could he be inside the cave? Where then, was Maryanne? Why was he lying down if he was looking for her and why was it so dark?* The stabbing pain in his head made it hurt to think. Adam was tempted to lie back down and let unconsciousness wash over him, but he resisted the feeling.

He had been at the cave with Abigail. Adam sat up against the chair and called her name with increasing urgency. The place was silent, apart from the sound of scuttling nearby. Bit by bit, pieces of memory returned.

With a start, he remembered that they had been locked inside a room. They then had tried to get out. There was a priest. One of the few people they had encountered. There was something very strange and unsettling about the memory. Everything was still very fuzzy. He touched his head again. The warm blood was congealing. Flashes reappeared of another man, another priest dressed like the first. He slowly looked around. He was sure he was now on his own. The first priest had taken Abigail away and then something — someone — had hit him. Adam groped around in the darkness until his hand met something smooth and wooden. Reaching up he felt the top of a table. Grasping the table leg he gradually raised himself from the floor and manoeuvred himself into a chair. He felt around in his pockets for his phone. It wasn't there. It must have fallen on the floor. He felt around near where he had fallen without success. He would wait until it got light before searching for it again.

He sat back. He was dehydrated. Hadn't the second priest brought them some water? Adam felt around the table until his hand met the pottery pitcher. It was still upright. He grabbed the handle and tipped it into his mouth, gulping greedily as the lukewarm water soothed his parched throat. Cupping his hand with what was left he cleaned some of the blood away from his wound. It stung. The water helped to clear his head and he sat, trying to order his thinking. He looked at his watch. It was well past midnight. He wasn't sure how long he had been unconscious, but he had to assume that Abigail had, by now, met up with her mother. At least something good had come out of this. Why hadn't she come back, though? Finally, he was close to Maryanne, but he couldn't see her. It was so frustrating. And why he had been attacked? This was a holy place, a sanctuary. These people were meant to assist others. It made no sense. He was suddenly worried for both Abigail and Maryanne.

Adam stretched out. It was impossible to get comfortable on the hard wooden chair — it would be a very long night. His head still hurt, but the sharp pain had receded. He hoped his injury was only superficial. Someone would have to answer for the assault. He shouted for help, but there was no answer. The place was silent. It was likely he would remain locked in the room until the morning. With the arrival of new visitors to the cave in the morning, the priests would surely have to let him out. Then he would look for answers to their treatment, but first he would find Abigail and Maryanne and take them to safety. This may be a house of God, but they would go straight to the police to report what had happened. He would also contact senior officials in the Catholic Church and tell them. They needed to know what this religious order, and Anton in particular, were doing in their name.

Eventually, he slept. He was exhausted. Despite this, he was woken several times by a noise outside the window. Each time he steeled himself to confront his captor, only to discover that it was the wind, blowing in gusts around the courtyard, rattling the window frame.

They came for him in the early morning. Three of them, dressed in their black cassocks and hoods. He was asleep and was woken by the sound of the key in the lock. The door swung open to reveal it was still dark outside, with only a glimmer of early morning light. He looked at his watch. It was four twenty — dawn was still more than an hour and a half away.

"Get up. It is finally time to go." Anton's voice. He

was the tallest of the three by a few inches.

Adam tensed but remained seated. "Hang on. Where is Abigail?" he demanded. "And where is Maryanne? I'm not going anywhere without both of them."

Anton moved in front of the other priests, who remained guarding the door. "That is not your choice. You are trespassing on holy property and we wish you to leave." He could barely control his anger.

"That's complete rubbish. It was you who locked us in this room, preventing us from leaving. I'll wait right here until you bring both women to me and we will all leave together when it is light. Please just go and get them."

The priests behind Anton made a move forward, but he put out his hand to stop them. "I am sure this man will eventually understand reason." He turned to Adam. "I have spoken to both the women and they do not wish to accompany you."

Adam shook his head. "That is bollocks."

Anton's eyes flashed with anger. "Enough of this. Get up."

"I am not going anywhere without them. I do not believe what you are saying. I will leave if I hear directly from them that they wish to stay."

Anton studied him. His lips were white. "That will not happen, I am afraid. They are staying with us and both are now asleep in one of our guest rooms. It has been an exhausting time for them as you can imagine. They now need to rest." He spoke slowly and deliberately. "We wish you gone from here before we open our doors to our visitors, so we are going to escort you from the sanctuary now."

Adam was getting nowhere. All he was doing was provoking Anton. He looked at the three of them. They would soon force him out. He looked around the floor of the storeroom.

"Can I at least look for my phone?" He pointed to one of the priests. "Can I use that light you have?"

"It is not here. We removed it earlier."

"You have no right to it. May I then have my phone back before I leave?"

"That is also not possible. It was damaged. We found it on the floor. It must have fallen from your pocket. All we could do was throw it away." The priest stared at Adam, challenging him to disagree.

"I fell on the floor when one of you bastards hit me from behind. Can you explain why you thought it right to assault me last night?"

"No one assaulted you. That is a serious accusation."

"Turn on the light and then explain this injury to my head?"

"You must be delusional. None of us has touched you. You must have fallen on the floor whilst you were sleeping. No matter. We should be going."

Adam shrugged. "You do understand that I will report you to the police the moment I get out of here — for assault and false imprisonment... and anything else I can think of. I will have the police up here to release Abigail and Maryanne before the end of the day."

Anton smiled. "I am sure you will. You do what you have to. As I said earlier, it is you who is trespassing. You have no right to be here."

"I will get them to thoroughly investigate your so-called sanctuary. They will go through every inch of this place."

"Fine. Let us be on our way then. The sooner you leave us, the sooner you get to the police." He nodded to the two priests standing by the door and they moved to the side to allow Adam space to leave the room.

Adam stood up without swaying and took a step forward. He was still dizzy, but he managed to walk through the door and into the cool of the courtyard. To the left, the door to the cave was firmly shut and the priory opposite was in darkness. There was no point in shouting out to Abigail.

The priests fell in behind him. The kerosene lamp illuminated the square, as they made their way towards the start of the steps down the mountain. Thin streaks of pre-dawn light were just visible in the sky. After the night in the dank storeroom, Adam gulped in the strengthening breeze. He half-stumbled on the courtyard's paving stones. The priest with the lamp laughed.

"Go down the steps to the right," Anton directed. "We will accompany you to the bottom of the cliff and along some of the pathway. We want to make very sure you have left the property."

The group paused at the iron entrance gate and waited in silence as one of the priests produced a large metal key and unlocked the gate. Then they began their descent. Adam took the uneven steps slowly. He was shaky and unsteady on his feet. He was leaving Abigail and Maryanne behind, but he felt a wave of relief to be away from the cave and priory. The lights of the *hostellerie* glittered in the plain below. The priest with the lamp moved past Adam to the front of the small group. Anton and the silent priest were at the rear. The wind had strengthened further and made the descent all the more precarious.

It felt considerably more than the eighteen hours ago that Adam had ascended the stairs with Abigail. With each step, he felt as if he was abandoning the women, leaving them to fend for themselves. He had no choice, but he would make sure that they were released as soon as possible. He had to get back to civilisation safely. That, he knew, would not be an easy task. His legs felt like jelly. He could not afford a fall on his way down.

Soon the grey outline of the shifting forest canopy below appeared. They were close to the bottom of the stairs and the base of the cliff. Strong gusts of wind now buffeted them, making it difficult to keep their footing. Was this the start of another mistral? Would falling branches present a new danger as he made his way down through the forest? He had to get to a police station in one piece.

As they reached the final flight of steps, Anton signalled quietly to his colleagues. They slowed. The kerosene lamp was placed on the lichen-covered stone wall that marked the commencement of the cobble and dirt pathway down through to the forest floor. Adam would need it to be able to see the narrow path that snaked down the mountainside. He stepped forward to take the lamp and turned away from the priests.

Anton reached into the folds of his cloak. Catching the movement, Adam turned to look behind him. The lamplight revealed an old wooden baseball bat. Adam stopped and turned around. Another of the priests produced a similar club. There was no misunderstanding their intent. In his present condition, he could not outrun the three of them. He had been naïve. He was not getting off this mountain alive.

"Why?" he asked simply. "What have I done to you?"

"Did you really think you would leave us alive?" Anton's expression was mocking. "If so, you are even more stupid than I thought. You are of no value to us, but we cannot have you interrupting our plans for Abigail. You know too much."

Adam turned to the others. "Surely you can see that this man is mad. He is obsessed—"

"Forget it. You are wasting your breath. As I said, you are incidental to our needs. They will not listen to someone like you." Anton took a step closer to Adam. By this time, all four were standing in a semi-circle in the clearing. In the dim early light, the cliff shone a ghostly white. Adam backed away, towards the edge.

He held up the lamp to reveal the ghostly tableau. "Please think about what you're doing. It should not be this way. You are meant to be servants of God. You should care for your fellow man." There was no response. "Can't you see that imprisoning innocent people is wrong? Please let us all go. We're not a threat to you. None of us are." There was not a glimmer of compassion among them. The two men holding the baseball bats advanced on him.

"Wait!" Adam desperately tried to buy time. A sudden strong gust of wind hit them and almost blew him off balance as he backed away towards the forest edge, eyes on the raised clubs. "What is going to happen to Abigail and Maryanne?"

Anton stopped. "What do you think we are going to do to them?"

"Please, just let them go." He accepted the fate that he knew was about to befall him. "They've not done anything to hurt you."

Anton laughed. "You do not understand. You have no idea. They are the reason that we are here. They are the reason for the order."

"You're right. I don't know what you are talking about. This is all crazy. Let them go. I will wait down here for them."

They moved in, encircling him, a look of determination on their faces. Adam desperately looked around. They had blocked off the pathway to the forest. It was much too early to expect anyone else to be around. Another fierce gust of wind hit the clearing and the group staggered away from the cliff, towards the path. He tried to break free by moving to the side, away from the edge. They continued to close in on him from three sides, so he swung the lamp, throwing it at as hard as he could at Anton in the middle of the group. The lamp arced through the darkness and hit Anton's head a glancing blow, causing him to stagger. The glass shattered and the light went out. The lamp rolled across the path before disappearing over the edge of the cliff. In the semi-darkness, with shadowy figures moving around the narrow pathway, Adam tried to slip by the unarmed priest to his right, but a hand grabbed his arm. He fought off the priest, freeing himself, before turning to run down the path. The tall priest to his side raised his baseball bat.

The first blow caught him around the midriff, making him double over. He staggered backwards and stumbled, his feet sliding on the loose gravel. Adam raised his hands to protect his head. The group advanced, pushing him further towards the edge. Below the path was a near-vertical thirty-foot drop down through the canopy of trees. The next blow caught him on the shoulder, sending him sprawling. He struggled to his knees as the priests closed in again, their weapons raised. Covering his head with his arms he braced himself for the blows to come. Adam felt that what strength he had disappear with each blow. He staggered back to his feet. He could not last long. He needed to take the fight to them. Grabbing Anton's cloak he landed a blow to the man's face. The priest raised a hand to the side of his face and Adam made a frantic grab for the club in the priest's other hand, wrenching it free. He stood back with the club raised and stopped the priest's advance. They looked uncertain. Adam got in another blow to Anton's head, this time with the baseball bat. The priest sprawled onto his knees, grabbing one of Adam's legs. Another fierce gust hit them, causing them to step back. The other priest advanced, distracting Adam. Anton lunged at Adam's club and hung on with both hands, then swung him around with considerable strength, forcing him to let go of the weapon. Adam felt the ground give way under his feet. As he flailed his arms backwards, the other priest raised his club above his head to finish him off.

Chapter 21

Blood seeped from the edges of Anton's plaster. He was limping and in a foul mood. Once they were in the corridor, he opened a wooden door, hidden in the dark beneath the staircase, and gestured for Abigail to enter. Had her mother been this close all the time that she had been held in the room? She had to stoop to go through the door and found herself in a dark passageway. Anton turned on a switch and the lamp illuminated a long gallery, empty apart from two clay urns. Above each of the urns was a wooden cross. The room smelt of damp and moss. At the end was a metal door with a small open grating at eye-level. Abigail recognised it from the day before.

"I don't understand—"

"Don't worry. You will soon." The priest paused at the door before opening it. "You are about to meet up with your mother. We will allow you to spend some time with her on your own."

Abigail followed Anton in a trance. The temperature fell by a few degrees as she entered the lower level of Mary Magdalene's cave.

"You are now in the crypt of the sanctuary."

She nodded mutely. Her mouth felt dry as she followed him across the cave. She cast her eyes around the shadowy walls of the lower cave. Surely her mother was not down here.

"Don't worry. You will not be disturbed. We have closed the cave to all visitors for two days." They came to the alabaster statue of Mary Magdalene, set in a dark recess at the back of the cave. Two rows of flickering candles surrounded it. Anton bowed to the figure and beckoned Abigail forwards. "Here she is."

"I don't understand."

"You are both finally reunited." His eyes shone with a fervour that was becoming familiar. "You can take your time with her."

"What the fuck...What are you talking about? Where is my mother? You said you would take me to her." She looked around blindly, willing her mother to be there.

"She is there, right in front of you. She has been waiting for you patiently for a very long time." He was looking past her, directly at the statue.

His face had the expression she had found so disturbing as a child. He continued with his fixed stare and she finally understood that he was insane. As the realisation dawned, tears slid down her face.

"You are mad," she whispered. "What have you done with my mother? Where is she? Please tell me. What you're doing is so unkind."

The priest was in a trance. "I will now leave you both. No doubt you have much to catch up on. When was the last time you saw her?"

She shook her head. "You complete bastard. Where is my fucking mother? I despise you. All you have ever done is try to destroy her."

He looked at her with bewilderment. "Look." he pointed. "She is on her knees, waiting to welcome you. Go to her."

"You're sick. You need help, don't you understand?"

He regarded her blankly. His voice was impersonal as he ordered, "Go on. Go. This will be good for you. You need to get to know her again. You have not always understood her. You have been very unfair. It is you who has hurt her."

Abigail sobbed openly. "Just leave me alone," she replied softly. She turned away from Anton and sat below the statue.

Rousing himself, he replied, "I will go. I will give you time together. But do not think of leaving. We have locked the door to the entrance to the cave. No-one will come to help you." With that he left, leaving Abigail alone with Mary Magdalene.

She sat there unmoving, as tears streamed down her face. All hope had left her. She was isolated and imprisoned by a madman. She didn't know where Adam was and was still no closer to finding her mother. She'd been so certain Maryanne was here, but now…

When she felt able to, she rose and took a drink from the rock pool. It was cold, with a distinct mineral taste. She splashed her face. It still ached and the cool of the water felt good against her skin. Little natural light penetrated this area of the cave and she was surprised to see it was still morning. She looked back up at the statue. The alabaster glowed in the candlelight, lending it a maternal warmth. Abigail took comfort from it and found a new resilience. She climbed to the upper chamber. The entrance door was locked and the stained-glass windows were protected by iron bars cemented into the stone. There was little point in calling out for help. The only way she was going to survive was to escape this cave. She tried the other door, on the far side of the cave, which led into the storeroom where they had been imprisoned. It too was locked and Abigail pounded on it, shouting out Adam's name. She hadn't believed Anton's claim that Adam had left the cliff, but he wasn't responding, so perhaps it was the truth. Perhaps Adam was on his way down to get help. The faint belief gave her confidence to carry on.

There were still areas of the cave, mainly the dark recesses to either side of the marble altar, that they had not previously explored. She climbed carefully over the damp black rock, looking for hidden passageways. She lit one of the larger candles to use as she clambered over the uneven rocks towards the rear of the cave. The fire damage and deposits of soot on the roofs of the smaller recesses suggested that these areas had been used for cooking over the centuries. The cave darkened and narrowed the further she went back. Climbing back to the main part of the cave she fell as she tried to clamber over a rock slippery with water that seeped through the ceiling. The candle went flying. Cursing, she inspected herself. The sharp rock had torn through one of the knees of her jeans. Carefully pulling up the one leg of the trousers she saw that the knee itself had been badly scraped and blood was starting to seep down the leg. One cut was quite deep. She looked around and found a white linen handkerchief left as an offering to the saint. Sitting down stiffly she manged to tear the material into two strips which she could bind around the knee. It seemed to stem the bleeding.

She tried the door once more, banging on it and shouting out to Adam. He surely must have left. She now tried the rest of the cave. Eventually she gave up, realising that there was no way out other than the way she had entered. By this time it was nightfall. The stained-glass windows remained black.

At the end of her search, Abigail returned to the crypt again. She crouched down and helped herself to more water and examined her knee. It had stopped bleeding and she dampened the cloth and cleaned the blood away. Finishing, she looked up above her, lit by the flickering candlelight surrounding the ghostly white of the statue of Mary Magdalene. The lights of the candles made the scene strangely soothing, as if the statue itself was offering up protection to her.

Adam must have reached the bottom of the mountain by now. Hopefully, help would soon arrive but she knew she couldn't afford to just wait for its arrival. She needed to try get as far away from this place as possible. With a start, she realised that Adam didn't have the keys to the hire car. They had been in her pocket, but had now fallen out, or had been removed. But Adam would have a phone signal the moment he got through the forest and would be able to call for help. For now, though, she would just stay close by the comfort and reassurance offered by the statue of the saint.

She must have drifted off. When she woke, she was lying on her side, her head resting on her arm, at the foot of the statue. Someone was coming down the stairs. A priest appeared, carrying a tray. She had not seen him before. He set the tray before her.

"My child, you must eat. I have brought you something to keep your strength up." His voice was soft, his English heavily accented. His face seemed kindly. He sat on a chair and indicated she should sit, too. The tray contained some coarse bread and cheese, a small bowl of tapenade and a banana. There was no knife, so she had to break the bread and cheese with her hands. Despite her anguish, she still ate hungrily. As she did so, she looked curiously at the priest. He was more in keeping with what she would expect of a priest.

"Who are you?" she asked.

"I am Brother Bonnaire, one of the senior friars of the priory of La Sainte-Baume. You have met some of the other brothers."

"I have. You seem different to them."

He smiled. "Thank you."

"Please can you tell me why I am being held here?"

"You must understand that we, as brothers, observe a vow of silence here. Normally we do not speak. But I understand that you have a need to talk, a need for questions to be answered about your mother and, importantly, yourself. It is understandable and the least that we can do for you. Unfortunately, at the moment, Brother Anton cannot help you."

Abigail nodded. "Let's start with which questions you can answer. Why am I here, in this cave?"

"Well, you are here to find your mother."

"Anton — Brother Anton — told me he was taking me to see my mother. And then he brings me in here to this statue. I don't understand. Please tell me what's going on."

The old priest shook his head. "Brother Anton is very spiritual. He has special gifts. He is able to see the world in ways the rest of us are not able to—"

"He thinks this statue is my mother. He said that earlier." She felt herself becoming tearful again.

"In some ways he is correct. He has visions. He sees your mother as our Saint Mary." The priest smiled.

"This is making no sense at all. His so-called visions are really delusions. He's sick." She shook her head and pushed the tray away. "And where is my mother? Is she here at all?"

"Brother Anton, indeed all of us, have a knowledge you do not possess." He leant forward and clasped her hands in his. They felt gnarly and arthritic and she recoiled.

"Just don't touch me."

"Your mother is directly descended from Mary Magdalene and her unfortunate union with Jesus." He paused, then continued. "Our order is tasked to ensure the end of this terrible bloodline. It must not continue, my child. It cannot and has to be eradicated — for ever, for all our good." He looked into her eyes. "It is only now that we are finally able to fulfil this holy undertaking."

Any hope that Abigail was dealing with someone rational all but disappeared with these chilling words and her fear returned. They were surely all mad. "This is all ridiculous. How do you know this?"

He sighed. "My child, I am very sorry."

"Stop calling me that. What possible proof can you have?"

"The order has researched this over many years. We have ancient texts and records here in the priory, going back over eight hundred years. With these we are able to prove the unbroken line over the past two millennia. Brother Anton has been heavily involved in this project for a long time, from the time he was sent to Ireland as a student."

She shook her head. "That sounds like a novel, not real life."

Brother Bonnaire smiled. "We have the records to prove the bloodline to your great-grandmother, on to your grandmother, and finally to your mother. Of course, there were times when we could not locate any living direct descendants, and we thought the bloodline had died out naturally." He paused. "Did you know that your great-great grandmother was born in Lower Saxony, in Germany? She was born into nobility and, as the only daughter, was the last remaining female descendant."

Despite the lunacy of what he was saying, he made it sound convincing. Abigail could not help listening.

"Her supporters became aware that the order had located her and she was moved secretly to a town in Brittany. She lived in a small town called Plouzané — in an area of the Pays de Léon — undiscovered for many years. Your great-grandmother was born there, the second of two daughters. She moved to Dublin in the 1890s after her elder sister had died of pleurisy in her thirties. We did not track her down to Ireland until after she had died. By that time, your grandmother was ill and had very little time left."

"I don't believe you. I don't believe any of this. You all live in your own deluded world."

"Brother Anton was sent to keep a close watch on your mother. She is the direct descendant. Did you know that she came to recognise this? These days we can, of course, use modern technology. She agreed to a DNA test that confirmed our understanding. She understood that she could not be allowed to live on."

"No!" she exclaimed loudly. "You are all wrong!"

"Unfortunately for you, we are not." He sighed. "We can prove the genealogy to you. It will not change anything, however."

"So where is my mother? What has happened to her?"

"Your mother was staying nearby, at the *hostellerie* below. She was under our care. Brother Anton has been looking after her for the past few years while we tracked your whereabouts. Your mother has had, of course, her own struggles — sometimes considerable ones — but has never been mistreated. It is important you understand that. Brother Anton has made sure that she has had everything she needed."

"I don't believe a word of this. She would not deliberately stay away from me — or Adam. She loved him. She would not get involved with anything like this."

"As I said, she came to accept who she was. As I would hope you will as well. Of course, her faith was remarkably strong and you should be very proud of her. I have known her only for eighteen months. She understood her position."

Abigail thought back to when her mother phoned her. Was she there at the *hostellerie* at the time?

As though the priest read her mind, he nodded. "She wanted to speak to you, and we thought it was a good idea. We believed that you would eventually come to us, as you indeed have."

Tears welled. "Where is she now?" Abigail asked quietly.

Outside, the priory bells pealed. The sound was more mournful from the depths of the crypt. The priest stood and picked up the tray. "It is late, and I have to go. I will leave you here for your own reflection but I will return in the morning to answer your remaining questions." He began his slow climb up the stairs. As the front door to the cave was unlocked and opened, there was a crash of thunder. Then the door slammed and she was alone once more.

Left alone with her fears, Abigail felt numb and powerless. The bells stopped and silence, punctuated by the constant drip of the water from the roof, returned. In the darkness her mind drifted back to Maryanne's words in their last, brief, conversation. It had sounded as if the call was being monitored. She was certain Maryanne had been about to say something when the phone was taken from her. What was it? Abigail recalled that her mother had asked for forgiveness. She had wondered at the time what it was for. Was it for her childhood, or for Maryanne leaving her? Tears had started to form at the corner of her eyes. There was something else she now remembered, something that her mother had said at the end of the call. She closed her eyes to concentrate, brushing away the tears with her hand. It was something about Adam. Then she remembered. Maryanne had asked her to tell Adam she would never be able to go back. She had told Adam this and he had been shocked. Now she understood what her mother had been saying. She felt a rush of love and pain for their shared hurt, and tears began their inexorable slide down her cheeks.

*

It was early morning. Hazy light filtered through the stained-glass windows above. Abigail must have dozed off, despite the hard floor. Surely Adam would return soon with help. Minutes later, the door rattled and Brother Bonnaire returned. He brought more bread and cheese and a mug of hot chocolate. He came slowly down the broad staircase with a look of complete sadness. Abigail wasn't taken in. The priest put the tray on the ground, sat down beside her and sighed. His cloak was spotted with heavy rain drops and he shook it dry. Abigail ate and he watched until she had finished.

"You want to know about your mother, naturally," he resumed, looking to her.

Abigail stared ahead in silence.

He waited and then continued. "It is fair to say that,

towards the end, your mother struggled. She was not well and it was decided that she could not remain on her own at the *hostellerie*. She had tried to leave a number of times. She was also saying strange things and disturbing some of the pilgrims staying there. For her own good, we thought it better to bring her up here, which is against our rules, but the circumstances were exceptional. As indeed, they are for you."

"Where is she? Is she all right? Please let me see her," she begged.

"I am very sorry. That is not possible."

"Why? All of you promised I would see her."

"When your mother arrived here at the priory, we thought she would calm down, that she would find the solace she was seeking. After all, she had accepted what needed to be done. We left her alone for a long time in the same room that you have stayed in. After two weeks, we brought her here when the sanctuary was closed to visitors." The priest's eyes lifted towards the statue of Mary Magdalene.

"What, you brought her to stay in this dark, damp cave. By herself?"

The priest ignored the question. "Brother Anton tried to help her, but she reacted badly to him. She became irrational. She even attacked him, saying that he was evil. Your mother accused him of all sorts of crazy things, shouting that he was not a Christian, that he was a liar. Brother Anton was disturbed by this, very disturbed indeed. In the end I was worrying about his health as well."

She shouted, "I don't give a shit about Brother Anton! Just tell me what happened to my mother." Abigail feared for her own mental stability.

He recoiled from her, as though she might attack him. "I can see your mother in you."

"Good." The priest was silent for a long while. "Take your bloody food away," she instructed. "I want nothing more from any of you."

Brother Bonnaire looked mournful. He stood slowly, stiffly and Abigail thought he was about to leave. He remained still for a moment, looking down at her. The priest then seemed to come to a decision. He spoke in a low monotone. "I will continue. You have the right to know." He stopped again, as if considering his words, before resuming. "It was about three weeks ago. Your mother had been spending a lot of time here in the sanctuary... the cave... after it was closed each evening. Brother Anton reported that she had started having visions and delusions. She believed she was an angel. She said to me that the saint had told her as much. She could fly and would be resurrected."

Abigail could only look at the priest in horror.

"Late one afternoon, after the main entrance was closed, she must have wandered out of the cave, into the square outside. We don't know what happened, but we think she actually believed she could fly: that she could fly from the sanctuary out over the cliff to the plains below. That is what we think happened. We did not see it. We looked everywhere for her in the cave and in the priory. Eventually, by the evening, we found her down there, at the foot of the cliff. What was remarkable was that there was not one mark on her from the fall. Not one single bone was broken." He held up his hands in wonder. "It was as if she had floated to the bottom." The priest looked up at the statue again before turning back to Abigail. "I am very sorry for your loss."

Abigail thought she might faint. She opened her mouth to speak, but no words came out. She was numb.

"In the end, it was for the best," the priest added.

"I don't believe you," Abigail said after a long silence. She had to force the words out. "You are lying, just like the rest of your colleagues. When Adam returns with the police, they will find out what you have been doing. You will not get away with it."

"That will never happen. We thought that there was no need to tell you, but I will now, as you raise the matter. Sadly, an accident befell your Adam early this morning as he was leaving and—"

"What do you mean by accident?" Abigail leapt to her feet and glared at him. The priest took a step back before resuming.

"It was still dark when he left. He was on his way down the path below the cliff. It seems that he slipped on the cobbles and, well, fell over the side and down the mountain. It was very unfortunate."

"No! This is all bullshit. You are lying."

The priest continued calmly, "Sadly, he did not survive. We did all we could." All this was said with the same cruelty and contempt she had seen in Anton.

"We haven't managed to recover the body yet. Where he fell is very steep and the vegetation is very thick. But rest assured, my child, we will find him and, when we do, we will inform the proper authorities." The priest straightened up. "You will stay here until we come for you. It will not be much longer. Our preparations are almost complete."

"I still do not believe anything you are saying. You can't be so completely cruel?" Her whisper echoed her feeling of defeat.

"It is what has to happen, my child. It was always going to be this way."

"No! No!" She shook her head. "You're wrong. Adam is fine and will be back soon with the police. Then we will see what happens to all of you."

His face was expressionless. "I am afraid that you are going to be very disappointed. You are understandably emotional. I comprehend that, I do. I am sorry that there is nothing more I can say that will make you understand."

"You are completely mad. All of you disgust me."

He turned to go. This time there was no disguising the coldness in his stare. "Let me be very clear." He paused. "You will not leave this sanctuary alive. You are in the holy cave to make your peace. Please take this opportunity to do so. You will not have another."

Chapter 22

Adam twitched as a bug crawled inside his ear to shelter from the heavy rain. He half-opened one eye. Raindrops penetrated the thick forest canopy, and water cascaded over the lichen-covered rocks of the steep mountainside. He twitched again, consciousness returning with the rain. Dark clouds slid slantwise across the angry sky. Branches and trees tilted and swayed sideways in the fierce wind. His thoughts swirled. He was lying on his back, looking upwards, and rainwater soon pooled in his eye socket, forcing him to blink and close the eye once more. He hurt all over and his arm hung at a strange angle. He moved his head sideways, keeping his mouth closed to stop himself slowly drowning. Desperately, he fought to hang onto consciousness. Blood rushed to his head as he realised he was lying upside down on the steep slope. His legs were entangled in thick bushes. He closed the eye again. He was surrounded by a symphony of noise. A continuous roar of wind accompanied the sudden, numbing, crash of thunder against a background of the incessant drum of heavy rain. Why was he here? What had happened to him? He couldn't think; he only felt, and it wasn't good. Every part of him hurt. He was dying. A drowsiness and sense of comfort enveloped him and his body relaxed and shifted slightly. Gravity took over and, inexorably, he resumed his terrible head-first slide. Extending his good arm, he clung to a branch to prevent sliding further into a deep ravine far below him. Gradually his grip slowly loosened and he relapsed into unconsciousness and resumed his plummet down the remaining sixty feet of the slippery mountainside.

Hours later, the heavy rain had relented, and night-time had almost departed. Adam groaned. He couldn't move. A low roar came from beside his head made him open both eyes. He was lying on his side, his body crumpled and half-submerged in a shallow pool beside a fast-flowing stream cascading down the mountain. He turned his head. The dark outline of the cliff-face towered above him. Disjointed memories returned. There was a fight, some faceless men. Why had he been attacked? He couldn't remember, but he had been thrown, or he slipped, over the cliff. He went over the edge backwards and then there was the weightlessness before he hit the mountainside. The crash into a thick bush had somehow slowed his fall.

Adam's throat was dry. He needed a drink. He tried to move his legs. His body had somehow twisted in the fall and one leg was lying over the other, which was bent at the knee. He struggled to free the trapped leg and then used his good arm to reach a sitting position. It was tortuous and a sharp pain wracked the left side of his body each time he moved. It seemed to take an age but, eventually, he manoeuvred himself to a sitting position in the shallow pool, beside the rushing water. He was parched and he gulped greedily as the cold mountain water soothed his painful throat. With each mouthful, his senses returned. He now remembered the monks in the priory above. They had attacked him and they had intended to kill him. Well, they had certainly achieved most of their objective. He had expended what little strength that remained and he slowly lowered himself back to the damp ground so that he was lying on his good side. The lower half remained partially submerged in the shallow pool. He felt his eyes close again.

Voices were calling from above. Daylight had returned. It was still windy, but the rain had stopped. Adam shivered. He was cold and wet. They were coming for him and he knew that he had to get away. They were still some distance above him. He looked around. The vegetation was thick. It was unlikely they would spot him from far above and their progress would be slow. Clambering down the side of the cliff would be treacherous. The wet earth and lichen that covered much of the rockface made descending precarious. It would be easy for his pursuers to lose their footing and plunge down the mountainside.

*

Snatches of voices above shouting directions came sporadically. They were getting closer. Adam knew that he would need to move soon from where he was lying. If the priests worked their way methodically down the mountain, they would eventually reach the spot at the bottom of the gully where he lay. In his present state, he couldn't fight off one person, let alone a group. He gritted his teeth and crawled towards the edge of the fast-flowing water, his body protesting with each movement. He was sure he had broken bones on his left side. His arm felt paralysed and his ribs screamed with the pain. With the volume of water cascading down the mountainside, the stream had fast become a river. The water coursed around a jumble of large boulders. He lowered himself, gasping, into the freezing water, and grabbed hold of the side of one of the rocks. The water surging around him reached the top of his chest. Clinging grimly to the slippery rock he just managed to stop himself being swept away in the strong current. Adam took a deep breath and edged forward to a smaller rock, collapsing onto it, his breath now coming in gasps. The far bank was in reach. With his good arm, he grasped an overhanging branch and, grunting with pain, pulled himself from the water and onto the bank on the other side of the river. Exhausted, he rolled onto his side and lay there panting, trying to recover. It was a small victory and he felt safer. There was a chance they might not think to look for him on this side.

Adam looked around, assessing his chances. His pursuers were less likely to look for him upstream, particularly if he could climb up the steep slope. The undergrowth around the river provided good cover. He hauled himself unsteadily to his feet. He could still hear the voices but there was no indication that he had been seen. The sun had risen and light was filtering through the thick forest canopy. Adam felt his body slowly warm, as the temperature increased, and with it, the numbness on his left side reduced. The wind still whipped the branches from side to side. That might work in his favour. His movement would be less likely to be spotted from above. He stumbled across the slippery ground. His legs were rubbery and, every few minutes, he had to grab a branch and stop and gather himself. Foot by slow foot, he climbed the far bank, working his way upriver. Fallen branches and loose rocks tripped him and debris, torn from the trees above, crashed to the ground around him.

Progress was slow, but after a while, Adam realised the shouts from above had been left behind. He rested on a boulder, hidden by a curtain of vegetation. He held his breath and listened. Apart from the wind gusting through the trees, there was nothing. Had his attackers reached the gully floor? Were they now trying to decide which way to go? Would they look at the fast-flowing water and follow the current downstream? Or would they think like him, and go the other way? He had to move away. He searched the debris lying around him and found a sturdy stick to aid his trudge up the hillside.

Around a bend, he came across a rocky outcrop where the river cascaded in a torrent over a ledge. The waterfall was partially hidden from below by bushes clinging to the surrounding rocks Behind the waterfall, he saw a small cave. carved over the millennia from the mountain. At the moment, the river was in full flow and he could shelter there, hidden by the wall of water. Adam edged his way cautiously along the narrow, slimy, ledge beside the waterfall. It would provide refuge. There was just enough room for him to wedge himself against the rock and remain relatively dry. He needed to remain hidden, in the hope that his assailants might believe he had been washed away in the downpour.

The cave was perhaps five feet deep and about the same across. Occasionally the water splattered where he was crouched, but in the main, the cave was dry. He lay down and rested his head on a small shelf. The roar of the waterfall drowned out all other sound. All he could do now was rest and to try to regain some strength. He was starving. He hadn't eaten anything for almost two days. He tried to put his hunger to the back of his mind but he knew he would need to leave the security of the waterfall eventually and search the forest for something to eat. For now, he would wait and hope his pursuers gave up their search.

Sleep was hard to come by. Escape from his pursuers had been his priority but, now that he was safe for the moment, he allowed his thoughts to return to the events of the past few days. Memories of Maryanne flooded back. Had all of this really happened? Where were Abigail and Maryanne now? Were they still in the priory above? Did they know that something had happened to him?

The cascade of water slowed to more of a steady flow. If it subsided much further, his hiding place would soon become visible. It was after midnight, though, and it was unlikely that the priests were still on the mountainside. He resolved to stay where he was for a few more hours, until after daybreak. He could then search for food and would also make a splint for his damaged arm. Only then could he turn his attention to climbing out of the gully. In the meantime, he settled back as best he could. For the first time, there was some hope of survival, but he would need to recover some strength before he left his hiding place.

Adam was woken early by the welcoming sound of nature reasserting itself after the storm. There had been a shift in the wind pattern during the night. The persistent growling through the treetops had become intermittent. The mistral was blowing itself out. Battling the elements would be less of a problem, but a new challenge faced him. His forearm was swollen, red and throbbing around the break, and infection was setting in. Meanwhile, the pain in his ribs made him feel faint. The priests had inflicted a methodical beating on him before he fell over the cliff. Without medical treatment, he knew he was not going last more than a few days. The respite provided by the curtain of water tumbling down the rocks was to be temporary.

Adam began the slow climb out of the gully, grabbing

hold of branches and bushes to help him. The forest floor was starting to dry. Even so, he had to stop every ten yards or so. His hunger pangs were growing. He searched around him for something edible and was rewarded when he emerged onto the flatter ground of a ridge and found a wild fig tree, half hidden in a grove. He gathered the fruit he could reach, sat down against a towering Scotch pine and ate. When he had finished, his hunger was far from sated, but he felt better. He had heard nothing from his searchers all morning and he felt more secure. Now his survival depended on him finding his way down from this mountainside. So far, he had not come across any paths, other than what looked like narrow animal trails criss-crossing the terrain. A wave of fatigue overcame him and he drifted off in the shade.

When he came round, the sun was now shining directly into his eyes from a gap in the forest canopy. The sun was much lower than it had been earlier. It must be the afternoon. There was an acrid smell in the air. Were local foresters clearing the dense woodland? Perhaps he was not alone, and he might find help. He got unsteadily to his feet. The sun was starting to go down and he needed to get off this mountain. He felt he would not survive another night. His progress on the flat was hampered by the thick vegetation and the lack of a pathway. It was impossible to follow a straight course and he zig-zagged his slow way through the forest until the ground started to fall away once more. The smell of burning came in wafts. Once or twice Adam caught sight of smoke blowing on the gusting wind. Ash and fragments of what looked like charred paper drifted across the clearing.

Just when he had given up looking for anything else to

eat, he suddenly came across a plantain bush, standing on its own. He recognised the fruit from a Caribbean holiday many years before. Hungrily, he peeled away the skin and bit into the flesh. It tasted like raw mushroom. He picked another and, as he ate, looked back up the way he had come. Through a clearing between the towering pines, he caught a flash of red, lighting up the evening sky. The red flickered for a while, then it vanished.

Going down was easier and he was able to manoeuvre himself between the scrub and the trees. He looked at his watch, which had somehow survived the beating and the subsequent fall. He had been walking, or stumbling, for almost four hours. He felt himself weakening, but he kept going, knowing that, with each step, he was putting distance between himself and the deranged priests. His destiny was in his hands. All bird song had disappeared, replaced by the sounds of the evening. From a distance came the croaking of forest toads. The sky had greyed but there was enough light left for him to see his way forward. He had only an hour at most before it would be too dark to see. From time to time, he looked back. A strange reddish glow was spreading across the horizon.

Dusk fell and the outlines of the trees and branches faded. The gusts were less penetrating, but a fine ash continued to fall. He needed to seek shelter soon. When he emerged from a dense clump of trees into a small clearing of bushes and scrub, he looked for a flat, protected patch of ground where he could spend the night. His mouth felt dry and he was lightheaded. He hadn't drunk anything since leaving the safety of the waterfall that morning so, before he found a place to sleep, he looked around for signs of a river or stream. At the edge of the clearing, beyond which the ancient forest resumed, he saw movement. It was followed by a rustle of bushes between two narrow beech trees.

"Hey!" His cry was tentative, his throat scratchy and sore. He couldn't believe the sudden change in his luck. Waving his arm above his head he cried again "Help! Help!" His call was answered by movement to the one side of a thick gorse bush. Squinting, he saw a figure, crouched over, just beyond the edge of the clearing. It did not reply. They must not have seen him. He tried once more. "Help. I need help. Over here." This time his voice came out as a stifled yelp. He must look quite a sight, standing there waving in the middle of the clearing.

Adam approached the area where he had spotted the movement. The ground and vegetation around the clump of bushes had been flattened. He could see no one, but they couldn't be too far away. There were no more signs of movement. Had it just been the wind playing tricks on him? He was about to try one last desperate shout when a large shape rose from a depression in the ground about twenty yards in front of him. The shape separated itself from the grey of the backdrop and he realised that he was staring at a huge wild boar. It emitted a low rumbling growl as it rose to its feet from a kneeling position.

"Jesus." Despite its short legs, the *sanglier* was more than a metre high and it weighed far more than Adam. With its matted greyish-black woolly fur and its muscular wide shoulders, it looked to be a powerful, fully-grown, adult male. Its razor-sharp tusks protruded from either side of its snout. Adam was in serious danger. He could not win this confrontation. The tusks could tear him apart. Even from this distance, it gave off a foetid smell of decay. His mind flashed back to Uzès. He and Maryanne's encounter with a *sanglier* preceded her disappearance. Was the same about to happen to him?

It took all Adam's strength to keep still. He hoped the beast would not see him as a threat. Its ears were pointing towards him as it also stood its ground. Its focus was fully on him. Adam had second thoughts and started to back away slowly. The wild boar watched him intently, shaking its heavy head from time to time, snorting and growling intermittently. Foot by foot Adam made his retreat, hoping the animal would eventually turn and leave, but, if anything it seemed more enraged. It pawed at the ground with its front hooves. The swaying continued. The animal was going to charge him. There was no way out. Turning sideways, he speeded up. The *sanglier* remained where it was. The distance between them increased. In the fast-fading dusk, a fine grey ash floated across the clearing. Adam stumbled on an exposed tree root, almost falling to the ground. The sudden movement was enough for the animal and, with a guttural roar, it charged. Its speed was terrifying and the huge animal closed the distance rapidly, its head lowered, the vicious-looking tusks aimed at his body. Adam crouched to face it, concentrating on the tusks as they bore down on him. The *sanglier* launched itself and he felt the crash of the massive impact and his ribs shatter as its body collided with his chest. The power was immense and the force threw him through the air. High above the clearing the sky erupted in a fiery red and yellow fireball as he felt his world darken.

Chapter 23

Anton came for her in the late afternoon. He escorted her up the staircase leading to the upper level of the cave, and then across to the open front door. The howling wind swirled in a vortex around the courtyard. Despite its strength, the fresh wind felt wonderful on her skin, cleaning away the hours of captivity. Abigail stopped to savour the freedom and the freshness. It had been raining hard. She had heard the drum rolls of thunder from inside the cave. He shoved her forward and pointed across the courtyard, towards the priory. Another priest emerged from the front entrance carrying a bundle of wood. He glanced in her direction and continued towards where a jumble of wood already lay, piled high, now covered by a tarpaulin to protect it from the rain. The wood pile was placed in front of the statue of the Virgin and her child, at the edge of the cliff. Behind it was the large cross set against the backdrop of the plain and valley below. She felt a chill and averted her eyes from the pyre.

Anton held the door for her as she once again entered the priory, she suspected for the last time. Not one word had passed between them and he looked gaunt and ill at ease. He had injured his side and moved stiffly. Once inside, Anton pushed roughly past her, as if her presence angered him. She followed. Halfway down the long corridor, Abigail glanced through an open set of wooden double doors. Inside was a large chapel with a marble altar, half-covered by a white cloth, on which three large candles flickered. In front of the altar, a dozen or so wooden chairs were laid out in two curved rows. Abigail inhaled the heady scent of incense. Anton stopped and waited; an expression of contempt played across his face. He indicated with a shrug that she could enter. Abigail took a couple of paces forward. Her attention was diverted by a large white cloth, emblazoned with the concentric circles she had come across in the *hostellerie* chapel, draped on the wall behind the altar. The inner circles were broader and darker, bisected top and bottom. She backed out of the chapel. She wanted no part of what was to happen.

Cooking smells drifted from the open kitchen door. Anton then unlocked the door to the room that had been her prison and indicated that she should go in. He slammed the door behind her and locked it. The room was much as she had left it, apart from a long white dress now hanging from a coat hanger on the cupboard door. She went over and touched the heavy linen fabric. What was it doing there? She sat heavily on the bed. She felt a sense of infinite weariness. Her scraped knee was bleeding again and her jeans were sticking to her. She took them off and went to the bathroom and stood in front of the cracked mirror. Her appearance horrified her. Her eyes were bruised and hollow, her cheek and lip were cut and covered in dried blood and her hair was lank and matted. She looked a hundred years old. To make herself feel better, she took a lukewarm shower and tried to clean herself as best as she could. She felt numb and hopeless. Life could be tenuous and unpredictable, but she had not expected it to end quite so early.

There was some shampoo, and the old bar of soap. She couldn't wash away her situation, but, being clean suddenly felt important to her. By the time she turned off the shower, the water was cold. She dried herself with the old towel that was still damp from the day before. She thought about wearing some of her mother's clothes — her own had seen better days — but she couldn't bring herself to do so. She put her bloodied jeans back on.

Abigail lay on the bed, staring at the wall, and waited. As exhausted as she was, she could not sleep. She knew her fate, but she hoped that what the priest had told her about Adam had been a lie. They wanted to take everything that mattered away from her. All she had left was a distant hope. She only had their word that Adam was dead. He was strong and resilient and there was the faintest chance he had managed to get away. Even so, it was probably too late to save her, but others would know what had happened and these bastards, these madmen, would receive their justice. No matter what befell her in the coming hours, she would hang on to that idea — and her dignity. She must stay strong.

She had to wait for less than an hour. The old priest knocked before sliding back the bolt and entering. He had brought some food and it smelled delicious. He put it on the table in the corner and sat on the chair beside it.

"My child."

"Do not call me that."

He sighed. "All right, have it your way. Please eat your food. We are not unkind men. When you have finished, we will take you to our chapel. It is fair that we explain what will happen tomorrow morning at first light. These things will not change. We will pray for you, and you may join us. We will be accompanied by two Masters of our Order of Preachers. One has made the journey from Rome, and one from Marseille. They will lead the prayers tonight. After, you may remain in the chapel for your private prayers and reflection. You understand?"

"I do. I also understand that you are mad. You won't get away with this."

Brother Bonnaire looked sad. "Very well. I will leave you to have your food and I will be back for you in an hour."

"Just before you go, what is up with Brother Anton? I don't particularly care, but he seems angry and can hardly look at me."

"He is very disappointed with you. He is very sensitive and, as I told you before, he has not been well. He has confused thoughts and we did not think it wise for him to spend time with you alone. At his request, we did, though, allow him to bring you up from the sanctuary. He is no longer allowed to visit you and will not bother you further."

"Good. I'm glad about that. He's been the source of huge unhappiness in my family. I will save a special prayer for him."

"That is your entitlement. I will leave you now." He turned to go.

"One last thing." She pointed. "That white dress over there, is it something to do with my mother?"

"No, my... That is for you. You will wear that dress tomorrow."

"And if I don't want to?"

"I am afraid that will not be an option," he replied sadly. "It was brought for you by the Master. If you do not put it on willingly, we will be forced to dress you. I doubt you will like that." With that, he turned and left.

Abigail sat for a long while in the semi-darkness, unable to move from the bed. She stared blankly at the bare walls, trying to block all thoughts from her mind. Eventually, feeling strong pangs of hunger, and knowing the priest would return soon, she forced herself from the bed. The chicken stew had cooled by this time. It was tasty but she could only pick at it, before giving up on it. It didn't matter anyway.

*

The smell of incense was even stronger when she entered the chapel, accompanied by Brother Bonnaire. A chair had been placed in front of the altar, facing the four priests who were already seated. She sat and regarded them. Low music, sung in Latin, played from the speakers in the corners. Behind her, the candles flickered.

Anton was seated at the end and was the only one not looking at her. He seemed ill at ease and his eyes were cast down at the flagstones beneath his feet. Brother Bonnaire she knew, and one other, seated next to Anton, looked familiar. He was the short priest who had accompanied Anton when she and Adam had been locked in the storeroom. There was something vaguely familiar about him. The other priest she had never seen before. He was younger than the others. Perhaps he was a priest in training. In the middle of the group were two chairs for the visiting priests. All were now dressed in white habits, hoods back, revealing their faces.

The door behind the altar opened. Inside, it looked like an office or library. The two visitors emerged and sat. They were dressed in white, too, but both wore a black leather belt with a large silver buckle. Both were in their sixties, tall, with steel-grey hair. One walked with a slight limp.

Abigail sat, looking straight ahead. It felt as though she were on trial, which she supposed she was. These were her inquisitors, about to make a judgement on her life.

Brother Bonnaire bowed to the visitors, cleared his throat and addressed Abigail in a low voice. "We have explained to you why you are here. We have also told you the sad circumstances surrounding the departure of your mother. It was not what we intended, and indeed was very regrettable."

The two Masters of the Order watched Abigail with considerable interest.

"As the Order of Inquisitors, we have a process that we follow. Your mother's sudden death prevented that from happening. This mistake will not happen again."

She found her voice. "I assume you're eager to torture me. Well, go ahead." She raised her head defiantly and looked directly at them. "After all, it is only the twenty-first century. And there are six of you. It must be lonely up here on this bloody rock. You must get bored. I'm sure you have been looking forward to this for a long time."

Brother Bonnaire looked pained. The visitors remained impassive. "We understand your hostility, but we have no intention of torturing you. But, in one way, you are right: we have been waiting for this moment for a long time. It is our sacred destiny — we are as unable to change this purpose as you are to change who you are."

"I don't need the justification. Just tell me what you intend to do with me."

Brother Bonnaire looked to the visitors. One of them gave him the merest of nods. "Very well, I will make it simple. You will be taken out at first light. You will be wearing the white dress that we have brought for you. We will say prayers for your soul and then you are to be burnt at the stake. Your ashes will be scattered across the mountain by the wind. It will end our journey."

"Do you have any questions?" One of the Masters of the Order spoke for the first time. He had a gravelly voice and his English was heavily inflected with an Italian accent. *So, he must be the priest who had come from Rome.*

"Would it not be easier for you to just let me go?"

He smiled. "No, we cannot do that."

"Is there anything at all I can possibly do to stop you committing this insane act of murder?"

The gravelly voice replied "No."

"Then I have no other questions. I don't wish to pray in here. Just take me back to the room."

"As you wish." Bonnaire got to his feet. "We will pray for you tonight, as we will tomorrow at first light."

"Don't bother with that. Where I'm going when I die is not a place you will ever know."

*

First light had barely broken when they came for her. She was woken by the slow mournful sound of the bells. They reminded her of the bells she used to hear in Dublin, as a child, before a funeral. Were these bells for her? Her head ached. She dressed in the white dress left for her. It was a bit tight. She chuckled at the grim humour when she realised the fit did not matter. All she could hope was that it was flammable. She had no wish to hang around.

Brother Bonnaire entered. When he saw her trainers, he instructed, "No shoes."

She left the room barefoot. The other five priests materialised from the chapel entrance and fell in behind her. Bonnaire led the way. As he opened the front door, a powerful gust of wind slammed against it and the priest struggled to keep the door open as the group exited.

Gulping in the fresh air, Abigail looked towards where the jumble of wood had lain under a tarpaulin the previous evening. The wood pile had been built up into a pyre. A wooden chair sat in the centre and a long wooden stake protruded some six feet from the top of the pyre. It reminded her of pictures she had seen in the National Gallery of the burning of Joan of Arc. It was ancient and elemental. Her gaze was drawn towards the edge of the square, protected by a low wall. So, that was where her mother had chosen to end it. For a moment, she thought about doing the same thing. Should she try to fly? It was a fleeting thought. She would not give them the satisfaction — or an excuse to explain away her murder. One way or another, they would be caught and would pay for their evil.

The strong gales of the past few days now came and went: interludes of moderate wind being followed swiftly by sudden, damaging blasts. The group struggled to maintain their footing. The Masters took control and the strange group gathered between the pyre and the statue of the Virgin and her Son. Abigail stood quietly to one side. The priests were in deep conversation, trying to decide which way she should be positioned on the pyre. Abigail was surprised that there could be a good or bad position for an effective death. There was an argument for her to stand and face the statue and the cross. Her last view would be across the treetops to the plain below. That seemed appropriate and she grimly hoped that they would settle on this. Another of the priests disagreed. He was pointing and seemed to be saying that the wind was coming from the one direction, before it then swirled around the courtyard. A side-on position would provide a more efficient cremation.

Meanwhile, the wind continued to strengthen. Some of the smaller branches had become dislodged from the pyre and were blowing around the courtyard. If they waited too long, there would be no kindling left. Abigail had given up all hope of rescue: it would have happened by now. She was ready and now wanted it over with. One of the priests brandished an electronic firelighter, as if it were his latest toy. The younger priest carried a heavy jerry can.

The priests had come to a decision. Abigail was half-pulled, and then half-pushed, until she was positioned, standing on the wooden chair above the pyre. Anton, she noticed, stood to one side, eyes down and distant. Her wrists were bound tightly to the back of the chair and the stake. Then they bound her ankles. The wind howled around them as the men discussed, with much pointing, how best to light the pyre. Abigail supposed that any suggestion from her would be rejected. Eventually they formed a group in front of the statue and prayed. They were led by the two senior priests, the others stood in front of them with their head bowed. The words were all in French. In any event, the wind drowned out most of what was being said, although the name Mary Magdalene was uttered several times. She was past caring and raised her eyes to look steadily out towards the horizon, lit by the pink and yellow of the sun's first rays.

Whilst the prayers continued, she intoned, "Please let this be over quickly," and prepared to close her eyes for the last time.

The gusts carried the words of the prayers away, lost

in the wind. Eventually, she looked down and they seemed to be coming to a conclusion. The priests bowed their heads in silent contemplation, then turned to look at Abigail. One of the Masters nodded to the priest with the firelighter and he stepped forward and lit the kindling. A strong cross-wind meant it caught quickly, so he had to hurriedly leap back. The still-damp kindling and the wood from the deluge of the past few days created a thick plume of smoke as the flames grew.

Chapter 24

The kindling curled then crackled as it was set alight. Knowing the end was close, Abigail focused on the cross before her. Beyond she could make out the plain below and the *hostellerie*, looking tiny in the distance. It was a world away. A world now from her past. The first blast of heat as the wood above the kindling caught fire took her breath away. It would not be long now. She knew she was likely to die of smoke inhalation before the fire reached her. All she could hope for was that the pain would be brief before she lost all consciousness.

Thick acrid smoke swirled around the base of the pyre as the wind caught it. It swirled and drifted upwards and enveloped her. She tried to twist away towards the wind, but she was forced to inhale and began to cough uncontrollably. Her eyes and throat burned. As the flames rose, the shouts and cries from the priests below were lost against the fierce crackling. Flames crept up the piled wood and the heat was intense. The smoke billowed all around and obscured the view over the valley. Abigail kept her head up, despite the smoke. She would not be cowed by their evil. The plume of smoke was by now rising high above the sanctuary and would soon be visible from below. As the loud sounds of the crackling subsided the shouts of the priests was replaced by the racking sound of coughing: they were now also choking as they watched her die.

The mistral chose that moment, on its single-minded journey southwards, to make a final gesture. A huge gust roared through the foothills of the Cévennes and Alpilles mountain ranges, and accelerating through the valley of the Rhône. It ripped across the shallow cliff shelf at Sainte-Baume and the tableau formed in the priory courtyard bore the full force of its fury. Kindling, sparks and burning wood were hurled high into the air. The priests were blown off their feet and the heavy door to the priory smashed open. The curtain of flames and sparks were swept away from the pyre and, funnelled by the sheer cliff face, carried upwards so that they climbed high above the courtyard, in the direction of the priory. There was a crackling sound as the surrounding bushes and trees ignited with the intensity of the fire.

The air seemed to leave the courtyard. There were shouts and screams, as the priests tried to get to their feet. Fire engulfed the priests standing closest to the pyre. Through the swirl of smoke, Abigail saw one of them, dark cassock now alight, flailing uselessly as he tried to beat down the flames. He staggered, then collapsed to his knees. The youngest priest tried to help, but it was hopeless. Screaming with pain, the priest rolled to the ground and curled into a ball as the fire consumed him. The young priest fell back and looked on in terror. Meanwhile, two others pointed, shouting out in horror, as the centuries-old wooden roof of the ancient priority caught alight. The fire had started above the portico at the front and the blaze had taken hold at the very edge of the roof, working its way slowly along its length.

The gust fanned the fierce flames away from Abigail, towards the sanctuary and priory. As the direction of the fire changed, the intensity of the heat lessened. Sparks swirled up the high cliffs above the sanctuary, setting more buildings alight as the burning sparks rained down on the courtyard. Fire tore through the storeroom in which Abigail and Adam had been imprisoned, and, with a loud crash, the old windows imploded with the heat. The end wall of the souvenir shop collapsed, falling onto the narrow pathway, in a hail of sparks and flames, blocking any exit down the mountain.

Black smoke billowed and breathing became more difficult. Abigail heaved and coughed, inhaling more of the suffocating cloud. She thought she would pass out and felt her knees start to buckle. She was kept upright only by her bindings. There was a movement behind her and a hand, clutching a knife, appeared at her side. The knife disappeared and she could feel the ropes binding her hands being sawn. Her arms were suddenly free and she brought them in front of her. Angry welts from where the bindings had bitten into her covered her arms and wrists. The hand with the knife slashed at the bindings around her legs until she came away from the stake supporting her. Collapsing forwards, Abigail would have pitched into the embers if strong arms had not grabbed her, pulling her down from the pyre. Her white dress ripped from the waist to the hem as she was dragged away from the fire and onto the cobbles. She lay on the stones, unsure what had happened. She turned, and then gasped. The arms belonged to Anton.

"What…?" she could only croak.

Instead of answering, he grabbed her under the arms and helped her to her feet. Smoke still engulfed the pyre and surrounding area, while the flames flared out towards the priory. Visibility was now limited to a few metres, at most, and there was no sign of any of the other priests. The cries and shouting that had surrounded her on the pyre had been replaced by more distant shouts. Did she have the strength to make a run for it? She was disorientated and confused.

"Why?" she asked fearfully. What awful ending did Anton have reserved for her, after all she had already endured?

He looked at her. His eyes communicated an infinite sadness.

Beyond Anton, a number of figures were stood before the priory entrance, looking upwards. The priests had turned their attention to saving their priory. Flames, whipped by the fierce wind, were running the length of the roof. The smoke was still thick and drifting. Abigail saw that the door to the priory was standing open. The inside had started to fill with smoke and soon she caught a glimpse of a flickering flame deep inside the dark building. Shouts came from within. The pyre, with the stake at the centre, was now fully alight, contributing to the flames and the searing heat and the flames.

Anton grabbed her by the hand. Repulsed by his touch, Abigail recoiled. Ignoring her response, he grabbed her arm and pulled her away from the fire and towards the cave entrance.

"You have to come with me. You need to leave." He was gruff.

"What are you going to do with me?"

"Come, please." *Was he pleading?* "You have to get away. They are diverted by the fire in the building, for now."

The door to the cave opened easily and Anton ushered her inside, shutting the door behind him. Were any of the priests even aware Anton had rescued her from the pyre? Visibility had been so poor, they may not have noticed and assumed her body was even now being consumed by the flames. The air in the cave was mercifully cool and clear of smoke. Anton shouted to her to follow him as he ran for the marble steps leading down to the lower cave. Abigail could barely stand and she struggled down the steps. When she had reached the bottom, she had to sit down to recover. Her breathing was ragged and she desperately needed to rest. Her white dress, as well as being torn, was scorched and burnt through in places. She was covered in soot and grime, her face smeared black.

Anton was at the door leading back into the priory. He turned and returned to her.

"I have to stop." She was straining for breath, her chest heaving.

"Just for a moment."

She pointed. "There's no way I am going back inside there. Please just leave me here."

"We have to go quickly, while we have time." He seemed to be listening for sounds from the cave above. No one seemed to have noticed their disappearance yet.

Anton waited for a few moments. Then he said, "Please, we need to go now." He raised her by the arms and led her over to the pool of water. He lowered her to her knees in front of the statue of Mary Magdalene. Abigail's throat was raw and burning and she drank deeply. Crouching there, she splashed water over herself, thinking she could just curl up in the cool calm and lie below the statue. She felt looked after, and strangely at peace.

Anton waited a while, then said, with renewed urgency, that they had to leave now. The priests would look for her in the cave eventually. He brought her to her feet and she followed him across to the door. He drew out a key and unlocked the heavy metal door.

"Stop!" Abigail had come to a halt.

"We have to be quick. There is no time."

"Where are we going?"

"Back into the priory. I will show you. I am trying to save you."

She was confused. She started to say something.

"I owe it to your mother," he added quietly.

"But the roof is burning. It will just get worse. And what about the priests? Some have gone inside."

"They are there to try to save the books and documents in the library. Some are priceless and they have to be saved. Without these records, the order is nothing."

An understanding dawned over Abigail. "OK. I see that."

"That is now their focus. Come. They may not even notice us."

Abigail followed Anton. As they reached the door at the end of the corridor, smoke streamed underneath it. Anton opened it cautiously. The passageway that ran the length of the priory was filling with smoke. Shouts of desperation came from the priests as they battled their way inside. One of the rooms to the front was ablaze. Anton instructed her to wait and he slipped off, into the smoke-filled corridor. Shortly, he was back, indicating she should cover her mouth and nose as best she could and follow him. They crept slowly into the corridor. To Abigail's left was the room in which she spent a couple of nights. The smoke made it difficult to see where they were going. They passed the stone stairs leading upstairs, the source now of most of the smoke pouring into the passageway. She looked up the stairs saw the hazy outline of flames flickering, and then a sickening crash as part of the roof fell in.

"Quick. There is little time left." Anton hurried

forwards. In front of them were two figures, outlined in the haze, coming out of a side door, weighed down by armfuls of books. Anton opened the kitchen door and hurriedly pushed her inside, shutting the door behind them.

"What the hell! What are you doing?"

He ushered her over to the far wall where a large iron wheel was mounted and bolted to a heavy beam. Handles on either side operated the pulley mechanism that brought goods up the cliffside to the priory kitchen. Below the wheel was a trap door. The wheel was grooved, allowing a thick rope to be winched up and down by the handles. It was a crude mechanism, but it had met the priests' needs over many centuries. The trap door stood open and Abigail gulped in the fresh air. A large heavy wicker basket was attached to one end of the rope, just below the opening.

The large kitchen was warm, despite the air from the open trap door. They heard the beams above creaking and expanding and they looked up. The ceiling was starting to glow a faint red and whisps of smoke were appearing from behind the beams. A crack, followed by a scream, came from upstairs. Smoke started to pour through the roof, sucked in by the draught from the trap door.

Abigail stared down. This part of the priory jutted out over the cliff. There was a three-hundred foot drop to the storage shed far below. The rope was thick but seemed worn and frayed in parts. She guessed Anton's intention.

"I can't do this." She was shaking. Fear had returned after the numbness of the past hour.

"You have to. It is the only way out for you."

Anton walked to the corner of the kitchen where three fire extinguishers stood. Grunting, he pulled one over and threw it through the trapdoor.

"What are you doing?"

"Most of the fire extinguishers are stored in here. There is one more upstairs."

"But the kitchen is starting to burn. Shouldn't we be trying to put the fire out?"

"No, this place is finished." He dragged another fire extinguisher across the stone floor and tipped it through the opening.

As the final fire extinguisher disappeared, he said: "You will have to go down by the pulley. You must leave now. Get into the basket and lower yourself by holding onto the other rope. Do not try to go too fast or you will lose control."

Abigail looked wide-eyed at Anton. "I'm not getting in that thing. It does not look safe."

"You have to. It is the only way down."

She shook her head. "I, I can't" she replied softly.

"You have to," he repeated. "Otherwise, you will die."

Abigail looked through the trapdoor and hesitantly crept towards the basket. "Will it hold my weight?"

"It will, there is no problem."

She touched the basket. "But won't it tip me out?" she asked.

He looked her directly in the eyes. "You will be safe, but you need to trust me. Please, this is what your mother would have wanted."

"OK. Here goes." She gave him an uncertain smile.

"Let me help you." Anton held the basket while she squeezed in. It was tight and she had to pull her legs up under her chin. It swayed disconcertingly.

"Remember, hold the other rope to make sure you do not descend too quickly."

Abigail nodded uncertainly as she positioned herself so she could grab the rope. "What are you going to do?"

Anton turned the handle and the basket started to descend below the priory floor.

"I wait here," he replied.

"But—" She met his gaze. "Thank you," was all she could offer.

With that, there was a loud thumping on the kitchen door and the door handle turned. Anton rushed over and grabbed the handle, putting his full weight behind the door. There was shouting from the outside, voices asking what was going on. The smoke had thickened and part of the ceiling was starting to give way.

"Quick!" he shouted. "Go now! Use the rope and I will try to hold them."

Anton's name was being shouted. Abigail's last sight of the room was of Anton putting his weight behind the door, as flames licked around the corners of the kitchen. And then all view disappeared as the wicker basket descended below the kitchen floor. The rock of the sheer cliff face suddenly appeared and the basket rocked alarmingly. A geared mechanism helped control the speed, but Abigail had to use all her strength to hold onto the rope and stop the basket accelerating uncontrollably to the bottom. As she did so, she could hear raised voices coming from the kitchen above, followed by a scream.

She was halfway down the cliff face when there was an explosion above and part of the kitchen caught alight. It would only be a matter of time before the fire spread across the room to the rope holding her. Burning debris fell past her, down to the clearing and the forest below. A blanket of smoke shrouded the forest canopy. Another explosion followed — the gas cylinders must have caught alight. A burning wooden beam from the kitchen ceiling threatened to disintegrate and rain down on her. She was two-thirds of the way down. Her hands burned from grasping hold of the rope. More and more debris from the priory fell past her and Abigail looked around her in desperation. She was still well above the tree line.

From high above came the whirr of helicopter rotor blades. She felt the downdraught as it hovered above the priory. A large water container was suspended below it. As the basket swayed dangerously, she could see that the entire priory was now burning. It had lost most of its roof. There was the faint sound of another helicopter coming up the valley. She looked back up towards the burning building and saw, to her horror, that the pulley rope had started to smoulder. It was just a matter of time before it caught alight and the basket, with Abigail in it, plunged the remaining hundred feet. The basket lurched and tipped to one side and Abigail fell across it, jamming herself in the corner. She lost her tight grip on the guide rope and her descent accelerated. She was still thirty feet from the top of the storage shed when the last cord in the rope burnt through, sending the basket spinning to the ground.

Chapter 25

It was a warm day, even for early summer. The sky was a deep Mediterranean blue and the barest of zephyrs ruffled the treetops lining the car park. The gentle breeze was a far cry from the recent mistrals. The couple got out of the car. This time there were no tour buses, just an old Volvo from Germany, two motorbikes parked side by side and a delivery van. They walked slowly past the sandstone buildings of the Boutique du Pèlerin and the Tourist Office and crossed the road. He still had a limp and his ribs hadn't fully healed. His left arm was in a sling from the break in his wrist. They stood, alongside each other, in front of the solid double wooden doors of the *hostellerie* entrance.

"Are you all right to do this?" he asked.

She looked up at the sky before nodding and following him inside.

From the reception area, they turned right and walked through the maze of dark corridors until they found the door they wanted. The sign on it said '*Cimetière – Privé*'. He grunted as he pushed open the heavy door with his good arm. They stepped outside into the bright sunshine and she took his hand as they entered the *hostellerie*'s quiet cemetery. It was enclosed on three sides by an ancient wall, shaded by pine trees, and looked out over the Sainte-Baume range, mountains they now knew so well.

He looked across at her. "Are you really sure you're all right? You know we can wait. We don't have to do this now."

"No. I can do this. I can do it with you beside me."

The cemetery was quiet. They walked along the three lines of neatly laid out graves, all outlined with small rocks and bearing simple wooden crosses. They came to the last grave at the end of the third row. There was no name or date, but they knew it was her grave. Abigail had brought a simple bouquet of peonies, signifying healing, together with a single white rose, Maryanne's favourite flower. She laid the flowers at the head of the grave. They stood silently, each with their own thoughts. Tears flowed down both their faces as they held each other's hands tightly. It had been a long journey, and this was an end, but also a beginning. They stood there for half an hour. Everything was still. No traffic went by outside, they heard no voices, not even surrounding birdsong. It was as if the world was holding its breath in that instance.

Eventually, Abigail raised her bowed head and gazed towards the mountains. They, in turn, looked down on her, unmoved by the scene. She could see the cliffs above the trees and could just make out the cave. Above it, the grey cliff face was still scorched black. The priory had all but disappeared into a heap of charred rubble. The inside of the cave was relatively undamaged, although two stained-glass windows had succumbed to the heat. The clear-up was progressing and the cave was due to reopen to visitors in a few months' time. Church services would commence later in the year, although their frequency would be reduced to twice a week. The talk in the village, and at the *hostellerie*, was that it was uncertain whether the priory would ever be replaced.

Abigail still had nightmares. The detail of her ordeal on the pyre remained etched on her mind all too vividly.

The hospital had advised counselling when she returned to England. She had been seconds away from being burnt alive. Had it not been for Anton rescuing her at the last minute, she would be dead. The nightmares included the burning priory, her escape through the kitchen and her frightening descent down the sheer cliff.

*

She'd had a miraculous escape, as if someone was looking over her that day. She recalled the perilous descent and then the freefall as the rope burnt through, sending the basket plummeting towards the ground. It had glanced off the roof, sending her tumbling out of the basket and into the dark storeroom below.

Abigail remembered that her landing was broken by sacks of fruit and potatoes and then there was nothing until she had regained consciousness, half-buried between the sacks. She lay there for a while, desperately trying to collect her thoughts. She moved onto her back and realised she hurt all over. Acrid smoke started to fill the storeroom and she knew she still remained in imminent danger. Forcing herself to sit up, she checked for broken bones before slowly clambering down from the sacks and lurching towards the door. Burning debris from above continued to fall and had set part of the roof alight. The heavy door was locked by a large bolt. Abigail shouted and banged against the wooden door as smoke billowed around her. Eventually she heard voices outside.

*

A fire crew had smashed open the storeroom door. They had been winched down to the clearing from a helicopter. She must have looked quite a sight. Her ripped white dress was scorched and blackened and her face and hair were covered by black grime and soot. All she remembered was the shock of seeing her rescuers. She couldn't believe she had been saved. She had collapsed and had to be carried, before being winched up to the hovering helicopter, and rushed to the hospital in Saint-Maximin where she was treated for smoke inhalation and burns to both feet and one arm. The doctors feared she may have permanent damage to her lungs and she was referred to specialists.

When she was well enough to answer the police's questions, they did not believe what she was telling them. The first interview was brief. They left, believing that she was still confused and traumatised from her ordeal. It took them time before they began to take elements of her story seriously. Bit by bit, though, they started to find evidence to support her story that she was the victim of an attempted murder by priests up at the sanctuary of Sainte-Baume.

A week after her rescue, she was visited at her bedside by a senior police officer. Heavily overweight, with a mournful look, he sat down with a sigh.

"At this stage of our investigation, we can conclude that the fire was not an accident. It seems to have been started deliberately," he said solemnly. Pulling out his notebook, he informed her that the findings substantiated her story. Her burns, and the forensic tests on her clothes, were consistent with it. Importantly, examination of the courtyard grounds had indeed shown evidence of the construction of a pyre, much as she had described. They had even found a charred piece of the stake and a burnt-out jerry-can.

"And what of the people... the priests up there?" she had croaked. "Have you interviewed any of them?"

"I am sorry, there are no other witnesses." There had been no survivors, but four bodies had been found. There was no sign of any others.

"But... but there were at least six people there!" she exclaimed. "I know there were six priests there. I saw them before the fire started."

He smiled sadly. "This is what we have found at the moment. But we have a lot of wreckage to sift our way through carefully. It is likely we find more... bodies. Perhaps now we may only find bones. The fire was very intense."

Abigail was compelled to also ask what state the priory was left in, and whether any of its contents of the building had survived the fire. She wanted to know whether the historic books and documents stored in the library had escaped damage.

Shaking his head, he confirmed, "I doubt it very much." He looked at her quizzically. "Why do you ask this question?"

"The priests were very proud of their collection. It went back many hundreds of years. They believed it to be priceless." She remembered the desperate attempts by the priests to rescue their treasures from the inferno.

"Don't forget that what the fire did not consume, the water used to douse the flames would have destroyed much of what was left in the priory." He looked doleful. "I fear that any books, papers and the like — these would certainly have been damaged irretrievably or burnt completely."

As the likelihood of finding anyone else alive diminished, the investigation changed into a forensic examination of the cause of the fire, the events leading up to it, and Abigail's claim that the priests had intended to kill her.

The police remained sceptical of this part of Abigail's story. She was subjected to exhaustive questioning about why these priests, dedicated men of the cloth, had the intention of murdering her. She had been careful in what she disclosed to the authorities, focusing more on the priests' state of mind and their isolation.

Understandably, the investigators found all this very difficult to deal with. It was well outside their training and their normal expectancies investigating crimes of violence. They had spoken to the church authorities in Marseille, who were still trying to come to terms with the loss of life at Sainte-Baume and the burning to the ground of one of their oldest and holiest priories in all of France. On hearing of the claims made by Abigail, the church authorities immediately denounced them as fantasy; a mythology that was entirely without foundation. The authorities were quick to threaten legal action if this woman persisted in such wild and baseless accusations designed to bring their church into disrepute, and to damage its reputation. The police chief shortly after received a strongly worded letter in this vein from the church lawyers.

At this stage, the police had been happy to conclude that Abigail was still overwrought by events, some of which she may have imagined. Later they did acknowledge that it had proved particularly hard to have any direct conversations with potential witnesses, including members of the Dominican Order itself.

Eventually, it seemed that both the police and the church had become reconciled to concluding that the priests at Sainte-Baume were renegades and what had transpired was outside the knowledge or influence of the church. Ultimately, they had to accept some elements of this extraordinary story when it was discovered that Adam himself had been found.

Abigail had reported that Adam was missing, but a police search, both on the ground and from the air, failed to find him. The initial conclusion was that he had also died in the fire. Abigail refused to believe this, or to give up on Adam. It was a few days later, after she had been moved from intensive care into a private ward, that news emerged of a man having been rescued from the mountainside, following a hunting accident. He had been found by a local hunter some distance from the fire, in a different area of the mountain range. It seemed he had suffered an attack by a wild boar. A local rescue team had been called and they had taken the injured man to a clinic in Le Plan d'Aups, where he was treated. When the authorities had been initially informed, it had been assumed to be a hunting accident, unrelated to events elsewhere at the cave.

When the man had been brought down from the mountain, he was unconscious. He was stabilised, placed on a drip, and in a neck brace, and treated for his external injuries before being transported to a bigger hospital specialising in brain trauma in Marseille.

When it was established that the rescued Englishman was indeed Adam, the police interviewed him and he confirmed being attacked by a group of priests on the mountain and left for dead. They were happy to report that Adam was making good progress at the hospital and that no brain injury had been found. Importantly, the brief details that he managed to recount matched with that of Abigail. He had no knowledge, however, of the fire that had razed the priory at Sainte-Baume to the ground.

Abigail's private room in the hospital looked away from the mountains and out over the motorway and the plains of the valley. It provided the privacy she needed to recover as she best she could. She had spoken a number of times to Adam on the phone. Caroline had visited both her and Adam twice, having returned to France immediately on hearing the news. An obviously pregnant Vivienne had also been to see her. Despite these visits, she often felt alone in her room, where she would find herself staring blankly out of her window, her thoughts elsewhere.

*

Two weeks later, they were released from their respective hospitals and Abigail picked up Adam from Marseille in a hired car. Navigating their way through the morning rush hour Marseille traffic, they emerged from a tunnel and passed the docks and the glistening blue of the Mediterranean. Leaving the busy city traffic behind, they headed for the A7 motorway which would take them to Orange, and back to Uzès, where Caroline was waiting. Adam asked Abigail about her work. They had agreed earlier to leave the important discussions about Maryanne and what had happened in the priory at Sainte-Baume to a later date.

Abigail grimaced. "I phoned them and apologised for not contacting them earlier. I should have done so. I told them I'd been in hospital, that I'd lost my phone, but they weren't too happy. It seemed very hard to explain, so I thought, bugger it, it's probably for the best and I resigned. They were startled by that and tried to backtrack, to talk me out of it, but I realised it was the right decision for me. I need time off, to sort myself out. Of course, I will get back into it eventually, but only when I feel ready. Vivienne and Emile have invited me to stay with them in Saint-Quentin when you go back. Vivienne has promised to teach me pottery and I will help Emile at some of the markets. I'm rather looking forward to it. I need to do something different for a while."

Adam looked across at her. She did look happy.

"And I want to see Jean. I need to talk to him about his brother, Anton."

Adam looked quizzically at Abigail.

*

Standing in the small cemetery, looking out over the Sainte-Baume mountains, it felt as if Maryanne were there with them. Abigail turned to look at Adam beside her.

Conscious of her gaze, he regarded the grave. "You know, I got it so wrong with Maryanne. It has taken me until now to realise that there was little I could have done to save her."

"I think she had known that for some time." Abigail wiped away her tears. "And now? What will you do?"

"I don't know," he replied eventually. "I haven't quite got that far, but I guess it will involve a new start."

"And…" she prompted, squeezing his hand.

He smiled. "I've no idea." He knew what she meant.

She turned away from him and returned to looking out

towards the far-off mountains. Abigail then added softly, "I know you are leaving soon." It was a statement more than a question.

"Yes, I've booked a flight for the weekend. I have been here long enough. And you?"

"I have been speaking to Vivienne. We are planning to take part in the festival that celebrates Mary Magdalene in Saint-Maximin. It's held at the end of July. I was reading about it whilst I was in hospital. It sounds wonderful. Vivienne has said she will do it with me, before her little girl is born."

Adam nodded. "Good for you, Abi. I'm afraid that, after all that's happened, I just couldn't do that. Not at the moment. Not for a while, probably. For now, I know I need to get away from everything here."

"I understand," she acknowledged, placing her hand gently on his good arm. "She's going to be called Mary, by the way," she added.

He was startled. "Who is?"

"Vivienne and Emile's baby. They told me yesterday. They want me to be her godmother."

"That's wonderful. I'm happy for you."

"Thank you, Adam. We will only do the two main days at the festival," she explained. "It starts inside the basilica. Mary's skull is then brought up from the crypt and placed in a gold reliquary. Then there's a concert, which is normally followed by a pilgrimage up to the cave. Obviously, that won't happen this year. The main event, though, is the next day — a Sunday — and starts with a grand procession through the streets of Saint-Maximin. It's meant to be a joyful event and it's how I want to remember Mary Magdalene. I want to celebrate with her. I want her to be held up high, so that she can look far beyond the crowds. And I want everyone to feel proud and special in her presence. After that I'll come home, I promise you."

There was nothing more to say. With one last look at the grave, they turned and walked away.

About the Author

Having qualified with an MA in Clinical Psychology, Robert Cole decided on a career change, moving into the business world. After a lengthy and successful time with a large multinational oil company in the UK and overseas, he moved on to senior positions in various large organisations. Since retiring in 2018, he has concentrated on writing novels, and travel. Mistral is his second novel and is a powerful and sweeping drama set amongst the vineyards and picturesque towns and villages of Languedoc and Provence. His first novel drew on his affinity with Greece and its diverse islands. He is currently working on a sequel to this first novel.

In addition to the UK, he has lived in Singapore, Cyprus, the Netherlands and South Africa. He currently divides his time between Surrey and Uzès in southern France.

www.blossomspringpublishing.com